TRAITOR
A TAINTED AGE

Ash Leigh

Paperback ISBN: 978-0-9965526-2-2
Hardcover ISBN: 978-0-9965526-3-9

Published by BookLocker.com, Inc., St. Petersburg, Florida.

The characters and events in this book are fictitious. Any similarity to real persons, living or dead, is coincidental and not intended by the author.

Printed on acid-free paper.

Booklocker.com, Inc.
2016

First Edition

Dedication

For my GCU family. You know who you are. Y'all mean so much to me! Your support, friendship, and love have been absolutely invaluable.

For my God, who remains ever the most trustworthy and constant companion.

CHAPTER ONE

I fastened my necklace and scrutinized my reflection in the mirror. The little electrobullet hanging an inch below my collarbone was supposed to be a constant reminder from one of my old friends about the supposed power I kept hidden inside, but lately it had been acting like a trigger for my most terrifying memories instead.

Every time I looked at the bullet I could feel my heartbeat quicken and I could see Attis, my best friend, falling to the ground. I could feel the panic, thinking that he was dead all over again. The bullet he had been shot with was only a slightly newer model of the one I wore. For days I had thought my best friend and the leader of our tiny caravan was gone forever, but I had been wrong. Attis was alive. We had made that discovery months ago, but we still hadn't found him.

I leaned against the sleek dresser and stared at my hands, glaring at the useless, ugly scar I'd gotten during my last attempt to find him. Since then I had added an irritating ex-Provincial boy to my caravan, been adopted for reasons of legality and protection by one of the richest families in the country, and was currently living in New Capil, the capital province, right beneath The Eye that wanted so badly to exterminate everyone like me. I shut my eyes tightly for a moment before lifting my head and giving my appearance a gloomy once-over. There was no doubt that my life had changed. I had to admit that some of it hadn't been all that bad, but now everything was about to change again in a much less pleasant way.

A knock at the door interrupted my thoughts and I turned around as Lasey poked her head into my room. She had been a Gypsy too, before the Micahs had adopted her, but with her long, pin-straight hair and flawless features no one would believe she had ever been anything but a Provincial.

"The party is starting," she said with a wink. "Just wanted to let you know."

I tried to smile even though I could feel my stomach twist in on itself. "Thanks, I'll be right up."

She left and I surveyed myself in the mirror one more time. As far as I could recall, this was only the second time I had ever worn a dress. I didn't enjoy it, but this was a birthday party and the Micahs were weird about those sorts of things. I would stomach it for them. It was the least I could do considering the news I had for them.

***

I surveyed the room silently from where I stood by the kitchen bar. The stark white furniture had all been pushed to the corners and the first song had just begun playing; it wasn't Provincial music though. I knew this instantly because my ears weren't ringing and my knees didn't feel like they were about to vibrate into jelly. This music was nice to listen to.

The birthday girl was already twirling around with Sacrif in front of the many enormous windows overlooking a province pulsing with bright lights and far less wholesome parties against a solid black sky. Sacrif and Appy were good parents. I was going to miss them.

A touch at my hip distracted me and I looked down at the little girl requesting my attention. Steffy was looking up at me expectantly – well I guess "looking" wasn't the right word considering she couldn't actually see, but she obviously wanted something. I looked curiously at the older girl standing behind Steffy.

"Steff wanted you," Nanda said apologetically. "I thought it would be okay to let her out of lessons early so she could be part of the dancing up here."

I used to find it ironic that the oldest of the Micah children felt closest to Steffy, the youngest of my caravan. In fact, I couldn't think of any time in the last two weeks when I hadn't seen Steffy's little brown hand clasped firmly in Nanda's slim white one. Sometimes I felt a twinge of jealousy in my stomach, like some insect gnawing away at my guts. I had to remind myself about Nanda's past. Her little brother died several years ago, so her attachment to Steffy as a stand-in younger sibling made sense.

"Okay," I said, smiling at Nanda and trying my best not to appear apprehensive. "The first song hasn't even finished yet, so I guess you're right on time."

Nanda and I weren't close, but to be fair she wasn't close to anyone except Appy.

I picked up Steffy and plopped her on a stool so we were closer to eye level.

"Hey kid."

She smiled and I once again found it hard to believe that this little five-year-old was the same baby Attis and I had rescued from a troop of Runners so many years ago. She had recently lost her first tooth and two more seemed nearly ready to come out as well. I had to wonder what he would think of her now. He had never seen Steffy without dirt all over her and her hair standing in all directions. Come to think of it, he had never seen me without dirt on my face either. He'd be shocked to see me now. I self-consciously adjusted my dress. The music swelled and I had to force my thoughts away from Attis.

"I like your party dress, Steff," I complimented her. "It's beautiful."

Secretly, I thought Provincial fashion was ridiculous. There were two kinds of acceptable dresses as far as I could tell. The kind with an inconveniently long, draping skirt like I was wearing, or the kind with a skirt that stuck out in all directions like a wheel stuck around someone's waist. Both of these styles were lined with tiny strings of different colored lights – because they weren't already attention-catching enough.

Steffy shook her head, making her tight little curls bounce all over the place, pointing to the colorful decorations on her head.

"The ribbons are nice too," I assured her. "Are you having fun?"

Steffy nodded, a little grin lighting up her face.

"Are you excited to give Magely her birthday present?" I prompted.

Another excited nod.

"And you know how old she's turning?" I asked slyly, wondering if Steffy had actually learned anything about numbers from all that tutoring the Micahs were providing.

She signed the number fourteen, to which I responded enthusiastically, clapping my hands because I knew Steffy would clap her hands too and I loved that. Right on cue, the speakers flawlessly transitioned into the next song and, before I knew it, eighteen-year-old Fil appeared, bowing to Steffy even though she couldn't see him.

"Steffy, will you please dance with me?" he asked dramatically. "I don't know what I'll do if I'm turned down by such a bewitching young lady."

I rolled my eyes and allowed Fil to steal away my little girl with nothing but a quick wink in my direction and a nod at something over my shoulder. I frowned at these signs of conspiracy and whirled around to see Keel standing behind me. I felt my breath catch, which was ridiculous because Keel and I had known each other for several months now and had escaped several near-death experiences together. I should've been bored by his existence at this point – or at least accustomed to it. I knew my current reaction to him was probably due to the fact that he had kissed me a few weeks ago and I had responded by running away and crying in the elevator like the tough Gypsy woman I am. The tension between us might also have been due to the fact that I hadn't spoken more than five words to him since that night.

"Hi Delle," he said softly, watching me cautiously, like he wasn't sure if I was going to run away crying again or simply turn my back like I'd been doing since the initial running-and-crying incident. "Will you please dance?"

I fully intended to say no, but instead I heard myself say "okay" as he took my hand and led me onto the dance floor.

"You look beautiful," he offered.

I frowned. "You've seen this dress before. I wore it to the Provincial party the night Steffy was kidnapped."

"I wasn't talking about the dress," he corrected, looking at me with those piercing grey eyes, probably thinking I would swoon like I'm sure all the Provincial girls used to.

I scowled as he took my hand and led me around the floor to the music.

"So are we ever going to talk about what happened?" he asked after several moments of silence. "Or are you going to keep pretending I don't exist?"

"I think Steffy's calling," I said quickly, trying to pull away, hoping at least a light joke might turn the direction this conversation was taking.

He pulled me back in one motion and laughed. "Steffy's mute. Besides, she's having a great time dancing with Fil and you don't want to ruin that."

I sighed and resigned myself to the dance. After another moment of silence, he pulled me closer and lowered his voice.

"You've been avoiding me," he accused.

"No I haven't," I snapped, even though it was a lie because I had absolutely been avoiding him.

"Yes you have."

"Why would I be avoiding you?" I asked, doing my best to sound skeptical.

"I keep asking myself the same question and I have to wonder if it's because I kissed you. Although when I trapped you last week to ask if that was the problem you frantically assured me it wasn't."

"I wasn't frantic," I shot back, wondering again why I had ever agreed to let this Provincial tag along with us.

He rolled his eyes and said, "My mistake then. I guess you just *looked* frantic."

I rolled my eyes and in my peripheral vision I could see Jag – the quietest member of our caravan – and Magely whispering to each other, watching us in what was probably supposed to be a discreet way.

"Are you scared because I kissed you?" Keel asked bluntly.

My mouth dropped open as I struggled to come up with a cutting reply.

"Why would that scare me?" I asked much too angrily.

"You're forcing me to guess, since you won't tell me what's wrong," he finally said, the frustration finally making its way into his voice. "If you're upset because I kissed you –"

"That's not it," I interrupted, fighting the panic rising in my throat. I was still trying to convince myself that the kiss wasn't a big deal and I didn't need him ruining all my hard work.

The frustration in his expression was instantly replaced with bitter disappointment.

"We're being watched," I pointed out, hoping to distract him.

He raised an eyebrow but followed my gaze when I nodded at Jag and Magely. Jag caught my eye and smirked. Magely instantly turned away when she realized we were watching them in return.

Keel pulled me closer and swirled us around so that they couldn't see my face anymore. He dropped his voice so our eavesdroppers had no chance of overhearing.

"Can we please be friends again?" he asked, ducking his head to look at me with his light eyes, hopeful like the sky after a storm.

"We were friends before?" I responded dryly.

He smiled ruefully and shrugged. "I like to think so. We were at least getting there."

I raised an eyebrow at him in response.

He sighed then and squeezed my hand. "I just want to help, but you have to tell me what's wrong."

I hesitated, thinking of all the things I wanted to tell him – to tell *anyone* – but never would.

"I don't want to talk about it," I finally muttered.

"You don't want to talk about it *right now*?" he clarified.

"I don't want to talk about it right now," I echoed firmly.

"Later then?"

"Okay," I heard myself agree, even though I had no intention of doing so.

I was suddenly exhausted as I thought about the announcement I had to make soon. I rested my head on Keel's shoulder out of pure fatigue, instantly realizing my mistake and trying to convince myself to move. The convincing didn't work though because Keel's shoulder was both comfortable and an excellent hiding place.

Honestly, I was scared of the decision I would have to share with the family who had so kindly adopted me and my caravan. For all his faults, Keel was one of the only people I wasn't afraid of disappointing with my decision. He would probably be upset, but he would understand. Jag was a different matter altogether. I was already predicting the backlash my announcement would incite.

"Okay," Keel said quietly. He slid his arm further around my waist, letting me hide for a little while longer.

***

I helped Appy clear away the dishes from breakfast the next morning and box up the leftovers for another day. As far as I knew, the Micahs were the only Provincials who bothered to keep their leftovers and were probably the only ones who would be healthier if they didn't. Considering how burnt these particular leftovers were, I doubted they would ever be finished.

Magely was sitting at the table chatting with Jag while everyone else was slowly drifting off to their own activities. If I was going to talk to the entire family, it needed to be now.

"Appy, do you think I could talk to everyone for a second?" I asked quietly as one of the kitchen drawers slid back into place.

The tall blonde woman must have noticed something unusual in my voice because she turned around and gave me a searching look. I was alarmed to see tears forming, accentuating the blueness of her eyes, but she quickly blinked and turned away again leaving me to wonder if I had just hallucinated the tears.

"Of course, Delle."

I rubbed my hand nervously and followed her out of the kitchen, around the bar, to the couches that Lasey and Sacrif were pulling back into place. Steffy was bouncing up and down beside Nanda while Keel leaned against the window with his arms crossed. He was already watching me, like he knew what I was going to say. I studiously ignored him as Appy gathered her family around then sat down beside Sacrif, waiting expectantly for me to speak.

I tried to remember the smooth opening I had practiced for this little announcement, but suddenly my mind went blank. I looked around at all of the people who had welcomed me into their lives and dreaded that I was about to give them the impression that I was ungrateful. Before I could think about it anymore I took a quick breath and forced myself to speak.

"I'm leaving." I guess I expected them to be surprised, but instead they all looked pretty unmoved. "And apparently you already know that," I said dubiously, realizing then that at least half of my worrying had been purposeless.

"You've been acting weird lately," fourteen-year-old Jorge commented. "More than normal."

"We knew you wouldn't stop looking for Attis," Magely piped up, giving me an apologetic look. "We were just waiting for you to decide when to start searching again."

"I should never have stopped," I admitted grimly, sitting down on the arm of Fil's chair.

"To be fair, a building did collapse on top of you three weeks ago," Keel said, raising an eyebrow. "I think Attis would understand the concept of recovery time."

I glared at Keel but was interrupted when Jag's voice cut through my irritation, sounding both offended and frustrated. "Were you going to consult me at all before we left?"

I swallowed. I hated when Jag was upset with me. Up until recently he had devoted all his time to honing his sulking skills but he was rarely ever angry. He had grown up a lot since Attis was taken. He'd even gotten taller. And he had more opinions.

"I didn't consult you because you're not coming," I said with an expression as neutral as I could manage. "And neither is Steffy or Keel."

Jag's lips pursed and I knew we were going to have a loud conversation about my decision as soon as this little family meeting was over. I didn't even bother to look at Keel, but I could sense his tension and the fact that he remained silent gave me a good idea about how he felt. Maybe I was wrong in assuming he wouldn't judge me too harshly for this.

"I was thinking," I began with a wince, turning to Sacrif and Appy. "That Jag and Steffy could stay with you until I get back."

"Of course," Appy said instantly, flicking back her perfect hair. "You know that you're all welcome here as often as you want to be here."

"Thank you," I said, hoping my sincerity was evident.

"Do you know where you're going?" Sacrif asked abruptly.

I nodded. "I think so, but I'll need a way to get there."

I could feel the tense energy of preparation starting to build in the room as Appy fixed me with a steady expression and asked, "Are you sure you want to run again?"

I looked back at her, meeting her blue eyes with my own even though her expression was intense and her concern was palpable.

"Running is something I'm good at," I answered coolly, trying to smile like I wasn't nearly as scared as I felt. "Besides, this time I'm not just running. I'm chasing something too."

CHAPTER TWO

"You're not going without me," Jag said stubbornly, for what felt like the twentieth time.

"Once I find Attis we'll come straight back," I said, focusing intently on packing my bag to avoid the penetrating eyes Keel and Jag were training on me.

"Right. *We* will come straight back," Jag said pointedly.

I shook my head and yanked the drawstring on my bag a lot harder than was necessary.

"Jag," I began, slinging the bag over my shoulder and turning to face him.

"It's his choice, Delle," Keel interrupted firmly.

I groaned. "Keel, *please.*"

"He's right, Delle," Jag snapped, fire dancing in his eyes like I'd never seen before. "I can take care of myself – and I need to find Attis. I owe as much to him as you do."

"What if things were turned around?" Keel asked bluntly. "If I had been taken, you would let Attis go with you to find me."

"You're *not* Attis," I snapped, realizing my voice was a lot harsher than was probably necessary. "And besides that's not the point."

Keel clamped his mouth shut and narrowed his eyes.

"I'm coming whether you want me to or not," Jag interjected. "If you try and leave without us we'll just follow you."

"I'm trying to protect you!"

"I don't need protecting!" Jag shouted, surprising me because I wasn't sure I had ever heard him yell before except during an emergency. "I'm as much of an adult as you are."

I groaned and flopped back onto the pillows.

"You can't do this by yourself, Delle," Keel said stubbornly.

I covered my face with my hands and stayed silent for another moment. I knew I couldn't do anything to stop them from coming, but I wanted to. I had thought that maybe if I wanted them to stay behind badly enough, they actually would. Clearly, that wasn't going to happen.

"Fine," I finally grumbled, sitting up and removing my hands from my face. "I know you don't need my permission; I was just hoping to keep as many people out of danger as possible."

Jag sat down beside me and nudged me with his shoulder. "We don't need it, but we appreciate it."

Keel didn't say anything. He just watched me silently, his arms crossed. I flushed and looked away, standing up suddenly.

"Well, I guess you'd better go pack."

***

We were standing by the lift and had already hugged the majority of the Micahs goodbye when a blonde creature whirled across the room and slid to a halt right in front of us. Magely stood there, hand on hip and bag over shoulder. She looked, in one word, determined. I noted the excited gleam in her eye with a frown.

Before I could open my mouth, she announced, "I'm coming too!"

I felt like someone had just slapped me in the face. I turned to the parents in bewilderment, wondering what they would say to their only blood-related child's announcement. Appy's arm was casually linked through Sacrif's as she calmly met my gaze.

"No," I sputtered, spinning back towards the eager blonde child. "You can't come, Magely. I'm sorry."

"Are you going to try and stop me?" she asked, giggling because she knew I wouldn't.

"Sacrif, you're condoning this?" I asked in disbelief.

Sacrif shrugged but I could see the tension at the corners of his mouth. He wasn't happy about this either. Maybe if I had more time I could convince him to stop her.

"I wouldn't say I'm condoning," Sacrif hedged, looking down at his slim wife for affirmation. "But we're allowing it."

"Why?" I asked, glancing over at Magely who was busy making steady eye contact with Jag.

Appy smiled at me and even though I knew she was trying to soothe me, I could see the hint of worry in her eyes as well – not as obvious as Sacrif's, but it was there.

"As a former Gypsy myself, I really don't have a leg to stand on here," she admitted with a rueful smile. "If not for Sacrif, I would probably still be a Gypsy. In some ways it's a lifestyle with more risks, but it has its benefits."

I turned desperately back to Magely, stunned that the only Micah child who had never been a Gypsy was the one who wanted to live like one now.

"Magely?" I asked helplessly, hoping she would see the insanity of her decision.

"I'm coming, Delle," she said firmly. "I want to help."

I looked over at Keel. His expression was neutral but I didn't miss the slightly raised eyebrow. Out of everyone there, it appeared that Keel was the only other one who disapproved of this decision almost as much as I did.

Jag interrupted my mental breakdown. "We need to get going, Delle. You can finish processing on the way."

I scowled at him and looked to Keel, hoping for some support in this. He dipped his head a little, acknowledging the rationale of Jag's suggestion. I sighed and let my crossed arms fall to my sides.

"Alright, okay, fine," I surrendered, ignoring all of the protests bubbling at the forefront of my mind.

Now that another person had announced their departure, the goodbyes had to start all over again. In a way it was nice because it gave me another excuse to hold onto Steffy. Leaving her behind was like tearing a piece out of my heart. I knelt on the ground, hugging her tightly, explaining to her where we were going, that we were going to bring Attis back. I told her how much I was going to miss her and not to forget me and to learn a lot. I had an awful fear that she wouldn't remember me when we returned. That she would adopt Nanda in my place and I would be irrelevant. I pulled her back into another hug and bit my lip to distract myself from the intangible pain so I wouldn't cry. She patted my hair with her little hands and I let out an unsteady breath, trying to regain my composure.

When I finally released her and stood up, Keel was behind me. He met my eyes and I knew that he understood. Leaving Steffy behind was the hardest thing I'd ever done. I did my best to smile, like I was still confident about this mission, but inside I had never felt so unsure.

***

"So where are we going first?" Magely chirped as we entered the lift station and waited in line for an empty lift to reach us.

I was busy keeping an eye out for patrolling Runners who might know about me. I had a secret fear that Presid Bertley, the lead Runner who had given killing me his best effort only a few weeks ago, would appear around every corner and shoot us all dead. I had no time to answer Magely's irritatingly cheerful questions.

"We're going to Kilso," Jag explained to her quietly. He understood the importance of staying under the radar in a way his new girlfriend clearly didn't. "If Attis isn't in Kilso, he'll probably be in Atken."

A troop of Runners stepped into line beside us and I felt my breath catch and heart start to race.

"He's not with them," Keel muttered, understanding my silent anxiety. "As far as they know, we're just a couple Provincials on our way to Kilso for holiday. We have our papers. They have no reason to bother us."

Despite the truth in Keel's words, I couldn't stop thinking about Presid. The man was crazy. What used to be a distaste for us as Gypsies had turned into an uncontrollable psychotic obsession.

"He won't try anything in public if there's another way," Keel added under his breath. "I know him. He won't do anything that could damage his reputation – like attacking a group of defenseless kids."

Recently I had been able to make myself forget the relationship between Keel and Presid. It was times like this though that I remembered Keel knew our enemy better than anyone. Presid was his father after all. I turned around and looked into Keel's grey eyes. They were similar to Presid's in color, but they lacked the manic light of barely contained rage and insanity.

"Legally, we now have every right that a Provincial has," Keel said with a dry smile.

"We're hybrids," Magely chimed in. "Gypsies, but Provincials too."

"We're mutts," I answered wryly, wondering with dread how long it would be before the cruelties of the world took away the blonde girl's persistent sparkle.

Magely laughed and I couldn't help smiling. I hadn't really meant it to be funny, but Magely's happiness was infectious. I noticed Jag watching Magely with a smile, but I got the distinct feeling he was smiling about something completely different than the rest of us.

Keel muttered my name, disrupting my musings. I looked over at him and his eyes flicked to the group of Runners next to us. They had grown silent. It was time for us to do the same. They didn't need to learn anything about us. I could only pray they hadn't already heard too much.

A few minutes later, a lift arrived and we climbed inside. As it ascended out of the station I was grateful for the invisible shield around the open top lift, keeping the cold air and the rain away from us. With four of us it actually became warm relatively quickly and I was forced to take off the high-necked blue jacket the Micahs had given me as a parting gift. Even the fake leather it was made out of felt sticky, like it had already soaked in the water from the air around us. The others did likewise with their outer gear. I eyed Magely's black undershirt with mild surprise. I had never seen the pale girl in anything but white. Although the black was a stark contrast against the rest of the girl, it did help to rough up the angelic-glow she seemed to cast wherever she went. Her long shimmery hair was pulled back in a ponytail, helping her to look more like the fourteen-year-old she was. Usually, she looked younger. It was hard to remember that Jag was only a year older than her. I stared at the two for a moment, sitting close to each other and talking in low voices. They were just kids. Did they know they were kids? I didn't when I was fifteen.

"It's weird, isn't it?" Keel said to me in a low voice, nodding at the kids sitting across from us, completely absorbed in each other's existence.

"They shouldn't be here," I muttered. "They're just kids."

Keel shook his head and looked at me with mild amusement. "Not really. Life made them grow up a lot faster than they were supposed to."

"Maybe Jag," I admitted with a sigh. "But Magely was sheltered from it."

Keel chuckled and when I raised an eyebrow at his misplaced display of humor, he explained, "As far as Provincials go, Magely knows more about Gypsies than my father does."

"Yeah, well, your father's an idiot," I said grudgingly.

Keel grinned. "I'd drink to that if there was anything to drink around here. Or eat for that matter."

I got the hint and dug out the bottles of water we had brought then passed the bag of skips around. The skips tasted especially stale after the fresh food we had been eating at the Micahs. I watched apprehensively as Magely bit into one of the crackers for the first time. She showed no sign of discomfort and her delicate little nose didn't even produce one wrinkle despite the fact that I knew skips tasted like dirt. Keel nudged me and I nudged him back. Maybe this kid would be okay after all.

***

"Who are we meeting here?" Jag asked skeptically, looking around the restaurant, probably the fanciest one we had ever been inside.

"A contact that Sacrif mentioned a while ago," I said tersely, doing my best not to look out of place around the brightly colored and stick-thin Provincials strutting about and laughing in their high voices. "I used Appy's Tab to track her down one day on The Eye's main database."

"A Caretaker?" Magely asked curiously.

"Unlike your parents, not a Caretaker," I corrected. "She doesn't take Gypsies in and feed them, she's more like a freelance informant."

"She?" Keel asked.

I nodded. "She's meeting us to give us information about Attis's current location as well as the best way to reach him."

"She's just giving this information to us freely?" Magely asked.

"Of course not," I responded, glancing towards the door as it opened and closed, admitting a woman with pastel purple hair and a dangerously low dress, practically dripping off the arm of a large man in a multi-hued suit.

"How are we paying her?" Keel asked skeptically.

"She heads a research division on Taints," I said as casually as I could, anticipating the backlash this would receive.

"She's a Tinker?" Jag asked grimly, his dark eyes flashing unhappily.

I nodded. "Supposedly she's both respected and shunned by her colleagues for certain experimental methods of research she uses exclusively."

"Well that sounds promising," Magely commented nervously. "What's a Tinker?"

"Where to start?" I asked dryly, looking at Jag who shrugged in response. "Tinkers are best known for dissecting people with genetic mutations," I explained shortly.

Magely's mouth made a small "O" shape as she realized the significance of this.

"Like Delle?" she asked in horror.

I nodded and leaned back in my chair to look at the door again. The woman should've already appeared. I was starting to fear that she wouldn't show up at all. Or worse, that she had sent a troop of

Runners to arrest us and was just biding her time until we left the restaurant.

"So what's her price then?" Keel asked, trying to make eye contact with me even though I was busy monitoring the door.

"She wants a demonstration of my powers," I said, doing my best to convince them as well as myself that this wasn't a terrible idea.

"That's a terrible idea."

"You realize that dissection is where all business with the Tinkers eventually ends up?" Jag asked incredulously.

I shook my head. "Not this one. Sacrif is the one who told me about her. I wouldn't say she's a friend, but she's not a direct enemy either. She's just interested in the science behind how we do what we do. Besides, supposedly some of her methods aren't technically legal. I doubt she would involve the law in any of this because it would shine a light on that."

This was a speech I had repeated to myself over and over again since I first sent my message to this mysterious woman. I was trying to make myself believe it. If we were caught, she would be caught too. I had to hope that would be enough to convince her to treat us fairly.

Jag pushed his water glass away and scowled. "I think we should leave."

"We're not leaving," I snapped, knowing this might be our only chance to gather any relevant information about Attis.

"You should have told us about this," Keel commented, watching me with a strange expression.

"This is the only lead we have," I insisted, leaning forward, addressing my whole caravan. "If we want to find Attis we need to talk to this woman. This is my risk to take and my choice. If anyone has a serious problem with it, then –"

Suddenly a cool presence at my shoulder warned me to stop talking. I slowly turned around and looked up to find the woman with the purple hair watching me with a sly smile. Her eyes were a startling shade of yellow to match her dress, clearly covered with the fake irises that were so popular among Provincials now.

"I do hope I'm not interrupting anything," she said in a wispy voice.

"Dr. Reece?" I asked, unable to stop myself from raising an eyebrow at her fluorescent dress.

"Yes. And I assume you are Delle? I might have guessed that blonde child, but she is, after all, a child and I wasn't under the impression that I was meeting with children," the woman said with a breathy laugh and toss of her hair. "I'm not meeting with children, am I?"

I simmered and was about to retort when Keel placed his hand briefly on my knee under the table, warning me to stop.

I sighed and gestured to the empty seat, saying, "Please sit down, Dr. Reece."

Jag kicked the chair out for her rather than getting up and pulling it away from the table. I shot him a look, hoping he would behave himself even though he clearly hated this situation and didn't approve of my decision. He was clearly still miffed about being kept in the dark.

Dr. Reece slipped into the chair and sipped her water before wrinkling her nose and waving at a server to bring her some sort of alcohol more to her taste.

"Now let's see," she began in her mildly croaky voice. "I know one of your names, but I am afraid the rest of us remain estranged from one another."

"You don't need their names," I intervened. "We agreed to an exchange of –"

"Power, my dear," Dr. Reece said with a tinkling laugh. "Knowledge is power after all and I am exchanging knowledge for a glimpse of your pure power."

I frowned, wondering how this vague creature was supposed to be one of the smartest humans on the continent. She laughed again, seemingly at nothing, as the server gently placed her curved glass of alcohol on the table.

"Where is the man you came in with?" I asked abruptly, suddenly remembering that she hadn't come alone.

She raised an eyebrow at me as she sipped her drink. "I left him at the bar, of course. He has no part in this."

"Who is he?" Keel asked, his eyes glimmering darkly.

She waved a hand dismissively. "You Gypsies, always so distrustful. That man is merely my bodyguard. He accompanies me everywhere as I have made some enemies as of late and require protection."

"How did you make these enemies?" Keel asked suspiciously.

Dr. Reece rolled her eyes. "My, what hostility. I am not referring to your kind. My enemies are more powerful than that, within the government. There are those who question my research methods and claim I am too lenient with my subjects."

I squirmed at hearing Taints described as test subjects, but swallowed my discomfort and nudged Keel's ankle with my toe, indicating that he should shut his mouth. Before I had a chance to open my mouth and try to pursue the topic of Attis, Dr. Reece suddenly seemed to snap to attention. I tensed instantly and followed her sharp gaze to Keel. Now she had the expression of a scientist, focused and alert, far different from her languid expression from a moment before.

"Do I know you?" the woman asked, cocking her head, some of her pastel hair covering her eye as she examined him.

Keel ducked his head and I loudly clattered my plate on the table to divert her attention.

"You're not here to meet my caravan," I said sharply. "If you don't have anything of value to say then we'll leave right now."

Dr. Reece flipped her hair out of her face and turned to me with a dry smile. "Or I could call the nearest troop of agents to arrest the Taint travelling through this beloved city."

I tensed at the threat.

"But then, of course, I wouldn't have the privilege of seeing your powers at work, so I think I'll not do that. I'd rather hold to our original agreement, wouldn't you?"

I pulled my chair closer to the table and crossed my arms, leaning on the table. When I arranged this meeting I knew there could be consequences, but I had already decided they were worth it.

This woman had the answer to the one question that had been consuming me.

"Dr. Reece, where is Attis?"

CHAPTER THREE

"Well he's not here, dear," the neon woman said flippantly, tossing her disturbingly purple hair again.

I felt the gentle pressure of Keel's hand on my knee again, a warning not to lose it with this frustrating woman.

"Well where is he?" I responded through my teeth.

Dr. Reece smiled at me. "I want to know why this young man is so important to you, dear."

"He's lead my caravan for as long as I can remember," I snapped. "That's all you need to know."

"So he's your friend then?" she said with interest.

Attis's face flashed in my mind for a moment. I had to get information from this woman. I had to get Attis back. I needed him. He was my best friend.

Suddenly, a light seemed to reach Dr. Reece's eyes and her smile broadened, stretching across her plastic face.

"No. He's more than a friend, isn't he?" she said coyly.

I stared at her, trying to understand exactly what she was implying.

"Come now, dear, you can confide in me. Just a bit of gossip between girls," she said with a wink. "This Attis is quite dear to you. You love this young man, isn't that so?"

"He's my friend," I responded hotly, trying to stamp down the surge of emotions rising in my throat. "He's family and we're just trying to get him back."

The woman laughed her tinkling laugh and rocked back in her seat like I'd made a fantastic joke. "Oh, he's family is he? Well, that makes your being in love with him much dirtier, doesn't it?"

Keel's hand was on my arm now. I just stared at the woman with the purple hair, watching me with an amused expression. I wanted to declare that I wasn't in love with Attis, but the words wouldn't come. I opened my mouth to try and spit out all the rebuttals I could think of, but I didn't have any. I glanced down at my hands and saw them shaking. I immediately dropped them into my lap. I didn't want it to look like she had a struck a chord with me, but she clearly had. It had never occurred to me... Not really.

"May I ask you a question?" a light voice interrupted my frantic thoughts.

I raised an eyebrow at Magely who was looking curiously at Dr. Reece.

Dr. Reece seemed amused. She cocked her head and considered the dreamy-eyed blonde child. I sighed. At this rate, the woman would never take us seriously.

"You're the youngest Micah child, aren't you?" Dr. Reece said, leaning forward and placing her chin on her hand, her long-nailed fingers tapping her lip. "You're just adorable, aren't you?"

"What is your name, Dr. Reece?" Magely asked, sitting up straighter, giving no sign that she felt patronized, although personally, I was insulted on her behalf. "Your first name," she clarified.

The doctor considered her for another moment before sighing and resuming her former posture. "My name is Jayni."

Magely smiled like this was the best name she'd ever heard.

I rolled my eyes and was just about to stop this nonsense when Magely's voice took on a more serious tone.

"Jayni, you didn't come to toy with us," Magely pointed out, meeting the colorful woman's gaze evenly. "Per your agreement with Delle, unless you divulge all relevant information you have, she is under no obligation to display her powers for you. You won't call any agents to your aid, because as soon as they discover that you were voluntarily meeting with us, you too will be under arrest. So, let's dispense with this meaningless conversation and continue on to the matters we're all here for."

I blinked. The blonde girl sitting so placidly across from me didn't seem capable of reasoning with anyone, much less a woman like Dr. Reece. She had done it though. Magely's words had somehow managed to stop Dr. Reece's never ending stream of pointless words.

Dr. Reece pursed her lips and narrowed her eyes at Magely for a moment before sighing and raising a hand in surrender.

"Well now, you children are no fun. Fine then." At this point she turned back to me and sipped her drink again. "What do you want to know, dear?"

"Where," I began frostily. "Is Attis?"

"Currently your friend is here in Kilso, but tomorrow he moves to Laylen," she said calmly, a smile twitching at the corners of her lips, which were painted with the same color as her hair, hinting that she was still thinking about my relationship to Attis.

"Where is he being held in Laylen?"

"I don't know if 'being held' is the right choice of words for –"

"Just answer the question," Jag interrupted.

Dr. Reece sighed dramatically and continued. "Attis will be staying in the Office of Retrieved Commodities."

"Where is that?"

Dr. Reece shrugged. "I'm not one of the many hapless fools who go on holiday in Laylen. In fact, I've never been there, so I don't know where it is. That's something you dears will have to discover for yourself."

"How long will he be in Laylen?"

Dr. Reece shrugged again. "It all depends on how cooperative your friend is. A week at minimum."

"What do they want with Attis?" I asked, voicing the question that had been burning me the most. "Is he imprisoned?"

Dr. Reece laughed again. "My dear, if your Attis was in prison he would be staying in Kilso or Atken, not going to Laylen. There is no prison in Laylen. If they're taking him there they want something special with your special friend."

I silently fumed against her insinuations about Attis and I, but swallowed my pride and tried to think if there was anything else of importance that I should ask.

"Will he be guarded?" I asked, glowering into the brilliant fake-yellow eyes of our doctor.

She grinned at me. "That is just another piece of information I'm not privy to." Suddenly she clapped her hands and the server walking by immediately set down a glass of murky blue liquid in front of Dr. Reece. She picked it up in two fingers, drained it, and then smiled at me again with her unnaturally white teeth.

"Now then, I have told you everything I know about your young man. I am a scientist, not a politician, therefore I don't have the clearance to gather any more detailed information than I have already given you."

I frowned and sat back in my seat.

"I have completed my part of this deal," the woman said calmly, holding my gaze. "Now, it is your turn."

***

Ten minutes later we were standing in the crumbling basement of an abandoned building. Dr. Reece's bodyguard waited outside the building upon her request as the colorful woman took out her Tab and opened a new screen, hovering in the air and flickering with its bluish light, waiting to be filled with incriminating information about me. Apparently Dr. Reece was preparing to take notes on what she was about to witness. Keel was concerned that she might try and record a video that showed me using the powers, so I told him to keep Jag and Magely with him and they could watch over her shoulder to make sure she didn't.

"Whenever you're ready, dear," Dr. Reece said in her wispy voice, though the attentive gleam in her yellow eyes made me wonder if she was much smarter than she seemed.

By some weird instinct I looked over to Keel, wanting assurance that I was doing the right thing, not making a terrible mistake. It briefly struck me how strange it was that I wanted Keel's approval. When our old mentor, Richy, had asked me to let Keel join our caravan I hated the idea. Somewhere along the way I had come to respect the former Provincial – at least a little bit – even if his father was the person who had ruined my life and taken Attis away.

Keel nodded ever so subtly and I let out a breath I'd been holding. I shut my eyes for a moment, emptying my thoughts and feeling the warm rush of blood through my arms as my fingertips began to tingle like they'd fallen asleep. I opened my eyes and felt my vision tighten as everything around me came into clear focus and the colors became more vibrant.

I lifted a hand and stretched out my fingers, watching as five streams of blue light appeared, curling through the air like smoke. I raised my hand above my head and the lights followed, growing taller. I curled my hand into a fist and the lights swirled around each other, forming a sphere. I tightened my fist as hard as I could and the smoky blue lights condensed and formed what appeared to be a dark glass-like substance before shattering. The shards of the sphere fell to the cracked ground beneath me before dissolving into a fine mist and disappearing altogether. The sharpness of my vision faded back to normal and the pins and needles in my fingers gradually eased until I couldn't feel them at all anymore.

I looked up to find Dr. Reece tapping furiously away on the projected screen of her Tab as Magely stared at me with an awed expression. I had forgotten that she had never seen my powers before. Keel was looking at me with another one of his unreadable expressions. I remembered the unexpected kiss he'd given me and I frowned to conceal the nervous twisting in my stomach. I looked away from him and crossed over to Jag who was quick to step by my side, like I needed some sort of protection. I didn't know why Keel had become such a constant visitor to my private thoughts, but it would be great if that stopped.

We waited for the purple haired woman to finish her typing and when she did she turned to me, intrigued.

"I must say, I've never seen someone with abilities at your level exhibit so much control before. How do you manage to control and suppress the powers as much as you do? And how much energy do you feel is used up when you use your power? Also can you sustain the second form of those powers for any significant amount of time?"

Jag nudged me and Keel closed in on my other side, probably trying to give me a completely unnecessary warning about the dangers of answering this woman's questions.

I shook my head and beckoned for Magely to join us, leaving Dr. Reece standing several feet away, isolated from us.

"I showed you the powers," I said firmly. "And you gave us the information we needed. This deal is over."

The woman sighed dramatically and rolled her yellow eyes at the ceiling. "Fine, fine. I'll relent for now. But next time I'll be insisting upon some answers, my dear."

"Hopefully there will be no need for a next time," I responded frostily.

We trailed behind the florescent woman as she ascended the crooked stairway. Upon reaching the top of the stairs, she took her bodyguard's arm and clung to him like a wet cloth from that point forward. As we exited the building and turned to part ways, I heard a soft gasp from behind us and whirled around to see Dr. Reece staring at us with a surprised expression. I quickly scanned the area for a sign of anything threatening, but came up blank. I narrowed my eyes suspiciously at the woman.

"You there," she said, fluttering her hand at my caravan. "The attractive dark-haired one."

Keel raised an eyebrow at her and I in turn raised an eyebrow at him.

"What do you want?" he asked warily.

She laughed her obnoxiously high laugh and smiled at him in what was probably supposed to be a charming way. "You're Presid's boy, aren't you?"

My breath caught in my throat and I could feel my hands forming tight fists as I instinctually stepped forward, ready for some sort of fight. This woman was the first person we'd run into who recognized Keel. If she told his father she had seen him here, he would be on us before our lift even made it to Laylen.

"My, I must say, you have his eyes, dear," she continued with a smug expression.

I glanced over at Keel and noticed that his jaw was clenched. If I felt this sort of anxiety hearing Presid's name, whatever Keel was feeling was probably much worse.

"Oh don't worry," Dr. Reece said breathily, winking at him. "Your father and I are rarely on good terms. I won't mention our meeting to him. The more trouble I can make for him, the better."

"Am I supposed to thank you for that?" Keel asked tightly.

Dr. Reece's bodyguard stepped forward in response to Keel's threatening tone, but Dr. Reece put a hand on her man's chest and stopped him with another laugh.

"Well, yes, dear. I certainly think it's something to be grateful for." She paused for a moment, watching us with amusement as if enjoying her own private joke.

Without another word, Keel turned to go. I followed him without a moment of hesitation. Usually I was the one who initiated the movement of our caravan, but in this situation I was happy to let him lead.

Dr. Reece's ringing laugh followed us, haunting us like an obnoxious ghost. Then she was calling after us.

"Life is full of cruel ironies, isn't it, my dear?"

At this point I wasn't sure who she was talking to and I didn't care. We kept walking and we didn't look back. No one spoke for several seconds before Jag piped up.

"Hey, at least you're attractive, Keel."

Keel snorted and I smiled. Magely burst into a fit of childish giggles and Jag put his hands in his pockets, content for the moment in his ability to make Magely laugh.

I let out a deep breath. With Keel's emotional distress somewhat resolved, I could focus on what we needed to do next. Somehow we had to get to Laylen and infiltrate the Office of Retrieved Commodities. *No problem.*

CHAPTER FOUR

I couldn't understand why The Eye would send Attis to a place like Laylen. Known mostly for its summer apartments and synthesized natural parks, Laylen was a place for Provincials to vacation when they were bored with their everyday lives.

I wondered what Attis had done to convince them not to throw him in prison – or worse. I couldn't imagine Presid letting me go anywhere except the morgue. I could tell that Keel thought this was another trap, but he mercifully kept his mouth shut. It wasn't as if the thought hadn't crossed my mind. They could easily be using Attis as bait, lying in wait for us to show up to try and take him back again – but it didn't feel right. They had already tried using Attis and even Steffy as bait before, and I had rewarded them by collapsing an entire building on their best Runners. I doubted Presid would try that again.

Besides, as far as The Eye knew, I was just a harmless Provincial strolling around their country, digitalized papers in hand to prove it. Presid was the only one who claimed to have proof of my powers. It wasn't my being a Gypsy that was illegal anyways – it was just my Tainted blood. That's why I couldn't believe that this was a trap. When Presid tried something again, it wouldn't be under The Eye's watch. The man was crazed with his lust for vengeance, and he was willing to go below the law to get it. He wouldn't attack us on government property – at least not after what happened last time.

I shook my head and pulled a hand through my hair, hoping to shake free some answers and relieve the tension all the questions crammed into my brain were causing. The closer we came to retrieving Attis, the more questions I had. I never realized how many secrets Attis must have kept from me.

When Attis first rescued me after my parents were murdered by a troop of Runners, I was eight years old. I didn't remember anything about my parents, but considering that Attis was older than me when it happened, there was a good chance he knew exactly what happened to them. Presid had accused me of giving him the long scar that circled his hand and wound up his arm. I didn't remember mutilating anyone at the age of eight, but if there was any truth to what Presid said, then Attis would know. Attis knew more about me than I did.

And of course, there was always that one persistent, nagging question in the back of my mind. *How did Attis know about the closet?* On the day we thought Attis had been killed, when he had, in fact, been shot to the ground on a rooftop in a different province on the edge of the country, he told us how to get out. Before he was shot, he gave us directions to walk through a door, down a hall and into a closet that we learned had a trash chute we could use for escape.

To my knowledge, Attis had never been inside that building before, so how could he know? I couldn't understand why he'd never told me or why it never occurred to me to ask, but lately there had been more questions popping into my mind than ever before. As these questions and a hundred more buzzed around my head I must have been making a strange expression because Keel kicked my shoe from across the lift.

"So are you going to tell me?" he asked in response to my questioning look.

"Tell you what?"

He nodded at Magely who was curled on the seat beside me, asleep. Then he gestured to Jag who was slumped against the invisible shield around the lift, also unconscious.

"When we were dancing you promised to tell me what bothers you about me," he said pointedly. "Well Magely and Jag are asleep so now is as good a time as ever to tell me what the problem is."

I looked outside at the bleak landscape passing below us. There was a long stretch of bomb land between Kilso and Laylen that still hadn't recovered from the last world war. In the distance I wondered if the hazy shape I saw was a Gypsy camp.

"Delle," Keel prompted gently. "What's wrong?"

I drew my legs up onto the seat and hugged my knees. "I'm just thinking, okay? We'll talk, just not right now."

"Are you going to say that every time I bring it up?" Keel asked skeptically.

I gave him my most charming smile in response.

He raised an eyebrow.

I rolled my eyes and sighed. "Fine, you want to talk? Tell me about yourself."

"Myself?" he asked skeptically.

"Sure," I shrugged. "What was your life like before?"

"Before?" he echoed, looking unenthusiastic about my choice of conversation topic.

"Yeah. Before you joined us – before everything went down with your dad," I clarified, wincing because I knew this probably wasn't something Keel wanted to talk about. I guess I only asked because I had been wondering about it. "I mean, what were you like before I knew you?"

He sighed and leaned back against his seat. He considered me for a brief moment.

"Are you really asking?"

I made a face. "Of course, I'm really asking."

"Well," Keel said, looking out at the sky, probably just to avoid looking at me. "I was going to be a doctor."

"A doctor?" I don't know why I was so surprised. It made sense, really. He was smart, capable, and relatively good with people.

"My mom was helping me look for a school – there are only two schools in the country that train doctors anymore," he said slowly.

I wasn't aware of that. Two seemed like too few. I guess that explained a lot.

"My dad, of course, didn't approve at all because he wanted me to be an agent. There's no expensive schooling involved with that career path, just a few months of training," I didn't miss the tone of disgust that had edged into his voice. "But, being a Caretaker, my mom was horrified at the idea."

"What did you *want* to do?" I asked, although I was pretty sure I already knew.

"I wanted to help people – I guess I got that from my mom. I wanted to keep her safe, which would mean diverting my father's attention and becoming an agent, but I also wanted her to be happy, which would mean becoming a doctor."

"Oh."

So Keel was almost a Runner. That was new.

"What were you going to do?" I asked quietly, shrinking a bit when his turbulent eyes flashed at me.

"I probably would've become a doctor," he said shortly, slouching back against the seat. "I started school a few months before –" I heard him catch his breath and I regretted asking him any question at all. "Before it happened. Before he killed her."

I waited what I felt was an appropriate second and a half before opening my mouth.

"I'm so sorry," I said sincerely, trying to put every ounce of just how sorry I was into my voice.

Keel didn't answer, he just kept looking out at the star-less sky. I thought I saw a glimmer in his eye, but if he was on the verge of crying I wasn't going to point that out. That was perfectly reasonable considering what his father had done.

"You would have been a great doctor, Keel," I continued, giving him a chance to collect himself. "And – even though you're not a doctor right now – you're still helping people." There was a long pause. At this point I was just really hoping he decided to speak to me again at some point. "You're helping me – I mean, you already have helped me."

I was surprised by the wry smile he flashed me. "Have I now?"

"Yes," I said firmly. "Remember when I cut my hand on that ladder? It was gross and infected and I was stupid about taking care of it, but you stitched it up."

"You cut your hand, you were stupid – Yes, I recall."

I raised an eyebrow, consciously deciding to ignore the specific points he'd picked up on.

"Besides that, you've helped me try to find Attis and you've kept my caravan safe – two things you didn't have to do," I continued. "I think your mom would approve."

Keel was looking at me with an expression I didn't quite understand.

"I think she would," he finally said.

When his gaze didn't waver but remained stubbornly on me, I scratched at the scar on my hand and found a reason to get distracted with my necklace.

"I assume you still don't want to tell me what's been bothering you?" Keel finally asked.

"You assume right," I confirmed, again smiling charmingly because I knew it would irritate him.

He rolled his eyes and exhaled loudly. "Well as long as you're in an uncharacteristically silent mood, I guess there's nothing left for me to do except try to get some sleep before we reach Laylen."

I nodded silently, feeling questions start to surround me again like a magnetic blanket, overwhelming me, sticking to me, and obstructing my view of the current situation.

"Delle," Keel insisted.

I looked over at him questioningly.

"You should probably sleep some too," Keel said quietly as he settled into a more comfortable position.

I shrugged noncommittally. I probably should. I probably wouldn't.

***

We reached Laylen in the early morning. Although it was raining everywhere else, the province itself was entirely protected by a large-scale weather shield. It wasn't at all what I imagined. I only knew about it from the rumors. Supposedly Laylen was the province that all The Eye's officials came to for their vacations. It was an expensive place to stay.

The whole province was chocked full of tropical looking plants and mist machines. I had expected Laylen to look fake – like most everything else the Provincials created. Instead, it was almost beautiful. If I didn't know that all of the plant life here was synthetic, I might even have been enchanted.

As we exited the lift station I startled as one of the misters hidden in a leafy tree spurted water into my face, bringing me back to reality and all the horrors that most likely awaited us in this place. Jag snorted with laughter and Magely acted horrified at my surprise shower. Keel laughed out loud.

I scowled and wiped the water off my face, muttering about Provincials and their ridiculous inventions.

"Why would they bring Attis to a place like this?" Keel asked, dodging the spray from a machine that turned on as we approached.

I grunted in response to Keel's question. I was disgruntled both because he had managed to dodge the surprise water attack from a harmless-looking bush and because I didn't have an answer to his question. His guess was as good as mine.

The false atmosphere inside Laylen's weather shield was irritatingly sticky. I sighed and blew a strand of stray hair off my forehead. The things Provincials put themselves through in order to feel wealthy never ceased to amaze me. Supposedly this province was designed after a tropical paradise. The last war had basically obliterated any of the natural places resembling a paradise.

"What should we do first?" Magely asked with a bounce in her step, shouldering her pack with impatient energy.

"We need to find the Office of Retrieved Commodities," I said distractedly, pausing in the middle of the crowded street for a moment to get my bearings.

"We could always ask someone for directions," Magely suggested.

I pursed my lips and didn't miss the look of amusement on Keel's face as he took note of my reaction to the Provincial child's too-sensible suggestion.

"We could," I said flatly. "But I would prefer not to draw any attention to ourselves."

"Are you sure it's not just because you don't like people?" Keel asked with a smirk.

"That might be part of it," I grumbled.

"It's that way," Jag said, appearing at my shoulder, nodding in the direction of a building that had invisible walls and floors, so that it looked like the people inside were floating and walking on air. "Past the translucent building."

I turned to Jag with a surprised look and he shrugged. "I asked for directions."

I rolled my eyes. Of course Jag would do whatever Magely suggested because Magely was his angel. His Provincial angel.

Keel was watching me with an expression that suggested he was trying to suppress his laughter yet again. Was I that easy to read? Attis always said I was. I flushed and looked away from Keel.

In some ways, he was so like Attis. I didn't tell him that though. Everything Keel did reminded me of Attis in one way or another. It was part of the reason I avoided him. The more I learned about Keel the more I noticed their similarities. It was disconcerting, painful, and confusing. Keel was *not* going to replace Attis. He wanted to know why I didn't like him? Well that was one of the biggest reasons.

Out of the corner of my eye I noticed a frown tug at the corner of Keel's mouth. My sudden shunning of him must have been obvious. I pretended not to notice his narrow looks as I tied my hair up in a messy style to let the artificial breeze cool my neck.

"Okay, let's go," I said, moving confidently in the direction Jag had indicated.

***

It didn't take long to scope out the Office of Retrieved Commodities. Unlike in New Capil, there was no electric fence surrounding the perimeter of the main building and the many warehouses behind it. I guess no one expected an attack on the ORC. From what little I knew about the place and what I learned from eavesdropping on the people walking in and out, this was where they kept track of the stuff they stole from Gypsies, Taints, and anyone else who got in their way. They brought the items here to be processed and then stored the stuff in different facilities around the country.

"Why are they keeping him here?" Magely asked.

Jag was silent and Keel eyed the building thoughtfully. I bit the inside of my cheek at her innocent question. If one more person asked why Attis would be here, my sanity was going to crumble into nonexistence.

"I have no idea," I finally said after making sure my voice would come out softer than it felt.

I repositioned my pack over my shoulder and looked up at the massive building that stretched almost to the top of the province-wide weather dome.

Provincials bumped into us and squeezed around us as we stood rooted to our spot in the middle of the street. They didn't seem to notice us as they carried on with their shopping and chatted in their surgically modified voices, sounding like a pack of mice squealing back and forth. It struck me how strange it was to be able to traverse the provinces without having to duck behind every building.

"So what do we do now?" Magely asked.

"We need a plan," Jag answered, frowning at the enemy building in front of us.

"We need to figure out how to get inside," I said, silently wondering if Attis had already arrived. Maybe he was already inside. Maybe if I shouted, he would be close enough to hear me. My throat tightened up at the thought and I clenched my fists. If that was true, this was as close as we'd been to him since we lost him.

"We need to figure out how to get inside," I said tensely, glaring at the extravagant and frail architecture, my obstacle to reaching Attis.

"And how to get back out."

"Preferably without collapsing the entire building."

At this I turned to my caravan and found them all watching me, Keel with a particularly pointed expression.

"That was one time!" I defended.

I turned away from them, pretending to ignore their laughter as I walked back across the street and they followed, still snickering. Somewhere along the way, Jag had learned to laugh. He never used to laugh much. Maybe that was why their teasing didn't bother me so much now. I hid a smile, wondering what Attis would think about seeing Jag so smitten.

I wanted to find somewhere to stay that was close to the ORC, but I doubted we would find any Caretakers in Laylen. As far as food and board went, we were on our own. After just a brief look around the province, I doubted we would find any Gypsies here either. This Province was basically an enormous resort. This wasn't a place any sane Gypsy would choose to hide out.

We had been sneaking around the buildings with the best view of the ORC for hours. Every building we stepped inside was packed with colorful Provincials, either going to have some sort of unnecessary surgery done or going to relax in some sort of spa room with questionable "health" treatments. I turned away from my caravan for a moment, noticing the lifts positioned along the walls of the lobby.

If only there was some way we could access the upper floors of the building without getting caught, we would have a perfect vantage point for watching the ORC. I sighed as a security worker passed so close to me that I had to step back. Our chances of making it upstairs were slim to none.

I turned back around and faltered when I realized my caravan was no longer in sight. I turned around twice, trying to spot them through the crowd. Keel was the tallest and in his bright green jacket should have been clearly visible. Then I remembered that he had taken his jacket off too, nearly suffocated by the fake humidity of this island-paradise themed province. I sighed. Now finding them would be even more difficult.

"Is that Claudelle?"

I whirled around at the sound of my full name, hoping to see my old friend Richy, the Gypsy who had taught Attis and me how to survive on our own. At the same time, I knew it wasn't him and a sense of dread seeped into my stomach. The last time I'd seen Richy was when he forced Keel into our caravan against my wishes. He was the only one who consistently called me by my full name. The person facing me instead with a sly grin spreading across his face was none other than Gerrit Stole, one of the richest people in the country who I wished I had never met.

"Uh, hello," I said, trying to seem less taken off guard than I felt.

"You remember me, don't you?" he asked, making eye contact, trapping me into a conversation.

"Oh, uh, yeah," I stammered, shoving my hands in my pockets in what was probably an extremely unladylike manner as I tried to appear casual. "Gerrit, right?"

Gerrit Stole and I had met only once at a party I attended with the Micahs in an attempt to gather information about Attis's location. I remembered with an uncomfortable knot in my stomach that I had given him my full first name. At the time I felt like it helped me blend in with the Provincials more. Now I just regretted it. When Gerrit had discovered I was with the Micahs, also some of the richest people in the country, he proposed marriage, saying that we could have whatever we wanted with the amount of money our combined fortunes would offer. Aside from Presid Bertley, this guy was the creepiest person I'd ever met. I had seen him one other time, walking into the capital building with a Runner I couldn't identify. Fortunately, he hadn't seen me then. Before that, I didn't even know he was involved with The Eye. Knowing he was did nothing to make me feel better about this chance meeting.

His shark-like grin broadened. "This is a coincidence, seeing you here, Claudelle." I squirmed as his eyes looked hungrily around the room. "Is your family here with you?"

"No," I said sharply, then smiled politely at his disappointment. "I'm here with friends. Speaking of which, I should probably go look for them."

He awarded my effort at escape by taking my arm and dragging me off to one of the pristine couches situated around the lobbies.

"I'm sure they'll be fine," he said dismissively. "Now, as I'm sure you remember, we have business to discuss."

"Business?" I echoed dumbly and suddenly found that I was sitting on the couch with Gerrit Stole's arm resting on the back of the couch behind my shoulders as he sat much too close.

"I'm sure you remember what I proposed," he said, giving me a look that made me wonder if he thought I was just stupid or if he thought I was trying to be smart. "We could both benefit enormously if our family's fortunes were to be joined," he said smoothly. "And we could be the catalysts that make that happen."

Not one for casual conversation, I thought dryly as he jumped straight to the point, as if our conversation from over a month ago had never ended.

"Oh, that, well –"

"We could do whatever we wanted," he interrupted. "There is no one who can't be bought. No rules would apply to us and we could live free of any restrictions. Doesn't that sound wonderful, Claudelle? A life free of restrictions."

I scowled at him. This kid was clearly a born con-artist. He had intuitively sensed the key thing I found appealing about wealth and now he was using it as leverage – a life without restrictions, under no government's totalitarian control. For a second I imagined that life, but with Gerrit Stole involved I had no doubt that nothing would be the way I imagined it. I was horrified with myself for even briefly thinking about what it would be like to accept his offer. He wanted the Micahs money and I had become to easiest path to attain that. That was all this was for him. A way to become even richer. I needed to find my friends.

"I'm actually quite content with my life right now," I said, not quite sure if I was lying or not.

"You're content running from a government that wants to exterminate you?"

For a second I thought I had just imagined the words coming out of Gerrit Stole's mouth. I stared at him, my stomach twisting in on itself as I realized the cold gleam in his eyes and the calculating smile were signs that I hadn't misheard him.

"What are you talking about?" I tried not to stammer as I feigned ignorance, but even I knew I wasn't doing well. Lying wasn't one of my best skills.

"Claudelle, really, please don't insult my intelligence like that," Gerrit Stole said, rolling his eyes. "I know why you're here and I know who you are. That's why *I* am here." He paused as if savoring the drama of the moment. "What I'm trying to say, love, is that I know what you are."

CHAPTER FIVE

I reminded myself to blink as my hands formed tight fists on my lap. I stayed silent. I wanted to think Gerrit was bluffing, but something told me he wasn't. He knew about me. He knew I was a Taint. He could ruin everything.

"By the way, your work on the DGA building, back in New Capil? That was impressive, I have to admit." I was surprised to find that his amusement seemed sincere. "To collapse an entire building." He paused and shook his head. "That must be some impressive power you have. And here all those government officials think the genetically mutated are good for nothing." He leaned closer and winked at me. "But you and I know better."

"What do you want?" I hissed, glaring at him with all the disdain I could muster.

He made a clucking sound. "Such hostility, Claudelle. Here I thought you were better than this. I have no interest in thwarting your rescue attempt, believe me."

"What. Do. You. Want?" I repeated slowly, my knuckles aching from clenching my fists so tight.

He shrugged his lanky shoulders again, adjusting his expensive suit, the fabric flickering with electricity under his touch. "I need a favor."

"Why should I do you a favor?"

He raised an eyebrow at me and laughed. "Besides the fact that I have attendants standing by with a picture of you and I sitting here, ready to send to Presid Bertley?" He laughed again like he had made a fantastic joke. "I can help you rescue your beloved."

"He's not my beloved," I said sharply.

Gerrit held his hands up in mock surrender. "Forgive me then, I just imagined that blush in your cheeks. So, are you willing to do me this favor?"

"That depends on what it is," I said, watching him as his eyes drifted lazily around the lobby, observing the ditzy and glitzy crowd go by, unaware of us.

"I'll tell you what I need done as soon as you agree," he said, his dark eyes drifting back to me and locking on mine.

"How would you help us find Attis?" I asked, lowering my voice as I noticed several curious Provincials looking our way.

Gerrit didn't seem to mind the attention we were attracting and, as if to encourage it, he brushed a strand of hair off my shoulder that had managed to escape the tie it had once been secured in. My fingers tingled and I could feel my powers coming to the surface. I wanted to knock Gerrit Stole's teeth out and get away from him as quickly as possible, but there were several reasons I couldn't do that. The most pressing one being that it would attract more attention than just the few glances from the love-struck passersby that we were currently receiving. I could only imagine the picture we were making, with Gerrit sitting mere inches away, leaning towards me with his arm on the back of the sofa, nearly touching me.

"I can't get you inside the Office of Retrieved Commodities," Gerrit said, his voice even lower than mine now as he looked me in the eyes. "But I can get you some tools that will help."

"In return for what?" I prompted.

He laughed and shook his head, flashing me a smile of unnaturally white teeth. "How foolish do you think I am? I won't tell you what the favor is until you agree to do it."

My fingertips tingled again and I swallowed my disgust with this entitled villain. All I wanted to do was use my powers to trap him in a bubble of light and throw him off the roof. I had done it before.

"Now, now, Claudelle," he said coolly, covering one of my fists with his hands. "You wouldn't want to do anything you might regret."

I tried to move my hand but he held it firmly against the sofa. I could feel the cheap, soft fabric of the sofa fraying under my fingernails. I wouldn't be able to move him without making a scene. I looked Gerrit in the eyes and saw a threat there, mingled with something else.

Fear? That's what it was. He knew what my powers could do – at least he thought he did. He knew I had collapsed an entire building and maybe he could sense that I was thinking about resorting to force yet again. I desperately wanted to. Not because I necessarily felt threatened by this brat, but because I wanted to punish him for making an impossible job even harder.

"I wouldn't?" I snapped coldly, feeling my powers subside as my fingers stopped tingling.

"Not while I have your caravan," Gerrit Stole said with a shrug, lifting his hand off of mine.

I blinked as I processed his words. Suddenly I had the front of his expensive shirt clenched tightly in my hand and we were nose to nose. I could feel my fingers tingling like crazy as my heart pounded irrationally fast.

"If you don't let them go I will kill you right now," I heard myself growl, not bothering to check whether or not I meant it, as long as I sounded serious.

"I will let them go," Gerrit Stole assured me in a smooth voice, although I didn't miss the edge of fear in his eyes grow a little more defined.

"You'll let them go *now*."

"Do you agree to do my favor if I help you find your boyfriend?" he asked, lifting his chin and looking down at me, probably trying to seem undisturbed by my show of aggression, even though I didn't miss the shake in his voice.

"You're going to let my caravan go right now." The tingling in my fingertips became a burning sensation unlike anything I'd ever felt before as I tried to restrain the powers bubbling beneath my skin, trying to jump out. "Regardless of what I agree to."

"Yes," Gerrit said finally. "I will let them go eventually. However, I'll let them go immediately if you agree. After all, you don't really have another choice, do you? I'm the only help you have."

I just glared, wondering if this kid could actually prove to be at all helpful. If he could actually help me find Attis, maybe this favor was worth it. Not to mention that he had my friends locked up somewhere.

"Fine," I snarled, releasing his shirt and shoving him away with one final stare into his eyes, trying to communicate all of my loathing with a single look.

Gerrit Stole leaned back and proceeded to smooth and straighten his rumpled shirt. To anyone else, it probably just looked like we were enjoying a close-range conversation. I, on the other hand, felt like I had just fought a battle. My adrenaline was through the roof.

"Well, then, glad that's settled," Gerrit Stole said with an air of finality, though I prided myself on the subtle shake that had appeared in his voice. He stood up and offered me an arm, to which I narrowed me eyes. "Come now, Claudelle. Don't be like that," he chastised me with an arrogant wink. "I'm taking you to your caravan."

I continued to sit on the sofa, glowering at him.

He sighed finally and said, "This isn't a trap. I have no doubt that you could break my neck in a moment if you had the desire."

I considered his words, and upon deciding they were true, I stood up and took his arm.

He didn't lead me out of the building, like I expected him to, but instead he guided me over to one of the lifts along the wall. When another couple tried to get on the lift, Gerrit stopped them and lowered his voice, muttering something that made them laugh. The girl with the orange hair raised her eyebrows at me and giggled. I raised both my eyebrows as the lift doors shut and Gerrit glanced over at me with a grin. I didn't bother to ask what he had told them. I didn't want to know. I watched as Gerrit tapped the top button on the control screen and a moment later we were stepping off the lift at the top floor.

My caravan was there waiting for me, pacing. Magely exclaimed in surprise when I came into the room, following Gerrit Stole. I quickly checked the room for threats and found several armed guards positioned around the windows, obviously put there by Gerrit to watch my friends.

"Stole," Keel said in disgust, addressing Gerrit.

I touched Keel's back as I passed him. It was a warning to stay calm. Keel hated Gerrit Stole – so much so that I wondered if they had some sort of history I was unaware of. I would have to ask. Keel had been furious when Gerrit danced with me what felt like ages ago.

When I reached Magely and Jag I noticed Magely's hands trembling and, with a frown, I asked if she was hurt. She shook her head and gave me a falsely cheery smile. When I asked Jag if he was okay, he just rolled his eyes and muttered that I'd better explain all of this soon. If only I had an explanation to give him.

During these brief moments, Keel and Gerrit appeared to be having a silent standoff. Gerrit's arms were crossed placidly across his chest as he leaned to one side like he was slightly bored. Keel's arms were crossed, but it was clearly in an attempt to restrain himself from punching Gerrit in the face like the rest of us wanted to. There were few times I had seen Keel's eyes flash with that terrifying gleam, like lightning in a storm. It was intimidating. I touched his arm as I stepped up beside him, facing Gerrit.

Gerrit shifted his attention to me with a cocky half-smile. I frowned at him before clearing my throat.

"Explain how you're going to help us find Attis."

***

"So," Keel said skeptically. "You're an informant for the Rebels?"

Gerrit grinned. "I am an informant for whosoever is willing to pay the right price."

I noticed Jag listening more intently than usual. Whenever talk of the Rebels down in Tac was brought up, Jag would become enrapt in the conversation. The more time we had spent at the Micahs', the more absorbed he had become in learning about the Rebels. For some reason, his admiration of the Rebels produced a strangling fear inside of me. I wished he would drop his interest with those idiots down in Tac, getting themselves killed every day for a cause that any sensible person realized was doomed to fail.

"How noble," Keel said with a snort, looking with undisguised disdain at Gerrit.

"Call it what you will," Gerrit said coolly, unbothered by Keel's obvious derision for him. "My moral fiber isn't the purpose of our meeting though. As I'm sure Claudelle will tell you in full once I depart, we have reached an agreement. I will lend you the tools you need to infiltrate the ORC and in return, you will do me a favor."

"What sort of favor?" Jag spoke up, and I didn't even have to look back to know there was a scowl on his face.

"I'm glad you asked, friend," Gerrit said, his mouth twisting into a smile on the last word, turning his back to us and clasping his hands, looking out the string of windows lining one side of the low-ceilinged room. "Come look out here with me."

We shuffled over to the window, silently grumbling at being ordered around by this egocentric rich boy.

"As I'm sure you know," he began haughtily. "That building across the street is the ORC. That is where Claudelle's one true love is waiting."

"He's not my true love," I snapped angrily. *People have got to stop saying that.*

"I will allow you to stay here, in this room, to keep your surveillance of the building and figure out a way inside," he continued, ignoring me. "I have already paid the owner of the building a handsome price for it." He glanced back at me as if he could read my mind, continuing, "The landlord doesn't know who you are, only that I want this room for my own private purposes. He has been instructed to not question any comings and goings from this place. I suppose you could call this room your headquarters."

We waited only somewhat patiently for him to continue.

"Once you are inside the ORC, I will need you to complete my favor. There is something inside that building that I have been paid quite well to retrieve, but have had no luck obtaining so far."

"What is it?" I asked, looking across the street at the window filled structure, which was currently as impenetrable to us as the prison I had assumed Attis would be trapped inside.

"I need three of the ID rings the security workers in that building wear," he answered, glancing back at me with a brief smile. "That won't be a problem, I assume."

We'll just have to knock out the guards.

Gerrit was looking at me with an expectant expression. I sighed and crossed my arms.

"We'll get them," I agreed, glaring at him.

Gerrit laughed and clapped his hands. "That's a good girl."

I clenched my fists and was considering trying to throw the brat out the window when I noticed the fury in Keel's eyes, ready to break over Gerrit's head. The energy he was emanating was even more lethal than mine. I put a hand on Keel's shoulder to restrain him from whatever he was considering. His eyes snapped down to my hand on his shoulder then travelled up my arm to my face. The burning anger in his eyes cooled a bit and when I raised both eyebrows, he nodded once then turned away from me as I let my hand drop.

"I also need a train schedule," Gerrit said. "Not a normal one. I need the master list." In answer to our unasked question he explained, "When the ORC is finished processing the commodities they retrieve, they send out shipments of the different items they have obtained all around the country by train. I need the schedule that has these shipments listed."

I heard Jag curse behind me and I felt similarly betrayed.

"How are we supposed to find something like that?" I asked angrily.

Gerrit chuckled. "You're resourceful, Claudelle. I'm quite certain you'll figure something out." He turned around and straightened his jacket. "Alright then, I had better be going. I wish you all the best of luck."

That's it?

Again, as if reading my mind, Gerrit paused before entering the lift and dug something out his pocket. He surveyed all of us for a moment before his eyes lighted on Magely.

"Ah, the youngest of the Micahs," he said with a smile. "Here. I imagine you'll understand how to work this tool better than your friends will." With that, he tossed her a small silver object and as she caught it and turned it over in her hands I realized it was a Tab.

As Gerrit Stole stepped into the elevator and his silent guards followed him, Magely tapped a button on the Tab and a holographic screen appeared in the air before her. The lift closed and then Gerrit Stole was gone without so much as a goodbye.

Keel snorted and turned away from the door. I knew exactly how he felt. *Good scrapping riddance.*

We were all silent for a moment before Magely piped up.

"Delle, how did he –"

I interrupted her with false optimism, because frankly, I had no idea how Gerrit Stole found us, and if I added that to my list of questions right now, I was going to lose all hope of ever finding answers.

"Who's hungry?"

CHAPTER SIX

Surveillance was a boring job and I hated when it was my turn. I had to tell Magely every time someone entered or exited the building and she would record it somewhere in the Tab. The idea was that after a week or two of our painstakingly slow observations, we would eventually have a good idea of what the best time to enter the building would be. Finding the right time to sneak inside was just one of our problems though. Once we were inside, we still needed some way to blend in. The ID rings would help get us through any of the locked doors, but if someone decided to report our suspicious behavior, there would be problems. Getting the ID rings was going to be especially challenging too since they couldn't belong to regular maintenance workers. Gerrit wanted rings with specific clearance levels, which meant we had to get them from trained security guards. That was going to be harder.

During one of my long stints at the windows, staring at the building across the street as the false light of the province began to fade, Keel sat down beside me. He had been joining me in my silent watch fairly recently over the past several days. Considering how rocky our friendship had been since he'd kissed me a few weeks ago, I was surprised he wanted to spend any time with me at all. I was surprised to find that I appreciated it though. The more I talked with him or even just sat in silence beside him, the more I wondered if my fears about him replacing Attis were nothing more than paranoia.

Keel was a good person, even if his father wasn't. Keel wasn't trying to take Attis's place in my life, it just looked that way. And although I hadn't decided whether it was fortunate or not, it was a simple fact that Attis and Keel had their similarities. Both of them cared about the caravan and wanted to protect it. They were both determined and persistent, probably Keel more so than Attis. Both of them could read me like a book, the kind of books Attis used to tell me about, made from paper. None of these were really bad traits to have. Especially when I considered what kind of life Keel had come from, I had to admit that his behavior was impressive. Despite my attempts to keep Keel at an arms-length, he had managed to know me almost as well as Attis, my best friend, who had known me since I was eight years old.

With nothing but time on my hands, I had ridden this train of thought over and over again with consistency. That's probably why I smiled at Keel when he sat down beside me this time.

"You're cheerful today," Keel said, giving me a quizzical look but returning the smile like he was pleased.

I shrugged and quickly returned my attention to the building. "Not really."

"Do you have something against being cheerful?" he asked.

"Not really," I replied, making a face. "It just doesn't seem like there's a lot to be cheerful about."

"Well, we're still alive," Keel pointed out, leaning back to watch the sun setting behind the ORC. "And to our knowledge, we've avoided detection this far."

I sat forward and rubbed my hand, thinking about it.

"I guess so," I said with a shrug, then laughed out loud at a grim thought that popped into my mind.

"What's so funny?" Keel asked.

I rolled my eyes but smiled at him. "First I'm too serious and now I'm not allowed to be cheerful?"

He raised an eyebrow but sighed, failing to hide his returning smile. "That's not what I meant. Why did you laugh?"

I returned my attention to the doors of the ORC and thought briefly about my answer. Keel waited, patiently. I couldn't tell if he was looking at me or the building across the street and I was too self-conscious to check.

"It's just funny that staying alive has become something to be cheerful about," I finally admitted, shrugging.

"It won't always be this way," Keel answered, his voice more serious than I had expected.

I took a chance and glanced over at him. The sunlight was reflecting off his grey eyes, making them look startlingly intense.

"You wanna' bet?" I asked, but I heard my voice falter at my own negativity.

"Okay," he said, flashing me a sly grin. "If you're happy with the way your life is after we rescue Attis – after all this craziness and running away is over – then you have to kiss me."

I think my mouth fell open in surprise at his forwardness. I struggled to retain my composure as I turned away from him, doing my best to radiate disgust.

"I change my mind, we're not meant to be friends," I said with a mocking roll of my eyes. "You can go away now."

Keel laughed and settled back on his elbows, a deliberate message that he was planning to stay for a while. "And now we're back to the subject of intrigue," he said lightly, ignoring my dismissal. "How about telling me what's wrong?"

I could feel my hesitantly sunny disposition instantly start to wane.

"When we were dancing, you told me you weren't afraid of our kiss," he clarified, glancing sideways at me before returning his attention to the sunset.

I wasn't sure I liked the way he said "our kiss". I didn't remember kissing him back. To be fair, the only part of my reaction that I remembered at all was the running away part. I glanced over to make sure that Jag and Magely were deep in their own conversation.

"I wasn't 'afraid'," I hissed, although even I could hear the uncertainty in my voice.

After a moment of silence, Keel sighed and suggested, "Maybe we should approach this from a different angle."

I glared into the bright light of the sun.

"Why didn't you talk to me for those two weeks after I kissed you?"

Every time he said the word "kiss" I had to stop myself from physically flinching. I felt like I had done something wrong even though it wasn't like I asked Keel to kiss me in the first place. But what if I had? It wasn't like there was anyone else standing in line to kiss me. There was no one to be jealous or upset by it so what did it matter anyways? There was no reason for me to feel guilty.

"The answer to that question," I began slowly, looking for the answer in myself even as I listened to the words come out of my mouth. "Is that I was confused."

"You were confused?" he echoed, raising an eyebrow at me like it made no sense. "How so?"

"I don't know," I said helplessly, crossing my arms over my knees and resting my chin on them. "Clearly I'm still confused, okay?"

I didn't have to look over to know that Keel's lips were pursed and his grey eyes had snapped sharply over to my face.

"If not for this mission, would you still be ignoring me?" Keel asked, and I could hear the frown in his voice as I avoided his persistent attempt at eye contact.

I shrugged noncommittally. "Don't know. I'm confused, remember?"

We were silent for several minutes. I rubbed my eyes tiredly, wishing they didn't feel so dry so I wouldn't want to close them. I had just started thinking about Steffy, missing her, when Keel's voice dragged me away from that emotional pitfall.

"You love him, don't you?"

Jittery energy filled my limbs and I felt the beginnings of panic start surging through my brain. At first I didn't know if I'd heard him right because his voice was so soft, barely more than a breath.

"What?" I asked, knowing my voice sounded too shrill to pass as nonchalant.

Keel didn't look at me this time, which made me wonder if he was as uncomfortable as I was. He didn't answer for a few moments, in which time I wondered if he was just going to pretend he hadn't said anything at all. Then he drew his knees up, mimicking my posture as we stared out at the fast-approaching night together. The air between us was electric with curiosity and discomfort.

When Keel finally spoke again his voice was calm with just an edge of amusement to it. "You were upset when I kissed you because you wished it would have been Attis instead of me. You love him."

I expected an automatic defense to fly from my lips without even having to think about it, but instead the words got caught in my throat and I couldn't find anything to say that didn't sound like a lie.

"Maybe," I finally admitted, feeling like maybe this whole conversation was a dream at this point, which was the only setting in which it wasn't completely intolerable. "It's not like Gerrit and Dr. Reece made it sound though. I'm not in love with him." *At least I don't think so,* I added silently. *How would I know anyways?*

"No wonder you were upset when I kissed you," he said with a snort, finally shifting his gaze over to me, making my cheeks burn as I continued to avoid his eyes. "You were thinking of him."

I shook my head and hoped my mess of dirty hair was enough to hide the terror I was experiencing at this topic of conversation.

"N-not like that," I stammered. "I mean, sort of. I mean I wasn't imagining that you were him or anything like that. I guess, I wondered what he would think of it. Of someone kissing me, I mean." *Stop while you're behind, Delle,* I warned myself ineffectually.

"Oh." For a moment I thought he was going to leave it at that. "So he's kissed you before?"

I physically jumped at Keel's question and looked at him in surprise.

"No!"

Keel was just as taken aback by my reaction as I was by his question. Well, maybe not quite as much, because he started laughing at my mortified expression.

"Our friendship was never like that," I insisted angrily when he didn't stop chuckling. "We're just friends. That's it. That's all Attis wanted."

Keel raised an eyebrow at me like he wanted to contradict me, but his mouth stayed shut.

"I mean, that's all *I* wanted too – that's what we both wanted," I continued. "Besides until recently with everyone teasing me about it, I never really thought about it. I always knew that Attis and I would stay together and take care of our caravan. I never thought it would change. It was the only relationship either of us had, so leaving it undefined never seemed like a problem."

I didn't know where these revelations were coming from, but nevertheless I heard them come tumbling out of my mouth right into the lap of the last person I should have been admitting them to.

"That makes sense," Keel said in a tone of voice that clearly meant it didn't.

I shook my head and kept my eyes trained on the doors of the ORC as I muttered, "You wouldn't understand."

"Not unless you explain it to me," Keel said pointedly, now giving me his full attention without pretenses.

The space between my eyebrows was starting to feel sore. I roughly rubbed at my forehead and tried to relax my eyebrows, hoping it might trick the rest of me into relaxing as well.

"You'd have to understand our past," I finally said with a sigh. "Attis found me when I was eight years old. He was twelve. I don't remember anything before that. I just remember him pulling me by the hand, leading me away from a house that was burning down. Attis told me how a troop of Runners had stormed the house and killed my parents, leaving them inside as they burned it down."

I glanced over and noticed Keel's hands had formed tight fists, the knuckles white. I felt a fresh sort of pain for him. His father had killed his mother because she was secretly a caretaker, hearing that his father was probably responsible for the deaths of my parents too was probably excruciating.

"Attis said they were killed because they refused to turn me over," I continued, listening to the sound of Keel's breathing, now the only sound in the room since Jag and Magely appeared to have fallen asleep a couple yards away. "When I first showed signs that I was genetically mutated – Tainted I mean – The Eye tried to take me away from my parents and give me to the Tinkers so they could dissect me. My parents hid me until Attis showed up. He had run away from parents – he never told me why." I realized suddenly that Attis's life before he met me was just one more of the many questions I wanted answers to. I frowned as I tried again to remember any minor detail about my life before Attis. I couldn't. "When they killed my parents and burned the house down, Attis took me away. We jumped the tracks and headed to Maricket where we met Richy and Jag. We picked up Steffy shortly after that, when she was just a baby. Her parents had just been killed too, you know?"

I could feel Keel's gaze hot on my face. It had never ceased, but now his voice faltered as he spoke softly.

"I didn't know that. Why –?"

"Same as my parents," I interrupted him, crossing my arms tighter across my knees. "Steffy was genetically screwed, being born blind in one eye and mute. Her parents were trying to protect her." *I did almost as poorly when I let those Runners turn her other eye blind,* I thought bitterly, remembering with a wince the tragic day a stray stun bullet had hit Steffy in her only good eye and completely fried it.

"I didn't realize," Keel said slowly. "You've raised Steffy since she was a baby – you and Attis."

I nodded silently, not wanting to speak until I knew my voice wouldn't betray me. I missed both of them so much that it physically hurt, like a weight in my lungs.

"Being away from her must kill you," Keel reasoned.

I didn't know how I felt about the sympathy in his tone. What if it wasn't sympathy at all, but pity? They sounded so similar. I didn't regret the decision to leave Steffy with the Micahs where she would be safe. I didn't regret saving her as a baby either. There was nothing to pity, so if that's what he was doing he could stop.

"It does, but it would be worse if she was here," I replied tersely. "I'd rather she be safe even if I can't be with her."

Now it was Keel's turn to silently nod.

"Attis used to tell us stories," I said ruefully, not entirely sure why I was admitting this. "About our future. He would look off into the distance and pick an object as far away as we could see, then tell us that we would find somewhere past that someday where the

Runners wouldn't bother chasing us. It was crazy, but it was the only future we planned. I think we knew we probably wouldn't live long enough to find a place like that, so it didn't matter if our plan for the future was vague and completely insane."

"I was never a part of that future," Keel commented, not like he was realizing this for the first time – more like he wanted *me* to realize it. "Your plan for the future didn't include me, so when I kissed you, it shattered the future you'd always banked on." He paused. "Attis was the only one you could picture your future with. Does that sound about right?"

I shrugged but felt the stinging pressure behind my eyes signifying that my emotions were trying to take over. I hoped it wasn't obvious that I was holding my breath to keep myself in check.

"Yeah," I finally answered, frustrated by the vulnerable croak in my voice.

Keel nodded like he'd assumed as much as he stretched out his legs in front of him, leaning back. I didn't miss how this new position had us sitting almost arm to arm. I wasn't sure whether to move or not. I felt like maybe I should move away to a more acceptable distance, but then again, he was the one who moved first so clearly he was comfortable sitting this close to me. I blinked and tried to focus.

"I guess," I began, stopping to let out a pent up breath again. "When you kissed me, I didn't run away because I was offended or scared. So, just, don't think that, okay? I know that's what it looked like – and I'm sorry. And I wasn't avoiding you because I was afraid you'd kiss me again either."

Again I had the sensation that maybe I was dreaming this conversation after all. I let my hands drop and sat on my knees so that I was angled towards Keel. I was too involved in the conversation now to back out without seeming like even more of an emotional wreck, so I was going to have to embrace this feeling-session, dream or not.

"I was avoiding you because you confuse me," I said bluntly.

Keel's eyes flickered over to mine and stayed there, waiting for me to elaborate.

"Before The Eye took Attis, I only had four people to worry about. Me, Attis, Jag and Steffy. Then we met you and the Micahs and the numbers grew. Out of everyone though, you're the most like him. You pick up on things about me that only Attis noticed before. You treat me like a partner, not like a parent or a child. Attis was the only one to ever treat me like that before – at least some times. It's not that I think you're trying to replace him –"

"I'm not," Keel interrupted, horror showing in his eyes as he realized that I must have been thinking of him as some sort of monster who wanted to keep Attis out of my life.

"I know you're not," I assured him. "But it's happening anyways. You naturally fill Attis's role in a lot of ways. Being around you makes me miss him and then it makes me wonder how things will function when he comes back. I can't seem to picture my old life with Attis reconciling with this new one, with you and the Micahs, but once we find him it's going to have to."

The sun was almost gone and the light was dim sitting by the windows now, but I could still see Keel as clear as day. His black hair was messy, almost in his eyes like Jag liked to keep his. I remembered that I had intended to cut their hair before we left New Capil. Still, his hair managed to soften the angles of his face and brought out the grey in his eyes even more. I flushed as I realized that I had been silently staring at his face, analyzing it, and liked what I saw. My cheeks grew even warmer as I realized that he was doing the same thing to me.

I cleared my throat and looked away from him.

"So long story short, you confuse me because you remind me of Attis and I don't like being confused," I said briskly, hoping my tone was lighter than it felt.

"And you love him," Keel clarified. "You love Attis."

I groaned and put a hand to my forehead. "You people have got to stop. Regardless of what people keep saying, Attis is not my 'one true love'."

Keel laughed softly and shook his head. "I didn't say he was."

"You implied," I muttered with a scowl.

He chuckled at my expression but there was a moment of silence before he continued, his voice softer. "Look, Delle, you do love this guy, right?"

Now I was glad the light was gone because at least he wouldn't be able to see me blush. I struggled to find words that wouldn't show how irritated I was while still being somewhat honest.

"Well, yeah, I guess – but not the way people keep implying."

I expected Keel to say something dismissive, like maybe telling me I was in denial. That's what the others did. It was exasperating. I was so ready to be irritated that his response surprised me.

"I understand."

I blinked and looked at him in surprise. "You understand?" This was especially unexpected because I wasn't even sure that I understood my last statement.

Keel nodded. The shifting lights from the buildings and parties going on outside reflected off his eyes, making them glimmer almost as intensely as they had in the sunlight.

"Just because you love someone doesn't make them your one true love," he stated calmly. "A one true love doesn't exist. At least, that's why my mother used to say."

I could feel my defenses start to fall at the mention of his mother. It had been less than a year since she was murdered. Keel had loved her. I knew that much. He hardly ever mentioned her, but from what he said about her I probably would have liked and respected her.

"She used to say that life is full of choices," he continued. "You can love a lot of people. However, eventually you have to choose which one you're going to love for the rest of your life, the one you want to love the most. Each person presents a different set of challenges you'll have to deal with and your life could go in completely different directions depending on who you choose. Obviously then, some choices are better than others." He nudged me in the ribs with his elbow and glanced over at me. "For instance, Gerrit Stole and Attis could both be choices, but your life would be radically different depending on which one of them you choose in this hypothetical situation."

"That's not even funny," I said darkly, Gerrit's snake-like grin flashing through my memory.

Keel continued as if I hadn't spoken. "But do you see what I mean?"

I thought about the life Gerrit would give me if I had accepted his proposal. I wrinkled my nose.

"Assuming you do actually love all your choices, there isn't always necessarily a right or wrong one, just different. And your life would be different depending on who you pick," Keel said thoughtfully, still watching me.

His constant gaze was making me uncomfortable, so I snorted and tried to dismiss his attention, saying, "Because there are so many people lined up to be my choices."

Keel grinned and shook his head, finally looking away from me. "Don't get me started, Delle. My point is that I think Attis is one of your choices. But don't be fooled into thinking he's the only one who cares about you."

I thought about his words as my heavy eyelids tried to close over my tired eyes. I hadn't spent a lot of time thinking about true love – or even love at all. I had certainly never heard anyone talk about it like Keel did. I hadn't really heard anyone talk about it all. Still, I got the feeling that Keel's opinion wasn't shared with the majority.

Something touched my hand unexpectedly and I startled back to wakefulness, looking over at Keel who was watching me with a worried expression. "Are you alright?"

I forced my hand to remain still under his touch. I didn't want him to see how conflicted I was about his sudden proximity.

I blinked a few times and rubbed my eyes with the back of my free hand. "I'm fine, I just nearly fell asleep. I didn't miss anything outside, did I?"

Keel shook his head. "No one has come in or out."

I knew that I needed to respond in some way, to prove that I had heard him and that I was awake, but the silence kept stretching longer and longer as my weary brain struggled to come up with a proper response.

"Well that's good," I finally managed to mumble, forgetting what I was responding to even as the words came out of my mouth.

"You can go to sleep, Delle," Keel said with a slight laugh. "I'll finish the rest of your watch."

I shook my head. I wasn't entirely sure what was going on. Was he still holding my hand?

"No, it's my shift. I can do it," I mumbled, forcing my eyes open wide to try and prove to both of us that I was awake enough to be productive.

He laughed again and lifted his hand off mine, reaching over to tousle my hair.

"Go to sleep already," he insisted.

At this point his voice sounded far away and it felt like it took me several minutes to turn the sounds into words.

I fully intended to protest, but instead my eyes closed and although I knew somewhere deep inside me that I needed to open them and finish doing something, I couldn't make myself put in the effort to figure out what that something was. At least in my sleep, all the questions of the day went away, and it was just me and Attis again – like it used to be.

***

I woke up disoriented, and after stretching my limbs and prying my eyes open to take in my surroundings, I realized why. I must have fallen asleep despite my protests and had – through no conscious decision of mine – ended up using Keel's lap as a pillow. One of his arms was draped over my shoulder, tracing the scar on my hand which was formed into a loose fist by his knee.

I waited for the inward groan of embarrassment I knew I should be feeling. After a second, I was confused but not displeased to realize it wasn't coming. More than anything I felt guilty, knowing that Keel had finished my shift for me and then had sat there all night with my head in his lap. His back was probably killing him from sitting up all night.

I struggled to roll off his lap and sit up, and as I did so I noticed that one of the chairs from across the room had been pushed over to us. Keel was using it as a backrest. I frowned, wondering how I hadn't woken up. I was usually a light sleeper. Jag must have moved the chair over for Keel when he got up to start his watch.

"Good morning," Keel greeted me, grinning as I blinked the sleep out of my eyes.

"Morning," I greeted him, cocking my head. I tried to read his expression for any thoughts he might have had about my choice of sleeping location.

His amused expression and mysterious grey eyes gave nothing away.

"Sorry I made you finish my watch," I apologized, standing up and stretching again, looking around for our food sack.

"No need to apologize," Keel said with a dismissive wave of his hand. "I actually enjoyed it."

Before I had time to puzzle out that response, Jag nudged me from behind with his shoulder, and when I turned to give him a quizzical look he gave me a cheeky smile. I scowled at him, but was again surprised to find that I wasn't as bothered as I might have expected. Jag shook his head and smiled, tossing me a bottle of water before dropping a couple skips into my hand. He sat down beside Keel as I started nibbling on one of the round crackers.

Eventually, I sat down beside Jag. Magely joined us on my other side. At some point I must have resigned myself to her presence in my caravan, because I wasn't irritated to find her sitting next to me. I handed her one of my skips and she turned to me with a look of delighted surprise, like I had just given her the sun itself rather than a barely edible cracker. I tried to smile back, but wasn't sure if my lips were making the right shape.

I looked out across the street along with Jag and Keel as Magely took out the Tab, tapped it, and scrolled down the first screen that popped up for her. We sat that way for a long time, sometimes pointing out the strange behaviors of the Provincials strolling by below us, sometimes discussing strategies to get inside the ORC. Sometimes we just sat in silence. I settled into the atmosphere with a familiar sense of comfort. It almost felt like the old days, except that Attis and Steffy weren't with us. Now it was Keel and Magely. It was different, but not too far off. I felt a twinge in my gut as I accepted that things would never feel like they had before, with my original caravan. Maybe things could still be good though. This morning was proof of that.

I had just reached this warm and cozy conclusion, when Jag's terse voice shattered my contentment.

"We have a problem."

CHAPTER SEVEN

"What is it?" I asked, feeling panic creep up my throat at the sight of Jag's morbid expression, usually reserved for especially terrible occasions.

His scowl hardened as he motioned me forward and pointed at something in the street below. I struggled to follow his direction, but the crowd of Provincials was impossibly thick and chaotically colorful. It was too overwhelming to pick out anything in particular.

"What is it?" I asked in frustration, hearing the pitch of my voice change as I fought off the feeling that something devastating was about to happen.

"Not what," Jag corrected ominously. "*Who.*"

A strangled sound came from Keel's throat and I whipped my gaze over to him to find his already pale face completely ashen, jaw tight, eyes wide with revulsion, locked onto a certain spot in the crowd below. He looked like he might be sick.

"Keel?" I asked, fighting to sound calm, not like my heart had just dropped into my stomach at the flash of rage in his eyes.

I exchanged a concerned expression with Magely who was clearly trying to hide her own fright as Keel's mouth moved, but words didn't come. When Keel's senses finally returned to him, I almost wished they hadn't.

"*My father.*"

I was leaning towards the edge of the window before I realized what I was doing.

His father. Presid Bertley. The man who had ordered us all killed, the one who had ordered his troop to shoot Attis. The one who took Attis away from us.

He was certifiably insane with a personal vendetta against me. I had tarnished his reputation when I slipped through his grasp in New Capil and he wasn't going to allow that to happen again. I shouldn't have been surprised that he was here now. Tracking us had been his main occupation since I was a child. The only protection I had from him was that he had no proof of my powers. Although it might be illegal to be a Taint, it wasn't illegal to be a Gypsy. He couldn't kill me without proof that I was Tainted – unless he managed to sneak under the radar somehow. However, I had the feeling that he wanted to do more than just kill me. He wanted to be vindicated first. He would wait until he could prove my genetic mutations to his colleagues so he wouldn't look like a violent idiot anymore.

Now that a name had been put to the object I was searching for, I saw him clearly. I couldn't imagine how I missed him before. Presid Bertley stood at just-below-average height, smoothing down his jacket, fingering the gun at his belt, probably loaded with blue electrobullets, the kind known for never leaving a person alive. Well, except Attis. Somehow he had managed to survive that, but I didn't want to try our luck. The crowd pushed around Presid as he stood motionless. He was the only figure dressed in black in the vibrant stream of Provincials. I don't know how I didn't notice him before. He looked up towards our window and all of us instantly reacted by throwing ourselves backwards, out of his sightline.

He knows we're here.

I felt the old blue electrobullet on my necklace cold against my fingers as I closed my hand around it. Supposedly I had saved Richy from being pierced by this very bullet using my powers – the powers that made me a danger to society in the sight of The Eye. I didn't have any recollection of the event, but I was only a child when it happened, so maybe I wouldn't remember. Or maybe I had just blocked it out. Apparently there were a lot of things I had blocked out – like all of my childhood before Attis found me. Richy had given the bullet back to me, telling me that I was strong enough to use the powers. He wanted to convince me that I could do good with them. I had disagreed with him at first; my powers were volatile and dangerous. They were too strong to control. But he wanted me to use them to protect my family – and that's exactly what I was going to do. Remembering Richy's faith in me and the bullet around my neck helped calm me. I released the little blue reminder and was pleased to find that I felt steadied.

"How did he find us?" Magely asked, her lower lip trembling like she was on the edge of tears.

Jag and I looked at each other for a moment and reached our conclusion in unison.

"Gerrit Stole," Jag said icily.

"He sold us out," I said, realizing how impossibly stupid I was to believe that wasn't his plan to begin with.

I looked over at Keel to see his jaw still working, eyes fixed on the window.

I stood up and backed away from the glass, leaning forward just a fraction of an inch to peer outside at the street below. I ducked back instantly to find Jag and Magely already on their feet.

"There are others coming," I said briefly. "Two more Runners just joined Presid on the street, so we can only assume there's already a troop surrounding the building.

"We need an escape," Jag said.

This wasn't the first time Presid and his troop had shown up somewhere unexpected.

"We need a destination," I said, pacing towards the center of the room. I shut my eyes for a moment and pictured the layout of the province in my head. Attis had always put me in charge of navigation thanks to my unusual talent for memorizing any map I set eyes on.

"If we go to Laylen's power district there will be more places to hide," I reasoned out loud.

"But also fewer witnesses if Presid and his goons try something," Jag pointed out.

I nodded, my eyes still closed. "I know. But in the wealthier parts of the province there are fewer places to hide."

"Are they going to storm this room?" Magely interjected.

I shrugged. "Maybe. More likely they'll wait a while to see if we come out. They won't wait forever though. Eventually they'll bust in here. So let's move fast. Why don't you pack the bags?"

With my eyes still shut I could hear her hurrying off to pack our meager possessions. I pushed away the instinct that it might be in vain.

"If they come up here we're completely trapped," Jag said somberly.

"I know, I know," I said, my eyes finally snapping open, unhappy with the only solution I could come up with.

"What are our options?" Jag asked, his hands clenched into fists at his sides, probably already sensing my answer.

"If they come up, we fight," I said, trying to sound much more confident then I felt, like we would actually have a chance, like this didn't resemble what happened on that rooftop when Attis was shot. "If they don't come up, we bide our time. Maybe try to contact Dr. Reece – we know she doesn't like Presid. Maybe she'll help us if we make another deal."

I didn't miss Jag's eyes flicking over to Magely, whose head was currently bent over my bag, shoving everything I had haphazardly removed back into place.

"Go talk to her," I said, looking over at the shimmery blonde hair of our newest Gypsy. "Tell her what to do if it comes to a fight. And see if she can use the Tab to find a live communication channel to reach Dr. Reece."

Jag tore his gaze away from the girl and looked back at me for a moment. "Thanks."

I nodded and as he moved quickly away to join precious Magely, I turned to regard Keel. He was still sitting on the ground, head in his hands now. I knelt down beside him, waiting for him to look up, to notice me.

He didn't look up, but his voice came out harsh and shaky. "I didn't tell him where we are. I swear."

I looked at him in shock. *He thinks we're blaming him?* It had been a long time since I had doubted his loyalty. Even when I had, that was before I knew anything about him. He had even more reason to loathe Presid than we did.

"I know you didn't," I assured him, surprised and sad that he didn't understand he'd proven himself.

It was partially my fault, I knew. Actually, it was mostly my fault. I had made it clear I didn't trust him from the start and had been mostly horrible to him. Still, I thought I had made it clear that I didn't feel that way anymore. I had even apologized for it one time.

He looked up then and met my confused gaze with an agonized one. "You do?"

"Of course," I said abruptly. "We know you wouldn't hurt us."

I waited for some sign of acceptance to cross Keel's face, but it was slow coming and hesitant when it finally did appear.

"Now get up," I snapped, trying to meet his eyes. "We need every member of this caravan to figure a way out of here."

I stood up and looked around the room. Reasoning with Keel had taken away the last edge of my initial panic.

I stationed Magely by the window, just out of sight of the people on the street, so she could keep an eye on the movements of the Runners outside while Jag followed her directions from across the room, trying to coax the Tab into contacting Dr. Reece. Keel was loading our only gun with the only bullets we had, yellow and red. I hated using the red ones though. If we had another option, I wouldn't even carry them with us.

I could feel the electric energy of the red lightning inside the gel casing when I picked them up. If someone crushed one of them, the explosion would be terrific and could set off the rest of the electrobullets in our store. I knew this from experience. Not to mention that I didn't really want to paralyze anyone – even temporarily – which was all these were good for.

I tried to direct my frustration at being helpless in a more productive direction, but until we got a hold of Dr. Reece or the Runners outside made a move, there wasn't much we could do. We had no way to act, only to react.

"When we find Gerrit Stole I am going to strangle him," I snarled, furious with the dirty Provincial for putting us in this situation.

"Can you kill a devil?" Jag wondered out loud, producing a harsh laugh from Keel.

"I'm willing to find out."

I was just revving up to continue this attack on Gerrit Stole's despicable moral character when there was a knock at the lift door. I whirled towards it and raised my hands instinctively, the familiar tingling energy running into my hands and out my fingertips in streams of blue light, curling away in all directions until I used my mind to form and mold them into a rectangular barrier.

The doors slid open and to my surprise, a women stepped inside with a bag slung over her shoulder. She wasn't wearing a dress like most Provincial women, but she wasn't dressed like a Runner either. I could feel Keel and Jag step up beside me as Magely backed away from the window. The woman held up her hands instantly and dropped the bag on the ground. I wasn't sure, but it looked like there might even be something like concern in her expression. Her eyes looked familiar. I shook my head just a fraction of an inch to dislodge these distracting observations. There was no way I had met this woman before. Still, her appearance was bizarre in more than one way. Even through the bluish film of my lights, I could tell that her hair was blonde and cropped short, very unlike the fashion of the times. However, it was streaked through with red, with little strands of lights glimmering against it, making it look like fire.

"I'm here to help," she said quickly, addressing only me as the lift door shut behind her. "I promise."

"How could you help us?" Magely asked, surprising me since she usually wasn't the first to speak.

The woman's gaze snapped over to her and she stared for a moment too long before nodding at her bag. "Everything you need to make it out of this building is in there. I can take you somewhere safe."

I could see the hard set of Jag's mouth out of the corner of my eye and I knew he didn't believe her. Out of the corner of my other eye, I could see that Keel was considering her story. He had noticed the same things. She didn't look like the Provincials who usually tried to kill us, but she didn't look like a Gypsy either. However, this could easily be a trick that Presid was using to convince us to come outside.

I separated my barrier, keeping one half of it up, hovering in front of us like a shield, I let the other half of the lights relax into their natural tendrils, one for each of my fingers, and made a motion with my hand like I was picking something up. As the tendrils explored the woman's bag, I closed my fist and used the lights to lift the bag off the ground and bring it closer to us. This was a trick Richy taught me once. I had to wonder if he somehow meant for me to use it for an occasion like this. Richy always seemed to know more than anyone else.

"Check the bag," I muttered to Jag as the lights let it slouch to the ground in front of him.

Jag scowled but knelt down and unzipped it, pulling out fistfuls of Provincial clothing, wigs included.

"What is this?" he asked suspiciously.

"Disguises," she answered, raising an eyebrow like it was obvious.

"Why would you help us," I asked, returning my attention to the strange woman across the room.

She grinned. "I made a promise once. Besides, we Taints have to stick together, don't we?"

I unconsciously clenched my left hand and the blue lights hardened into a sphere of blue glass before shattering and dissolving as the pieces clinked to the ground.

"Who are you?" Keel asked in a low voice.

The woman's eyes never left my face even as she answered his question. "My name is Mona." Her eyes finally flicked over the rest of my caravan. "And we need to go now."

I could tell my caravan was waiting for me to respond. I knew what the votes would be on this one. None of them liked it. This Mona woman was suspicious and she knew too much. However, we literally had no other option except for fighting our way out or waiting for Dr. Reece to be helpful – if she even could be.

"Okay," I said slowly, letting the other half of my light harden and dissolve as Mona finally dropped her hands. "What's the plan?"

***

It wasn't an intricate plan. It was stupidly simple in fact. All we had to do was put on the Provincial costumes over our own clothing, then exit the building like some of the hundreds of colorful people who came in and out every day. We just had to act like we belonged and move fast enough to not be recognized, but not fast enough to be suspicious.

I clung to Keel's arm like a magnet, trying to look lighthearted and carefree, like the other Provincials swarming around us. Magely and Jag followed closely behind, and if their grimaces looked anything like the expression on my face, I doubted we would make it past the door.

To my surprise, we did make it out the door, despite the fact that the long blue wig I was wearing severely impeded my vision. I reached up to brush the plastic hairs out of my eyes long enough to just miss making eye contact with the devil himself; Presid Bertley was looking in our direction. I focused on keeping my breathing even and looking as vaguely happy as the next Provincial.

"He's seen us," I muttered as Presid started shouldering towards us, shoving unaware bystanders out of his warpath.

I glanced around quickly and caught sight of Mona, our mysterious possible-savior. She was striding some distance ahead of us, leading the way while managing not to associate herself with us. All of our belongings were shoved into the bag she brought with her, slung on her back. She didn't know we'd been spotted.

Unless this was the plan all along.

Presid could have sent the woman in just to draw us out so they could snatch us as soon as we hit the street.

"No, he hasn't."

I flinched at the voice right by my ear and turned to see Magely's eyes focused on something far away, even as she continued speaking. "He sees a blonde girl at the corner of the building. Her hair is up, like you usually wear yours. She's turned away. I believe he thinks the girl is you."

"How do you know that?" I whispered, glancing over at her then back at Presid to see that his gaze had indeed passed over us and continued on to something behind us.

Magely dropped her eyes and Mona, who had broken free of the crowd ahead, finally glanced over her shoulder to check on us.

"Magely?" I asked, confused and frustrated by her obvious unwillingness to explain.

"Not right now," Jag snapped at me, which felt like a slap in the face considering Jag hardly ever snapped at anyone.

"I asked Magely, not you," I snarled back, glaring at him, more upset by his tone than by Magely's inability to explain what was happening.

As we passed another Runner we fell silent and I tried to relax my eyebrows enough to look calm if not happy.

"It's okay," I heard Magely mutter to Jag and didn't miss her squeezing his hand out of the corner of my eye.

I turned to Keel and he met my eyes, also confused although not as suspicious.

"I'll tell you when we reach Mona," Magely assured me, now reaching over and putting a hand on my arm.

We couldn't have reached Mona soon enough for several reasons. She was waiting for us in the alley behind a building down the street, out of sight of Presid and his troop. It was also outside of the river of Provincials, flowing up and down the busy walkway. More than anything though, I was curious about Magely's hesitancy to explain how she knew what Presid was seeing. I had been certain that he had seen us. For a split-second I had pictured our arrest and felt the weight of our failure. Except, according to Magely, Presid had never seen us at all.

Before I could say anything, Mona was already turning around to lead us in a new direction and we were walking again, this time hidden from the eyes of the public. I looked over at Keel and suddenly realized I was still holding onto his arm. I dropped it and diverted my attention from him even as he turned to glance at me with a quizzical look.

Magely said something to Jag and he nodded, falling out of step with her and into step with Keel as they paced a few feet ahead of us, still several yards behind our mysterious guide. Magely stepped up beside me and slipped her arm underneath mine, linking us at the elbow.

"Delle," she started abruptly, her high voice almost too soft to hear.

"Yeah?"

"There's something I probably should have told you before now," she admitted.

I tensed. I didn't like secrets, but I wouldn't pretend I didn't understand the necessity of them.

"Okay," I said coolly, waiting for her to continue.

The silence between us stretched on for a moment too long before Magely's words finally spilled out. "I can see what other people see."

I would have asked for clarification, but she provided it on her own.

"All I have to do is focus on someone and suddenly I can see through their eyes."

It took me a second to understand that she wasn't just saying she was an extra-perceptive individual. For the millionth time that day, I felt like the wind had been knocked out of me.

"Magely," I didn't miss the shake in my voice as I said her name, seeing the flawless Provincial girl in an entirely new light. "You're Tainted?"

CHAPTER EIGHT

I was so stunned to learn that Magely was Tainted I hardly paid attention to where Mona was leading us. In the wake of Magely's confession, I was struggling to feel threatened by this woman. I was becoming sloppy. The Delle from a year ago would never have agreed to follow this strange woman in the first place. A lot had changed since then. I couldn't imagine what Attis would say about some of the choices I'd made in the last three months.

"Does Jag know?"

Magely nodded. "He guessed it yesterday. That's part of the reason I came with you. I really couldn't chance using my power when I lived in New Capil. Especially not now that my family is being watched so closely. There were already rumors about how odd I was circulating among my parents' friends. I just don't have the self-control not to use my powers. I can't help it and it was becoming obvious."

Clearly not to all of us, I thought unhappily.

"I don't know how you do it, Delle."

I took me a moment to realize the girl was looking for a response. I was still in a daze over this new information, trying to process what it meant. If Mona was a Taint as well, that made three of us in one group. We were practically begging to be exterminated.

"Do what?" I managed to ask, as I knew she expected me to.

Magely was the youngest of the Micah children. She was the only biological child that Appy and Sacrif had been able to conceive. Out of all the children, she was the last I would have expected to be a

Taint. All of the other kids were former Gypsies. Magely wasn't. They had all been on the run from The Eye at one point or another. Magely's record was spotless. How did the only child with a spotless record end up being Tainted?

"The way you suppress your powers," Magely continued, pulling me abruptly out of my thoughts again. "It's a constant battle to stop mine from taking over. I have to fight it back every day so I don't start staring into space, seeing what other people are seeing, in the middle of a conversation. I have to make sure I don't say anything that could lead someone to guess that what I see isn't what everyone else sees. Using my powers comes as naturally as breathing. I don't know how you resist yours. I only managed to live in New Capil for so long because my power isn't immediately visible like yours."

I frowned, uncomfortable with this slight diversion of topic. Attis was the one who helped me understand the importance of resisting my powers. I had spent the better part of my life ignoring them, shoving away the urge to let the extra energy building up in my fingertips explode into streams of blue light. When I was younger I didn't control the powers well and bad things happened – at least, according to Attis. I had no memory of those things. Hiding the powers, even from myself, was essential.

"Me either," I mumbled, hoping she would drop the topic.

There was silence between us for a few minutes, before I forced my mind to leave this new information alone and turn to things I could better understand to keep from going insane. I glared at Jag's back, irritated that he hadn't felt it important to tell me about Magely. Channeling this feeling of betrayal was much simpler than trying to understand the implications of having a second Taint in our caravan.

We had been walking for what couldn't have been more than ten minutes when Mona stopped. I tensed at the change in pace and looked around, expecting to see Runners lunging at us from every direction. We had turned down several different alleys, away from the fake plants and mist machines that attacked out of nowhere with jets of water. The steep walls of two surprisingly drab buildings rose up on either side of us, but I didn't see a doorway anywhere. If I had to guess, I would say we were on the outskirts of the power district. The smell of poverty hadn't quite reached us yet, but there were thickening signs of it all around us.

I peered ahead and strained my eyes. I wasn't surprised to see the dully gleaming dome of the power plant that created energy for this province, probably only a few miles away.

"Where are we?" I asked abruptly, narrowing my eyes at our mysterious guide as she turned around to face us.

"You can take off your disguises now. It will be difficult to get where we're going while you're wearing those."

I scowled at her evasive answer, but didn't hesitate to slide the bright blue wig off my head and slip the dress off, revealing my own clothes underneath. The rest of my caravan followed suit as Mona unzipped her bag and tossed us our jackets and packs.

"You'll want those," she said, nodding at my jacket as she started stuffing the disguises back into the bag. "Where we're going is a lot colder than this."

"And where exactly is that?" I snapped, shoving my arms through the sleeves and glaring at her.

"I told you I could take you somewhere safe," she answered as she zipped the bag and slung it back onto her shoulders.

"And?"

She crossed her arms and met my glare with one of her own, widening her stance, daring us to challenge her. "We're here."

"This is safe? Standing in between two random buildings in full view?" Jag asked, voicing my own skepticism.

I didn't miss the hint of a smirk on the woman's lips. That expression, like so much about her, looked familiar. I scowled even more, reminding myself that there was no way I could know this woman.

"Not in between the buildings," she corrected Jag, looking at him sharply for a moment before her eyes drifted to me. "Below them."

I felt Keel looking towards me, like I might understand what she meant. I assumed Jag and Magely were doing the same. The truth was, I had no idea what this woman was talking about, but I didn't want to make my caravan nervous by admitting that. Instead I crossed my arms and tried to look unimpressed and unconvinced.

The woman shook her head and the smirk widened before she turned to one of the walls and grabbed the handle of what appeared to be an old, rusted, trash chute, leading into the ground. We had used a trash chute twice now as an escape from The Eye in near-death situations. Needless to say, I wasn't happy to see one again. I was even less happy when the strange short-haired woman motioned us through the door that slid open to reveal a black abyss.

"Strangers first," Keel said dryly, raising an eyebrow at her and sweeping a hand towards the dark hole.

I silently applauded him for his unaffected tone and the forethought to make the woman go in first. She shrugged as if this was no problem and turned around, stepping backwards into the hole and beginning the descent down what appeared to be a ladder. We surrounded the chute with mutual feelings of mingled dismay and curiosity, looking down as the top of her head disappeared from sight.

Mona's voice rang out clear as a bell from somewhere below, echoing off the walls of the chute. "Are you coming or not?"

I scowled and could feel a rude response coming to my lips when Keel's hand on the small of my back stopped me.

"I'll go in first," he muttered, stepping around me, his hand brushing against mine as if by accident.

I could feel the memory of the gash in my hand itching again as I remembered the last time I climbed a ladder. The metal was rusted and broke off under my hand, tearing it to ribbons. It had become badly infected, but Keel saved it using some of the tricks his mom taught him to care for injured Gypsies. All that was left now was a neat scar along the side of my hand.

As soon as Keel's head disappeared down the chute, I turned to Magely and Jag, crossing my arms and nodding at the rusty hole.

"You two in next. I'll go last."

I didn't want to say that this could be a trap. Runners could come storming in as soon as we were all precariously clinging to the ladder leading down into a strange pit. I didn't need to say it. They knew. Even Magely for once, in all her Provincial ignorance, seemed to understand that much.

I didn't miss the quake in Magely's step and the shakiness of her breathing as she made her way toward the ladder. I didn't miss Jag putting a hand on her arm to reassure her as he helped her find the ladder that neither Mona nor Keel had needed help finding. I managed to maintain a neutral expression as Jag descended the ladder after the blonde girl and I followed suit. As I stepped down two rungs and my eyes became level with the top of the chute, I realized there was a symbol scratched into the side. It was a fish. I paused, considering what this could mean. I had only ever seen the fish used as a symbol to mark the location of a Caretaker.

Why is it here?

From somewhere below, I heard a voice echo up to me, ordering me to close the door of the chute. I stepped back up a rung and reached over my head. After several attempts to make my short arms reach far enough to catch the door, I managed to grab the edge of the handle and yank down with all my strength, the rusty wheels clicking and screeching on the tracks as it slid to a firm close, throwing us into complete darkness.

We continued our descent through the pitch black and just as I was wondering how terrible of an idea it would be to use my powers to brighten the space up, Mona's voice reverberated up to me.

"You know, Delle, you could probably give us some light."

I scowled and shook my head. I certainly wasn't going to use my powers while Mona wanted me too. For all I knew there could be cameras hidden in this shaft, waiting for me to produce damning evidence of my powers. That's all Presid would need. A moment later I heard a thud and a surprised grunt.

"Jag?" I asked instantly, alarmed.

"We're at the bottom," he replied, even as my foot searched for a rung and found flat ground instead.

"Now what?" Keel asked.

As if to answer his question, there was a dull clunking sound before several lights hanging from the ceiling started flickering to life. Keel's arm stopped me from moving further into the cavernous area. I frowned at him then followed his gaze and realized why he'd stopped me. I instantly held out my arm to stop Magely and Jag as well. Right on the edge of where the light reached was a group of about ten men, dressed in black, leveling guns at us. I wish I could say the situation was unfamiliar.

Just as I was about to curse and use my powers to throw Mona into a wall, our traitorous guide held her hands up and shouted, "Weapons down!"

I didn't unclench my fists even after all of the guns had been lowered and the posture of our almost-attackers relaxed. A man and a woman from the armed group holstered their weapons and approached Mona, who met them with a tired smile.

They spoke in voices just above a whisper, but, with all of the littlest sounds echoing off the walls of what I could now see was a tunnel, I was too distracted to catch every word. I did take note of the words "refugees" and "ORC". Keel and I exchanged bemused looks.

I looked over at Magely to see her taking in every detail of our surroundings with a mystified expression. Jag, on the other hand, appeared to be thinking deeply about something, like he was right on the edge of finding an answer to something. I watched as understanding dawned in his eyes. I had to read his lips since I couldn't actually hear the word he spoke.

Rebels.

"Keel," I whispered, darting my eyes at him then at Mona and her new friends. "These people are Rebels."

He was silent for a moment.

"What does that mean for us?"

I eyed the motley crew of dark-clad strangers blocking us from continuing down the tunnel.

"I don't know," I admitted, something I didn't like to say. "I've never actually met a Rebel before."

Keel turned to me and raised an eyebrow. Maybe I was just being paranoid, but he looked amused by the fact that I didn't know what was happening. I gave him a narrow look and returned my attention to Mona just as she turned to face us.

"We know why you came to Laylen," she said calmly. "And we want to help you."

I stepped forward, feeling the eyes of my caravan on my back.

"What do you think we came here to do?" I asked, again realizing that my own overly-confident stance was mirroring Mona's, who only stood an inch or so taller than me.

"To retrieve your friend," she responded, cocking an eyebrow at my accusing tone.

Jag's voice sounded deeper than I remembered and I nearly jumped as his voice filled the tall, narrow tunnel.

"Why would you help us? Don't you have better things to do?"

Jag always did have a talent for voicing exactly what I was thinking.

"You'll be helping us as well," Mona said with a slight smirk.

"How so?"

"There are certain items within the ORC that we were going to pay an informant of ours to retrieve. However, circumstances have changed and now we need someone else to retrieve them for us." Mona's voice changed from business-like to dry and humorless about halfway through her explanation. It was a tone that I myself used when discussing a certain individual we knew.

Gerrit Stole. He had admitted he was an informant for the Rebels – or anyone else willing to pay him an absurd amount of money. I didn't have to look at Keel to know that he had come to the same conclusion. I could feel it.

The couple who had approached Mona moments before now faced us. The man first looked at his partner then at us, frowning. Apparently he didn't like what he saw. I met his eyes and hoped he was getting the same message from me.

"We can get you in," the woman beside him broke in. "And we can tell you how to get out."

Mona sighed, like she was tired of this negotiation. "Look, kid, either way you're going into the ORC. It's pretty clear at this point that nothing is going to stop you. Let us make it easier and safer for you."

I could feel the hesitant agreement coming from the rest of my caravan. I looked around at them and waited for some sure sign that they wanted to take this deal. They nodded at me, almost imperceptibly. I turned back to the small army still blocking our path.

I squared my shoulders and looked directly at our strange new allies. I wondered what Attis would think about what I was about to say.

"Okay."

CHAPTER NINE

As Mona and her people led us farther down the tunnel, the air became colder and damper. I was once again grateful for the jacket the Micahs had given me. The tunnel was lit with the same unusual lights we had first seen inside the tunnel. The lights I was used to gave off a bright white shine, while these gave off a dingy yellowish glow.

"This is just one of the many tunnels created at the beginning of the last world war," Mona said in a hushed voice, even though the entire company could hear her voice echoing. "Very few are even aware that they exist."

I thought I detected a note of pride in her voice. I saw the man from before at the head of the group. He looked back at Mona and shook his head disapprovingly. If our guide noticed, she didn't let on.

"Do all the provinces have these?" Magely asked, not even bothering to disguise the awe in her voice.

I rolled my eyes at her childishness and Keel hid a smile.

"Most," Mona said, flashing her a quick grin, her eyes lingering on the girl for a moment longer than was necessary.

The man from before appeared beside us. He scowled at Mona and said pointedly, "Perhaps we should discuss the items that need to be retrieved."

I found the man's rough attitude both threatening and irritating. I also didn't like that he seemed to disapprove of Mona telling us what was going on.

"Let me guess," I piped up, putting on my sweetest expression. "You need three ID rings from the security workers and a master train schedule."

The man's face didn't change at all, except for hardening just a bit. His eyes went to Mona, and although the expression didn't change, it was clear that it was an accusation.

"She didn't tell us," I assured him with a smirk, while at the same time wondering why I felt the need to defend this woman. "Your flaky informant – Gerrit Stole, right? He told us what the items were. We were the ones he blackmailed into doing his dirty work. He mentioned that he was working for a group of Rebels."

Now the accusing eyes were turned to me. Keel scowled, seeming to grow taller at my side.

"Of course you're Rebels," I said frankly. "Who else would live in hidden tunnels and plan to break into one of The Eye's favorite facilities?"

The man gave me a hard look, but was distracted by Keel looming closer. The man narrowed his eyes then looked back to Mona, giving her a look that made it clear we were *her* problem now. Then he turned and began making his way back to the front of the ranks.

"He doesn't like you," Mona observed.

"I hadn't noticed," I said snarkily, feeling a slight rush of adrenaline now that the tension had passed.

"And you're such a pleasant person, I can't imagine why," she muttered, just loud enough for my caravan to hear.

Jag snickered and Magely hit him on the arm in my defense. I knew that Keel would be smiling too, so I didn't bother to look in his direction.

"So," I finally began. "How are you planning to get us into the ORC?"

"We've been surveilling it for the past few days," Magely added. "I guess that might be a pointless effort now."

Mona shook her head. "We can always use more data on the ORC. We'll compile what we know when we reach the base."

"The base?" I echoed.

Mona gave me a sideways look, and the strands of lights in her hair glimmered. "It's not much, but it acts as our headquarters for this region of the country."

"How many people are there?" Jag asked curiously.

"Several hundred at this base," Mona said over her shoulder. "It's one of our smaller operations."

"No," Jag said, quickening his pace to keep up with her. "No, I mean how many of you are there in all?"

Mona looked over at him and smiled slightly at his interest. "Several thousand."

"How does someone enlist?"

Jag's question scared my heart into my throat. Why was he asking questions like that?

"Not that any of us want to," I interjected fiercely, desperately hoping that Jag was just curious and wasn't actually considering something as crazy as enlisting in a hopeless fight.

Mona seemed surprised at my outburst. She looked over her shoulder at me for a moment and seemed to be considering something. She pursed her lips and returned her attention to Jag.

"That's a question I can have someone answer for you later. For now, we're here."

Just as I was about to ask where "here" was, we came to the end of the tunnel. There was an enormous cavern in front of us. It was the size of a small town, and there were people everywhere. There were walkways suspended above our heads and buildings several stories tall, even though we were obviously still underground.

As we cut through the busy rush, I realized that there was something similar about all of the people moving about. They all seemed to be moving intently in their own directions, single-minded, determined, probably off to save the world. They were all dressed in similarly dark clothes – rags really – except for Mona. With her red-streaked hair and Provincial clothing, she was a splash of color in a sea of greys and blacks. I looked at the blue leather of my jacket and then around at my caravan and realized that we probably stuck out here as much as she did. That was a new one.

The group of armed Rebels who had met us at the tunnel now dispersed amongst the crowd, and the couple who had spoken with Mona and briefly addressed us split off in a different direction. The man gave one more glance over his shoulder at us before disappearing from view.

"This way," Mona directed, motioning to the metal stairs bolted to the side of one of the buildings.

Keel led the way this time and when the stairs finally ended, we found ourselves on a railing-less platform at the top floor of the building. Mona let us into the poorly built structure through a door I hadn't noticed before. Once inside, she nodded at a plastic table with mismatched chairs drawn around it.

I sat down beside Keel and he touched my hand under the table. I felt my cheeks warm and hoped I wasn't visibly turning red. I looked over at Keel to see what he wanted, but he wasn't looking in my direction.

Mona brought a pitcher full of lukewarm water to the table and asked Jag to grab a few of the cups off the counter behind him.

"I guess you could call this the dining room," Mona said with a wink.

I looked around at the walls that were obviously pieced together from scrap metal, covered with a thin layer of off-white paint that was probably meant to keep the rust away but was peeling off in jagged curls, doing little good.

"There's no one in here," Magely observed.

"Everyone's busy," the woman answered with a shrug. "When people come in here, it's usually not for more than a few minutes. Just enough time to use that old microwave in the corner and grab a beer out of the fridge."

"Beer?" Jag asked dumbly.

Mona grinned and passed him the pitcher of water. "Fill up those glasses and I'll get one for you to try. It's hard to find now, seeing as it's contraband, but beer used to be the drink of choice for the masses."

I gratefully accepted my water from Jag and when Mona popped the metal cap off the glass bottle she had taken from the fridge, I vaguely remembered Richy once fantasizing about the beer of old. I watched as Jag took the first sip. His expression was confused at first, then pleased. Magely seemed fond of it as well. I wrinkled my nose.

"Now the masses have had the sense oppressed right out of them so they think that syrup they drink tastes better than this," Mona added, watching with an amused expression as Keel swallowed the drink with an unhappy expression and shook his head.

"I take it you don't like it?" Mona asked him.

Keel shook his head. "I can't say I do."

She shrugged and dismissed him. "It's not for everyone."

I considered the glass bottle that had been passed into my hands. I smelled it and wrinkled my nose again. I didn't like the smell. I looked at Keel who gave me a pitying look in return before I took a sip. The taste was less offensive than the smell, but it probably wasn't something I would choose to drink. I shook my head and slid the bottle across the table into Mona's hand.

"So," Mona said, pulling out a chair and sitting down, looking at each of us in turn. "I'm guessing you have questions. I'm probably one of the only people in this place willing to give you answers, so you'd best ask them now before the general shows up."

"That guy from the welcoming party?" Keel asked, raising an eyebrow.

Mona nodded. "He comes off a little unfriendly because he is. He's a good leader though."

Keel's other eyebrow lifted to match the first. He obviously wasn't convinced.

"So, questions?" she prompted, her eyes returning to me as if I was the most likely to ask them.

"Is Mona your actual name?"

I looked incredulously to the short blonde girl who seemed younger than ever with her random question hanging in the air.

Mona just raised an eyebrow in response.

Magely blushed her delicate pink and continued, "Sorry – that was dumb. I've just never heard that name before. I wondered if it was a nickname or something."

Mona laughed and shook her head. "I guess I can understand the curiosity. My full name is Monalise Corentine. But please do me the favor of never calling me that. I only go by that name when I want to blend in with the high-class Provincials. It's too fancy for my taste."

"You said you're Tainted?" Magely asked, surprising all of us again since she was generally the timidest.

Mona nodded, seemingly undisturbed by this question. I, however, was only growing tenser. Maybe Magely didn't understand yet, but sharing information about yourself – especially if you happened to be a Taint – was never a good idea.

"What's your gift?" the blonde girl asked, leaning forward eagerly.

I blinked. Richy always referred to the powers as a gift. So did Magely's parents. I don't know why it hadn't occurred to me that Magely would too. I, on the other hand, was more likely to call it an enormous pain in the neck.

"I can sense others like us," Mona responded easily.

"You can sense them?" I heard myself ask in disbelief, even as I flashed back to the moment that Mona burst into our room above the spa, when she stared at Magely for a second too long.

Mona nodded.

"How did you know where to find us?" Keel asked.

I was more interested in how she knew about us at all and why she decided to save us, but I somewhat patiently waited for an answer to Keel's question.

"Gerrit told me," Mona said wryly, finishing off the rest of the beer and setting the bottle aside, drawing her cup of water closer. Now she looked directly at me, as if I was the only one at the table. "He told me he had a group set up for the job we needed. He told me where he stashed you. He also told me of one particularly high-risk individual in the group who was rumored to have the impressive ability to create blue lights and use them as a weapon."

I raised an eyebrow. "I'm guessing Gerrit heard that from Presid."

Mona shrugged. "He did admit that it was only a rumor. I knew it wasn't though, as soon as I stepped out of that elevator."

If it was possible, my frown deepened even more.

"How are you planning to get us inside the ORC?" Jag broke in impatiently, his curiosity about our rescue more than satisfied by this point.

Mona redirected her attention to Jag a moment before Keel touched my hand again under the table. I was grateful that the woman was distracted, although I didn't know why I cared whether she knew that Keel was holding my hand or not. I didn't expect Keel to keep hold of my hand, but he did, pulling it over and resting it on his leg, our fingers intertwined. I carefully didn't look at him and he didn't look at me. I did look at Magely though who was pretending she hadn't noticed our joined hands. From the little smirk on her mouth and the pinkness of her cheeks, it was obvious that she had. I imagined that Keel was probably somewhat amused, knowing I was flustered.

"What do you need ID rings and a train schedule for anyways?" Magely added, innocently nosy.

"That's classified information," a gruff voice interjected.

We all turned to see the man and woman from before striding towards us from the doorway across the room, bringing a trail of three more people behind them. Mona stood up to greet them, nodding respectfully to the general and the other unnamed people. I discretely pulled my hand out of Keel's and placed them both on the table in front of me, palms down, waiting for the offensive man to begin our meeting.

"Which one of you has the data from your surveillance?"

Magely raised her hand meekly into the air. I rolled my eyes.

The general turned to one of the unnamed and nodded at Magely, who held out her Tab like she was afraid she might get bitten. The unnamed took the Tab with a muttered thanks and nod of his head, then he was gone.

"He's going to add your data to ours, to make sure we plan the infiltration most effectively," Mona explained, sitting down as the general and his right hand woman sat down, along with the other two strangers who still hadn't spoken a word.

Magely nodded, still shyly, like a child. For just a moment I felt a sharp twinge in my chest as I thought of Steffy, also shy. I wanted her to be here with us, but that was just a feeling. In my head I knew that was the last thing I *really* wanted. I wanted her to be safe, no matter how badly I missed her. I bit the inside of my cheek to distract myself and returned my attention to the gruff man eyeing us, calculating.

"Let's get this over with," he finally said, exhaling heavily.

We spent the next hour discussing how we were going to infiltrate the ORC and then get back out with an extra person if all went according to plan. I silently thrilled at the idea that I could be mere hours away from reuniting with Attis but I kept my mouth shut for the most part. Throughout the meeting, I caught Mona watching me with a thoughtful expression. I didn't know why, but whenever she looked at me her expression became almost sad. I still had the nagging feeling that there was something about this woman I should recognize.

"Any questions."

It was more of a statement than an invitation to clarify the plan. The general clearly thought our entire mission was foolish and doomed to fail, but Mona had already admitted that they badly needed the ID rings and the train schedule.

We were a risk they would have to take.

CHAPTER TEN

The infiltration plan was built for two. I, of course, was one of the lucky winners and Keel was the other.

Keel had been watching me all morning with a concerned expression that I didn't fully understand. Jag's expression had been especially dark as well, so much that it even infected our ever-cheerful Magely who looked on the edge of a nervous breakdown when we said goodbye to them at the end of the tunnel.

I, on the other hand, was feeling nothing but energetic and hopeful. Today I would see Attis again. It had been months since we thought he was gone forever. Now we were going to get him back. We could finally go to that place at the edge of everything we could see and live safely and peacefully. Or even if we didn't do that, at least we would be together.

Attis.

I wasn't usually a sentimental person, but as we crawled out of the trash chute and into the muggy false-atmosphere of Laylen, I couldn't help but think it was a lovely day to break into an important government facility.

It was early in the morning – too early for any of the Provincials to be awake yet. The sky was barely light and the weather hadn't yet decided what course it was going to take for the day. The air smelled like opportunity – and the fake perfume of the mutated flowers growing on every corner. Keel was strangely silent for most of the morning. He didn't speak a word to me from the time we left the trash chute until we were within sight of the ORC.

He stopped me suddenly, grabbing my arm so that I almost stumbled mid-step.

"What is it?" I asked urgently, instantly searching for some sign of a threat to the mission.

"Are you sure you're ready to do this?" he asked quietly, stepping closer to me, forcing me to focus on him and nothing else, his hands resting firmly on my arms.

"To save Attis?" I asked, feeling like his question alone was a near-betrayal, not sure how he wasn't infected with the same enthusiasm I was.

"Not exactly," Keel said, shaking his head. Before I could rudely criticize his lack of faith, he continued. "The Eye has had him for weeks now, he might be a different Attis than the one you remember."

I looked up into Keel's eyes. I was used to seeing them turn stormy when he was this intense, but instead they looked hesitant, kind of like the sky looked when you couldn't tell if it was going to rain or not.

"I know, Keel," I said, surprised by the sheer sincerity of the concern in his voice. "Believe me, I know. A day hasn't gone by that I haven't imagined what they might be doing to him."

Keel searched my eyes again, as if he didn't quite believe me. Then he surprised me again by pulling me closer and resting his forehead against mine, closing his eyes.

"What's wrong?" I asked, feeling a sharp, new concern – this time for Keel's sake. He didn't answer for a moment and I fidgeted. We were on a tight schedule. "Keel, what is it?"

"Nothing's wrong," he said, but I didn't miss the silent "yet" at the end of his sentence. He opened his eyes and looked at me intently. "I just want you to be prepared. You don't know, Delle. My father used to tell me about what they do to Gypsies they capture."

"Those were the Gypsies they put in jail," I corrected him. "They keep moving Attis around – it could be different."

"But what if it isn't different?" he asked, lifting his head and looking into my face, apparently wanting a real answer.

"It's not something we can predict," I said, feeling the tension in my throat as my brain mentally ticked away our remaining minutes before the plan went fully into action. "If Attis is different than before – if he needs more help with –" I was struggling to find the answer that Keel wanted. "We'll be there for him. I mean, I will," I added. "I hoped you would too –"

"I will," he assured me. "I know you love him, so I'll do whatever I can for him."

I felt just the hint of a smile coming to my lips. Keel was really a wonderful human.

"Thank you," I said, putting every ounce of the sincerity I felt into those words.

He surprised me then by cupping my chin in his hand and kissing me briefly on the mouth. I flushed when he pulled away and turned, taking my hand without another word, guiding us down the street.

This kiss was different than the last one. It wasn't so desperate. It was sweeter. It felt natural. It was even – nice. I wouldn't have minded another.

I mentally slapped myself. We had a job to do. We were going to get Attis back and I could deal with everything Keel-related later. I might not be able to turn the clock back to the way things were before Attis was taken, but I could at least get part of it back. I didn't have to let all of it go.

Keel reached into his pocket and turned on the black box the Rebels had given us. It was a camera-killer, just like the one Sacrif had given us when we broke into the capital. By the count of ten, all of the cameras in the vicinity should be knocked out.

We moved quickly and silently around to the back of the building, where the security workers were just changing shifts. There were no witnesses, just like we counted on. The workers saw us approaching, but didn't have any reason to assume we were anything but normal Provincials, lost, asking for directions. They didn't see it coming until we were too close to stop. I felt the tingling in my fingertips and the blue lights appeared, giving them just a split-second to react before they both lay unconscious on the ground.

90

Keel slipped off their ID rings and handed me one, which I put around my thumb since it was too big to stay on any of my other fingers.

"Two down," Keel said.

I stood watch while he dragged one of the security guards back into the chair in his security station by the door, leaning him against the wall and taking the dark glasses out of his jacket pocket to put over the man's closed eyes.

The other guard was less fortunate. We dragged him through the backdoors, entering with the power of the ID rings and shoving him into one of the stalls in the nearest bathroom. We were just about exit the bathroom, and I was feeling more encouraged than ever that we were going to get away with this, when a third, enormous female security worker entered.

I briefly recalled what someone had once told me about how men and women used to have separate bathrooms. They had changed that during feminism's fourth big wave though. Still, the well-muscled woman looked confused to see Keel and I standing there together. She quickly went the way of the first two guards and with all of the guard's unconscious for a limited amount of time, part one of our job was complete.

"That makes three," Keel said, pocketing the last ID ring as I slowly opened the bathroom door, looking around to make sure the room was clear and no one was about to appear from the hallway we'd come from.

"Time to split up," I said, stepping out the door with Keel right behind me.

I turned to go in my planned direction, but Keel said my name and I turned back around.

"What?" I asked, feeling the jitters of nervousness starting to quake through my bones at our separation.

He shook his head and said, "You're not going to ditch me like last time?"

I smirked, even though it was ridiculous to smile in a situation like this. The idea of ever leaving him behind just seemed so ludicrous, it was funny he should even ask.

"Promise," I said firmly, forcing myself to put on a more serious expression so that he would know there was nothing to worry about.

He raised an eyebrow at me and then shook his head, giving me a crooked half-smile, like he didn't entirely believe me but he appreciated the sentiment.

"Good luck," I added as he turned away.

He shook his head again, but I saw the special, hidden smile he only used around me. Then he walked away.

***

The door of the lift slid into place and I tapped the icon for the top floor of the building. We didn't know exactly where they were keeping Attis prisoner, but the only living quarters in the ORC were on the highest floor. I doubted they had him gagged and stuffed into a corner of one of the offices, like they did when they kidnapped Steffy. She was small and easy to hide. Attis was less so. If he wasn't there, I would have an entirely new problem to deal with.

I tapped my foot impatiently, even though the lift was extraordinarily fast. I hoped Keel hadn't run into trouble. The only weapon he had was our gun and there weren't many electrobullets to go with it. The general had refused to lend us any weapons, saying they were in short supply and we could do without if anything Mona had told him about my powers was true.

The door to the lift slid noiselessly open to reveal a large, white room. I looked out of the elevator and peered upwards to see that the entire ceiling was a skylight, flooding the room with a pale, early morning wash. I carefully stepped off the elevator, expecting to find myself in a hallway, but instead it looked like I was in someone's luxuriously spacious living room. The only furniture in the room was made up of some sort of translucent material, besides the couch which appeared to be made of the same stain-dissolving material as the Micahs's. There were clear bowls stacked high with too-perfect apples, their skins just a shade too red to exist naturally. I took one more step away from the elevator and a movement from the corner of the room caught my eye. I whirled to face it, knowing that my fingertips were probably glowing blue light even as I forced myself to restrain the powers.

The figure across the room was dressed like a Runner, although the suit jacket that was part of their uniform was carelessly slung over the back of the chair at his side. I hesitated as the figure began to turn. The man's hair was blonde and there was something about his height and the broadness of his shoulders that seemed familiar. A moment before he lifted his eyes to me, I knew who it was.

"Attis!"

Even as I cried his name I knew I was being too loud, that I needed to remember we would still be in trouble if we were caught. As I watched the recognition and then surprise in his eyes turn to happiness I felt invincible. I had found Attis. Nothing could be wrong.

I ran across the room and wasn't at all surprised when Attis swooped me into a hug that lifted my feet off the ground. My heart was pounding ridiculously fast and I wasn't sure if I was breathing, I was clinging so tightly to him. I buried my face in his neck, refusing to loosen my grip even when he set me down.

"Della," he said, laughing and peeling my fingers from his shirt, pushing me back a few inches so he could look at me.

I knew I was smiling from ear to ear. I didn't realize how much I'd missed the special name only he called me. He captured my face in his hands, observing me with excited blue eyes – the eyes that I had seen every day for so much of my life and knew I could depend on no matter what.

"How did you get here?" he asked, dropping his voice, lifting his eyes from my own to look towards the lift, another reminder that I needed to ground myself and deal with the situation at hand before I continued my rejoicing.

"It's complicated," I said. "I'll explain later, but we need to leave now."

Instead of answering me, he pulled me back into a bone crushing hug, one hand tangled in my hair at the nape of my neck. "I missed you so much."

"I missed you too," I said softly, feeling like my heart might burst from the relief of finding my best friend, the person who had guided me through life and stood by me for the past eight years.

We stayed like that for a moment and I slowly felt myself relaxing against him before I remembered that Keel would be waiting, that we needed to leave or risk being arrested.

"So much has changed, Attis," I said, pulling away again, grabbing his hands and trying to pull him towards the lift, not sure why he was resisting. "I'll explain everything once we're out of here."

He pulled his hands out of mine and sat down abruptly in the chair behind him.

"What's wrong? Are you okay?" I asked, feeling my smile falter.

He rubbed a hand over his face and was silent for a moment before he lifted his eyes to me and smiled again, although this time it was a different smile – one I wasn't sure I had seen before.

"How's Jag?" he asked.

"He's fine. He's good," I stammered. "He'll be much better once we get you back."

"And Steffy?"

"Not here. She's safe," I assured him, glancing over my shoulder at the lift again, knowing that a security worker could burst through the door at any moment. "She misses you."

He nodded and a little bit of the smile I remembered returned. "And you, Delle? How are you? You look... great."

"Oh, thanks," I said, bewildered again by his questions that I definitely felt could wait for later. "You too."

Now that I really looked at him, I realized it was true. The sun was just starting to rise outside, and the first rays of sunlight were shining through his hair, which was neat and trimmed shorter than I remembered. It wasn't the shaggy mess I was used to, but his eyes were the same crystal blue.

"So we both look good," I joked and was pleased to hear his short laugh in response. "I would be happy to discuss just how good we look in much greater detail once we leave."

He laughed again, but it was a sharper sound than before. "You don't know how much I want to go with you."

I didn't comprehend what he was saying for a moment. When I did register it, I knew I must not have understood.

"What?"

It was a small sound to describe the icy feeling in my veins as Attis looked at me with the expression he reserved for especially hopeless occasions. It was the same expression he'd worn when we were facing Presid and his troop on the rooftop where he'd been shot. He averted his eyes then and dropped his head.

"I can't come with you."

I suddenly had the awful feeling that I was in a nightmare and had never actually woken up that morning or started our mission to save Attis. I wanted to argue, but his expression told me it wouldn't do any good. The relentless pounding of the air conditioner against my back was too real. The sick feeling in my stomach as my entire world came crashing down was too genuine. This wasn't a nightmare, no matter how much I wanted it to be. It was a feeling I recognized; it was the same feeling I had when I thought Attis had been killed.

I tried to swallow and choked. My brain struggled to find a different way to interpret Attis's announcement.

"Why?" I sounded like I'd just been punched in the stomach; the word was almost soundless coming out of my mouth.

"This is how it's supposed to be," Attis said, shutting his eyes and pinching the area between his eyebrows, like he was trying to recall something he had memorized a long time ago.

I didn't respond. I just continued to stare at my best friend with a stupid expression, not understanding – maybe not wanting to.

"From the beginning, I was never supposed to stay with you," he sighed, dropping his hands and lifting beautiful, defeated eyes to me. "It wasn't part of the plan."

I was certain now that gravity was shifting. The sky creeping closer and closer would eventually break through the glass ceiling with no other purpose than to utterly crush me.

"The plan?" I echoed dumbly, still not able to form fully coherent thoughts, much less words.

Attis dropped his hands to his knees and followed them with his eyes. He didn't say anything, even though I waited for what felt like an eternity. In the back of my mind I was aware that my situation was still risky, that time was an important factor in making it out of this alive. It didn't matter though. Maybe being shot would feel better than the turmoil I was currently experiencing.

"The plan," I repeated, hearing my own voice grow stronger as a switch snapped in my brain, channeling all of my fears into anger. "– was to find somewhere for our caravan to live in peace, away from The Eye and the Provincials and everyone else who wants to hurt us." I could hear my voice rising but didn't stop myself. "You promised we would find that place, Attis – *together. That* was the plan. *That* is the only thing any of us ever wanted."

The tone that Attis responded with was so empty that it froze my anger for a moment.

"I know," he said, still not looking at me. "That's all any of you ever wanted."

"*Us?* You wanted that too, Attis," I insisted, hearing the desperation in my voice, knowing in the back of my mind that there were too many unexpected factors involved to assure that future now. "We can still have it. Just hurry up and come on!"

I tried taking his hands and pulling him out of his seat, but his hands fell limply out of mine and he remained firmly seated.

"I can't," he said, shaking his head, his voice stronger, his shoulders straightening as he found some internal resolve.

"Why not?" I asked, the anger rising again to disguise the terror I felt at losing him again, especially now that I was only inches away from getting him back.

He shook his head and stood up, looking down at me before half-turning away, like looking at me was painful or maybe just disgusting. I grabbed his arm, unaware of my actions even as my fingers dug into stiff muscle.

"No, you're not doing this," I insisted, forcing him to look at me by stepping back into his sightline. "If you're not coming with me after everything I've done – that we've all done – you'd better have a scrapping good reason."

My blood was pounding in my temples at this point as I stared into his stony face. He looked back at me with matched determination. *Matched.* That was us. We were always perfectly matched from the start. At least I always thought so until this moment. Now it was clear that the scales were tipped. Something was horribly unbalanced. I didn't know how much or by what, but something was horribly, terribly different.

"You want to know why I won't come with you?"

His voice was flat and his eyes were glimmering in a dark, dead way I hadn't seen before. I thought I knew Attis as well as I knew myself. Had I always been wrong or had something changed?

"Yes," I snapped, despite every inch of my being telling me that I didn't want to know.

He shook his head and made an awful sneer, turning his face away from me.

"I deserve the truth!" My voice sounded shrill, but I didn't seem to be in control of it anymore. I wasn't even in control of the words coming out of my mouth, begging for information that by all indications was likely to tear me to pieces. "After all of this – everything we've been through together – everything I went through to find you again – you'd better tell me the truth, Attis, or so help me I'll –"

"Stop," he commanded, narrowing his eyes at me. "Stop it, Delle. We both know you can't do anything drastic here without getting caught. If you want the truth, I'll tell you, alright? It doesn't matter anyways."

Despite what he said, all of my nerves were telling me that the truth *did* matter. A lot. I tried my best at a fearless, determined expression, but wasn't sure if the face I was making resembled anything close. Whatever my expression, my body was shaking uncontrollably and that was a dead giveaway.

"The truth," he said, spitting out the words like they were bitter. "The truth starts with a lie."

A lie? I wasn't sure if I echoed this out loud or in my head.

"Do you remember when I found you?" he asked, looking me in the eyes, like he was waiting for me to give the wrong answer.

"Yeah, sure," I stammered. "It was in Harris. My parents were killed protecting me before you saved me from the Runners."

"Is that what you remember?" he asked, his voice dropping to a softer level. "Or is that what you remember me telling you?"

I was confused. I didn't know anymore. There were so many things I didn't remember – things I had blocked out.

His voice was even softer when he continued, making the entire confession even more gut-wrenching. "Part of what I told you was true," he admitted. "Your parents died protecting you. Their name was Corentine. That's all I remember about them, so don't ask me anything else. I wasn't the one to save you though."

I blinked as a little crack appeared in the mirror of my life. I had the vaguest feeling that I should remember that name from somewhere.

"Your father's sister was there. She wasn't supposed to be there, but somehow she found out that The Eye was coming to take you. She didn't get far. Scars – his real name is Presid – and his troop found her and took you. Not before you went ballistic with your powers though and nearly tore Presid's hand off when he tried to take you away. They mixed up your memories then gave you to me."

I cocked my head as two more cracks appeared in the mental picture of my childhood. *Mixed up my memory?*

"It was an experiment," he said coolly. "I was planted, Delle. They knew you were Tainted. I wasn't an orphan or a runaway. My parents are both alive and well, still living in New Capil. The Eye wanted me to watch you, to examine what you would do left on your own, what your powers would do. It was a test designed by some of their top scientists. They thought you would be a good candidate, since your powers were so easy to monitor. They wanted me to test your capability for control – when you were little you had none. Then at an appointed time, once they felt like they had all the information they needed, I would fake my death and the Runners would arrest you in order to hand you over to the team of scientists who designed the experiment." His mouth twisted into something resembling a smirk now. "Although I guess only half of that last part was accomplished."

There were so many cracks now that there was no more room for a picture. Everything I knew about myself shattered and I felt myself physically stumble back. I didn't know where to look. At Attis, at my trembling reflection in the enormous window behind Attis, at my traitorous hands, the blue, smoky lights curling around my fingers despite all the effort I had put into controlling them over the years. I stepped back again unsteadily, thinking for a moment that I might actually vomit. Attis didn't stop me, or catch me. He just watched me. He observed me in a distant way, apparently like he'd been doing for most of my life.

"You were planted?" I heard myself breathe, my voice scratching painfully out of my throat as I tried to combine the Attis I thought I knew with the one in front of me, telling me he'd been a traitor from the very start.

Attis shrugged, like it was of no importance. "You wanted the truth, Della."

I shook my head and reached out, hoping my hand would find something, anything to steady me as my world swirled down into a dark pit I couldn't see the bottom of but could feel waiting to swallow me whole. It hit me then like just another blow to the heart: Maybe I had been in love with him. Surely I must have been, to be so blind to who he really was.

Jag, my brain gasped, because I didn't have enough to think about. *Steffy.*

"You lied to us," I heard myself croak.

The break in my voice horrified me so much that I felt myself reaching for anything that could prevent me from making a greater fool of myself. Anger was the only thing I found, the only thing that could stop this unfamiliar pain bleeding out of me.

"All of us," I snarled. "We cared about you and the whole time you were just pretending."

Now that some of my reasoning skills had turned back on, it all seemed unbelievably dumb. I always wondered how Attis knew so much more than me. He knew the layout of the building we escaped from when we thought he was dead even though he claimed to have never been there before. All of the questions I'd been pondering were answered with the one undeniable fact that Attis, the only person in the world I had ever completely loved and trusted, was a traitor.

"You never felt anything for us," I accused savagely. "You were planning to betray us the whole time."

Attis didn't say anything. His jaw was hard and clenched. It was obvious that he didn't plan on responding to me at all. I stepped quickly away from him. It was clear that there was nothing left for me here, even though my emotions were screaming at me that I couldn't leave Attis, my best friend whom I loved. Every other part of me was sending off more practical alarm bells, telling me I needed to go.

"I should have known you were a traitor," I snarled, even as I backed away, towards the lift that would take me back down to where Keel waited by a backdoor. "I guess it's on me," I said in disgust, ignoring the part of my brain that insisted I could see a sharp spark of agony behind Attis's angelically deceptive eyes.

He doesn't care. This is what he wanted all along. He never wanted a future – at least not one that involved me.

"If only I had realized sooner," I said, forcing myself to look back into the cool eyes I would never see again. "I could have saved you a lot of trouble and stopped you from saving my life all those times."

His expression didn't change, but his fists were clenched so tightly the knuckles were white. There was a moment of silence so long I finally assumed he wasn't going to respond. I reached out and tapped the icon for the bottom floor as I stepped back into the lift.

The lift door was already descending when he finally replied, "Maybe you could have."

The lift door locked into place and I gasped for breath, feeling like I had been holding my breath for the last ten minutes. His last words stung more than they should have considering everything I'd just heard. Still, it felt like the final blow, struck to a person who was already fatally wounded and bleeding to death. It was one more kick, just for good measure.

I felt like there was something else that needed to be said between us, but I couldn't think of one more word to say. The Attis I thought I knew was dead. He had died that day on the rooftop and it was unbelievably idiotic of me to believe that I could ever get him back. The only thing I could think as the lift made its swift descent, was that I wished I had never found out Attis was alive.

CHAPTER ELEVEN

I shifted between feeling enraged to walking on air, disoriented and unaware of my surroundings, sick at my stomach and not quite sure if I was walking in a straight line as the floor tipped under my feet. I had slipped back into a daze when Keel found me, wandering aimlessly near our meet up point. He grinned and held up a Tab and I numbly remembered the master train schedule we were supposed to retrieve. At least Keel had gotten what he came for. As his steps towards me quickened, I knew I needed to respond, but my brain might as well have been a rock inside my skull, heavy and unthinking. As he looked at me, I knew there was something wrong with his expression, something I was supposed to react to. His eyebrows were coming together in that way was supposed to mean something to me, but it didn't.

"Delle?"

His voice sounded far away. He looked far away too, even though he was standing only inches away now.

"Delle, what happened?" His voice was tense – no, it was urgent. That was the word. He was alarmed.

I shook my head and could feel the rock that was my brain colliding against my skull with each small motion. I noticed that Keel straightened up and looked around. How long had it been since we started our mission? Not more than thirty minutes, surely. It felt like days. The guards we had left in the bathroom stalls weren't even missed yet. The plan couldn't have gone off more perfectly – except in one way.

"Where's Attis?"

This time I couldn't even shake my head. I just stared at him, surprised and furious in a distant sort of way that there were tears stinging behind my eyes.

"Is he –"

"Not coming," I whispered, dropping my eyes, just like Attis had when he refused to come with me, when he admitted that he had been lying to me about my entire life.

Keel didn't say anything for a moment. I didn't lift my eyes.

Finally, I heard him exhale a heavy breath and say in a pained voice. "We need to go."

He was right. I knew that. When I didn't move, he put an arm around my shoulders to try and guide me in the right direction. My mind flashed back to the last embrace I'd experienced. The daze disintegrated and I jerked away from Keel, once again fully aware and fully furious.

"You knew!" I accused. "You tried to warn me before we came, saying that he would be different. You knew something was wrong!"

Keel held up his hands and stepped away from me. I didn't miss the surprised look that flashed across his face, the hurt in his eyes, but at the moment I didn't care how he felt.

"Whoa, Delle, I never –"

"How did you know?" my voice came out in a desperate cry that I instantly wished I could take back. "Did your father tell you all about it?"

Keel's hurt expression instantly closed off. His eyes stormed as he looked back at me, completely silent. I knew I probably looked insane, as I glared at him with eyes that I'm sure were bloodshot with the effort it was taking not to burst into hysterics.

"You can blame me once we get back to the base," he said in a perfectly neutral voice, leaving me to wonder how offended he really was.

I didn't respond. Instead I whirled away from him, crossing my arms over my stomach as I stomped away from the ORC, where the security worker in the booth was just starting to stir and Provincials were just starting to approach the building to begin their work day.

***

I returned to my dazed, unfeeling state on the walk back. I remained that way even when my feet hit the bottom of the chute, sending a painful shock through my knees and ankles. We still hadn't spoken as we began our hike back into the tunnel to reach the base. Keel didn't try to talk to me. He was probably furious at me for accusing him of communicating with his father. I knew it was wrong and the small part of me that hadn't died with the Attis I thought I knew felt terrible for saying it, knowing I had only said it to hurt him, not because I actually believed Keel was talking to his father.

The anger came back when I noticed the bright light ahead that meant we were about to come upon the Rebel's underground base. I froze, realizing I would have to tell Jag that Attis wasn't ever coming back. Even worse, I would have to tell him why. I reached out and steadied myself against the wall. I was sure I was going to throw up.

"Delle?" Keel asked warily, stepping closer but not attempting to touch me.

I didn't blame him after what happened last time. I shut my eyes and tried to steady myself, to keep from being sick. I wasn't angry at Keel anymore. I didn't know if I was actually angry at him before, or if he was just a convenient target. Surely even if he had known something was wrong with Attis, there was no way he could have known the full truth.

"I hate him," I spat, leaning heavily against the wall, trying to shut out the memory of the cool blue eyes. The words were just reflex, they didn't make me feel any better, no matter how fervently I meant them. "I have to tell Jag." I was only fairly certain I was talking out loud at this point. "What am I going to tell him?"

Keel was silent for a moment. "The truth would be a good place to start."

I practically snarled at this response, as wise as it probably was. "It's going to hurt him."

"It won't hurt any less if you wait," Keel said.

"I know." My voice was cracking again, so I cleared my throat and crossed my arms, leaning against the wall and looking at my boots through the dim light. "I know that, it just doesn't make it easier."

Keel sighed and ran a hand through his hair. "I'm so sorry, Delle. I really am. If there's any way I can help at all, please tell me."

I nodded and stood up straight. The blind anger was cooling now, the nauseated feeling in my stomach wasn't as overwhelming. I waited for the daze to replace it, but it didn't come. I wondered if I had narrowly escaped a complete mental breakdown. The world seemed to be coming back into focus around me. I shut my eyes that felt itchy and dry from the effort of holding back pointless tears.

"I'm sorry," I muttered, pressing my fists against my eyelids. "I'm sorry I yelled at you and accused you. I shouldn't have."

Keel's cool fingers wrapped around my wrists and pulled my fists away from my face. I tensed at his touch, but I didn't have the urge to start screaming at him again.

"It's okay."

I pulled my hands out of his, suddenly uncomfortable with him touching me even though I could clearly remember enjoying it the day before – or even that morning when he kissed me.

"There is one way you can help," I admitted, knowing that I was grasping at air, since nothing could make this situation any less horrid. "After I tell Jag, just be there for him. You know, in case he wants to talk or something. Jag used to worship him when he was a kid."

Not just Jag.

Keel nodded. "I will."

"Thanks," I said, trying to put emotion into the word, but failing.

"And who's going to be there for you?" Keel asked as I squared my shoulders and prepared to enter the base.

"I'm going to be busy," I said, remembering where I knew the name Corentine from as my brain clicked and whirred back to life. "After I talk to Jag, I need to talk with my aunt."

There was a long pause between us as I took a deep breath and Keel processed my words.

"Your *what*?"

***

Telling Jag went better than I expected. He didn't yell or curse. He didn't even look on the verge of tears. He just stared into space as I listened to myself repeat everything Attis had told me. It didn't sound any better coming from my mouth than it did from his. I didn't vomit though, which was more than I expected of myself considering my gut was twisting and knotting so violently that it was almost debilitating.

The general and his second in command listened silently, accepting the Tab and the ID rings from us with a brisk nod that was probably supposed to express their undying gratitude. Magely, on the other hand, was leaking silent tears in a constant stream. I couldn't look at her. If I did, I knew there was a good chance I might start crying too. Keel was listening silently, probably starting to understand why I had acted the way I did before. Mona was the last person in the room. She didn't nod and she didn't cry. She didn't even appear to be listening. Her face remained impassive as she leaned against the counter, staring at a spot across the floor, never lifting her eyes.

The general and his second in command turned to go once it was clear that I was done debriefing. They thanked us again and commended us on our swift work. They didn't mention Attis. I was glad they didn't. Once they were gone, I hugged Jag. I expected to be the strong person in the embrace, the one supporting the other. That wasn't the case though. Jag's arms were strong and unwavering around me. He didn't seem shaken at all. As our hug ended I pulled back and looked up at him, realizing that he was taller than I remembered.

I stepped away and turned around, remembering the only other thing I needed to complete before I could surrender into the internal chaos waiting for me.

"Mona," I said frigidly, meeting her indecipherable look with one of my own. "Can I talk to you?"

"Sure, kid." She stretched as she came away from the counter and gestured for me to lead the way.

Keel nodded at me as I left the room. He would do what I asked. He would be there for Jag – even if it didn't seem like Jag needed it. Jag had Magely too now, who was already stroking his hand in a comforting way that made me strangely jealous.

"Who's going to be there for you?"

Keel's question wasn't even something I could allow myself to answer. I didn't deserve anyone to be there for me, not when I'd been so completely fooled by a monster like Attis.

"I'm sorry about your friend," Mona said, sounding sincere even though I knew better.

I shrugged and didn't answer as we walked down the steps, heading towards another one of the quickly-fashioned buildings across the way that contained our rooms. We stopped to let a semi-organized line of Rebels jog past us before continuing on our way again.

"At least I learned the truth," I said, knowing this sounded like a wise and controlled response, even if the caged anger inside of me was fighting to come out again. "About a lot of things actually – I even learned something about you, Mona."

Her innocence would have been more believable if she had acted surprised, instead she remained silent, keeping her eyes focused straight ahead of us.

"Were you ever going to tell me that I'm your niece?" I snapped suddenly, letting the anger lash out for just a second. "That you were there when my parents were killed?"

Mona finally looked at me, and as I stared back into her conflicted eyes I realized why I always thought she looked so familiar; she looked like me. She had my eyes, my hair, and even my height. Somehow, even her mannerisms were similar.

"I didn't tell you because you didn't need to know," she said firmly, even though I caught the gleam of uncertainty in her eyes. "You have your own life and I'm in no place to pretend to be family to you."

"You tried to protect me as a child," I continued, ignoring her. "Did you know I was alive after they took me? Did you just stop looking for me?"

Mona's eyes flashed at me. "Yes, Delle. Alright, yes. I knew you were alive. I had no idea where you were and no idea how to find you. I couldn't spend my whole life trying to find someone The Eye was doing their best to hide from me. It was an impossible mission."

"As impossible as finding Attis?" I shot back. I didn't give her enough time to answer before continuing. "Did you know about him too? Did you know he was the one The Eye assigned to watch me?"

She didn't answer. She didn't look surprised. She didn't even look at me.

"You knew he was a plant and you didn't say anything?" I asked furiously. "You sent me in there knowing what was going to happen, didn't you?"

"We needed those items," she said, her expression hard. "Sacrifices have to be made sometimes. We couldn't risk you not going in just because your friend let you down."

Her response chilled me, even though I really should have maxed out my emotional limit for the day already. Mona was right. She was in no position to pretend to be family to me.

"I would have gone in anyways," I growled, knowing it was true.

Mona shrugged. "We had no way of knowing that."

I shook my head silently and we trudged on towards the rickety stairs that led up to our living quarters. I stopped at the bottom and turned to look at Mona. She was my father's sister. That meant I must have gotten my blonde hair and my blue-green eyes from him. Mona didn't have freckles though, so I could only assume those were from my mom.

"What?" Mona asked, narrowing her eyes at me as I continued my observation. "Why are you staring at me?"

"I was thinking of my parents," I said bitterly, looking away from her. "You knew them."

Mona's expression softened when I chanced a quick look at her. "They were good people. After you were born they moved around constantly, trying to keep you safe. As you got older, your powers became more uncontrollable and more noticeable. Soon they had to move every few weeks. By the time you were eight years old, it was clear that a confrontation with The Eye was unavoidable. That's why I was there. Your mom had a feeling – she was an intuitive person – that something was going to happen. So they contacted me and asked me to come stay with them. I got there only a few minutes before the Runners did. They told me to take you away. They wanted me to bring you to the Gypsies and find a caravan for you to join. They thought you might be safe in a Gypsy camp. I had just made it to the edge of the province when the Runners found us." Mona's expression turned wry as she crossed her arms and looked at me.

"You were extremely uncooperative," she said dryly. "You didn't want to leave your parents. Your eyes were glowing and you were wreaking havoc on anything that came close to you. I had to step back. That's how they took you. I couldn't stand next to you because your powers were expanding in every direction, like a dome. Except it wasn't blue light then, it was white. I guess that changed when you got older or something, huh? Anyways, you knocked out an entire troop before they managed to restrain you. There was nothing I could do to stop them. I barely got out. I wouldn't have made it at all if another Gypsy hadn't seen what was happening and helped me get away."

Her story sounded similar to something I had heard once before. I had no memory of making a light dome or fighting a troop of Runners and I had no memory of ever seeing Mona before, but it made sense. Besides, what other choice did I have but to believe this story. It was all just depressing enough to be my life.

"I joined the Rebels not long after that," Mona said with a sigh, looking around at the bustling hidden base. "I wanted to ruin the government that did that to my family."

"But you didn't come after me," I said, raising an eyebrow.

Mona ran a hand through her hair and pursed her lips. "I thought that finding you was a lost cause. Besides, I knew they would've altered your memories. You wouldn't have remembered me."

You could have found me! My thoughts screamed at her. *You could have told me, convinced me of who you were – who I was! You could have seen through Attis.*

Finally, I nodded. After waiting a moment and seeing that she wasn't planning on saying anything else, I turned to climb the stairs.

"Delle," Mona called after me.

"Yeah?"

"I'm glad I did eventually find you," she said with her weird smirk. "Your parents would be proud of you."

I frowned at her and turned to leave again, calling over my shoulder without any enthusiasm, "Thanks."

Mona's words followed me up the stairs and through the rusty door that I slammed behind me.

Your parents would be proud.

What a cliché line. What was there to be proud of? I, Claudelle *Corentine*, had been happily swallowing lies for the last eight – almost nine – years. I had been stupid enough to believe in someone like Attis, a complete fraud. I hadn't accomplished anything. I hadn't even been able to keep my caravan together in the end.

I sunk down on one of the mattresses and curled onto my side. I shut my eyes and waited for the flood of tears. Nothing came except more of the sick feeling in my stomach and a pounding headache. I had waited too long and now all the feelings that my brain was saying I needed to experience were locked away somewhere inside of me, likely to make their appearance at the most inconvenient time.

If I never found out Attis was alive, would I feel this dead right now?

I let my mind wander along the shallower topic of why I wasn't drowning in tears. I felt empty and stuffed full at the same time. Empty of trust and full of truth.

CHAPTER TWELVE

I woke up blearily, thinking it was morning. Someone had put a blanket over me while I slept. I was so exhausted I hadn't even heard my caravan come in. I stood up and saw Jag and Magely still asleep. Keel was nowhere in sight.

I wrapped the blanket tighter around me and combed my fingers through my hair, wavy and matted from sleeping on it. I tiptoed across the room and opened the door quietly. I wanted fresh air, but since we were underground I was hoping that at least the freer air outside would do the trick. As I lifted my head and pulled the door closed behind me, I realized two things. First, it wasn't morning yet. The Rebels had turned down the artificial lighting over the base to simulate nighttime. Could my whole life really have fallen in apart in less than a day? Second, I realized that Keel clearly had the same idea. He was already there.

He looked over his shoulder at me and moved over a few inches to make room for me at the railing. It wasn't a balcony like the Micahs had, but there was a little landing just big enough for two people to stand side by side and look out over the makeshift base.

"I would ask how you're feeling," he started, looking out over the base. "But that seems like a dumb question."

I knew I should've responded with a short laugh or some sound to show that I agreed with the ludicrousness of it all, but I couldn't summon the memory of how to do that.

Instead I said, "Yeah." There was a long stretch of silence between us that wasn't exactly uncomfortable, just tense. I cleared my throat as the events of the day came back to me in pieces. "I'm really sorry for what I said to you earlier."

"You were upset," he said with a shrug.

"I was," I said dully. "But I still shouldn't have said it."

Keel turned to look at me then, concern in his eyes. "I forgive you, Delle. You don't need to keep apologizing."

I nodded and sighed, looking away from him to escape his gaze. He didn't stop looking at me though. I could feel his gaze on me for a moment longer before he settled down on the railing again, our arms touching as I looked up at the faintly glowing bulbs overhead.

"I wonder if those are what stars look like," Keel commented, following my gaze.

I shrugged. I used to dream about seeing the stars. Attis had shown me a picture of them once, from before we had weather shields over all the buildings, obscuring the already too-polluted sky. I used to think the idea of them was beautiful, but now, like almost every other memory I had, the stars were tainted – like me.

Keel nudged me and I turned to look at him.

"Do you need to talk about it?" he asked quietly.

I looked into his warm eyes and considered him dully. He hadn't given me any reason not to trust him – not since I first met him. Then again, I hadn't thought Attis did either. They were so similar. What would happen if Keel left too? I couldn't take that. If he turned out to be untrustworthy, I wouldn't just be on the verge of a mental breakdown – I would lose my mind and in all likelihood dissolve into a puddle of whatever it was that I used to be.

"Probably," I finally said in a cool tone, returning my gaze to the disenchanting bulbs.

Keel didn't press and I was glad for it. Attis would have. We stood in silence for a few more minutes before I forced myself to act like a human again, with the appearance of human feelings and concern.

"Why are you awake?" I asked, turning to Keel, leaning against the railing. "You should sleep."

Keel didn't look at me, but his hand covered mine on the railing. I resisted the urge to pull it away as the nervousness in my body threatened to make me sick again.

"I couldn't sleep," he said with a heavy sigh. "I was worried about you."

"You don't need to worry about me," I responded automatically, if not a bit robotically.

Keel shook his head and looked at me with a twinge of annoyance.

"Really, I'm okay," I insisted, but I couldn't quite find the enthusiasm to make it sound convincing. Keel shook his head again and looked like he was about to contradict me, so I hurried to amend, "I will be. I will be okay, Keel."

He nodded and some of his annoyance faded. "I'm so sorry, Delle."

I withdrew my hand too quickly as I sensed a hug coming and turned my face away as the tears I had tried to summon earlier decided to show up. I bit the inside of my cheek and waited for them to go away. Maybe I would have cried in front of Keel before, but I couldn't risk it now.

Not when he could turn out to be like Attis.

I couldn't get attached. That would mean gut-wrenching, soul-splintering pain if he turned out to be a traitor too.

"You should go to bed," I said, wishing I sounded a little less breathless. "You need to sleep."

Keel stepped away and I didn't turn to see his expression, which I knew was probably wounded – or angry. I heard the door to our quarters open and waited for it to shut again before I sat down hard on the landing and gasped, inhaling sharply and trying to hold back the tears. All attempts to control myself were ineffectual now. All I could do was lock my hands over the back of my head, hide my face in my knees, and shake as I tried to keep my pitiful sounds and gasping breaths to a minimum as my tears sunk into the fabric of pants. I was grieving all over again. I was grieving for Attis, and now for Keel too who, through no fault of his own, I could never envision myself trusting again. Attis hadn't just taken away the future involving him; he had stolen any future I could have had with anyone else.

***

Morning was numb. Morning was easier. When I finally managed to staunch my flow of pitiful tears, I had tried to go to sleep, but rest wouldn't come. I lay on my mattress, staring at the flaking ceiling until I heard the bustle outside pick up. I waited for the others to wake up, knowing that we needed to make a plan to get back to the Micahs in New Capil. I stared at my small bag, mentally counting every item I owned, all packed inside. I did this obsessively and repeatedly until Jag finally stirred. I was glad that he was the first to wake up.

"How are you doing?" I asked as he sat down beside me and rubbed the sleep out of his eyes.

He shrugged and made a face. "I could be worse."

I nodded. Jag had never been the optimistic type, so this minimizing of something terrible seemed strange to me.

"What about you?" he asked, looking sideways at me.

Somehow, despite my unaffected manner, I was pretty sure he knew I was a complete mess.

I gave him what I hoped was a dry smile. "I could be worse."

Jag nodded. "So, Mona's your aunt?"

I raised an eyebrow at him, only vaguely surprised. "How did you know?"

He shrugged and answered, "Last night when you disappeared Keel said you were going to talk to your aunt. I just assumed."

I stayed silent, wondering if he was upset that I had "disappeared" last night.

"Besides," he continued, apparently not bothered. "She looks just like you."

"I noticed," I said, shaking my head. "Apparently she was my dad's sister."

"So your last name?" Jag asked curiously.

"Corentine," I replied, wrinkling my nose.

"Claudelle Corentine," he said thoughtfully. "Sounds cool. I wish I knew my last name."

"I wish you did too," I said slinging an arm over his shoulder, like I used to when we were kids.

He put his arm over my shoulder as well, but it wasn't the skinny, light arm I remembered. It was heavy and sure.

"Man, I miss Steffy," he said suddenly.

"Me too." I missed her so much that it physically hurt. "We'll be back soon." *And when we're back I'll have to tell her about* him.

Jag stretched and stood up. "You keep saying you're going to cut my hair, you know."

I groaned. "Sorry, Jag. I know I do. I'll cut it when we get back to the Micahs. I promise."

Jag shook his head. "I like it this way. I can tie it back now."

I didn't miss his eyes dart over to the little blonde figure, sleeping on a thin mattress in the corner. Somehow I was pretty sure Jag's new attachment to his hair was because a certain girl liked it this way. I pursed my lips and consciously made the decision not to roll my eyes.

"Whatever you want," I murmured.

Keel and Magely woke up a few minutes later and we commenced the planning of our return trip. No one mentioned Attis. Even though I could now think of his name without falling into a pit of complete insanity, it was probably for the best that we avoided the topic. I let Jag take the lead on planning our trip back. I was having difficulties staying out of the avalanche of my own thoughts long enough to discuss things in an intellectual manner with people. I was an observer, not a participant. For now, I was content to stay that way.

As we repacked our bags, I could feel Keel and Magely watching me. Neither one was subtle about it, although I think Keel was trying to be. Magely, on the other hand, kept trying to make eye contact. I was past my dislike of her, seeing as she had done nothing to deserve it in the first place besides express her positivity with annoying frequency. I had to admit that I even appreciated her at this point. I just couldn't take her sympathy filled eyes or her definition-of-sweetness attitude, so I avoided her.

The general and his second in command weren't sad to see us go. They seemed relieved to have us off their base, despite the fact that we had retrieved their items in less than an hour without being caught or leading anyone back to them.

"The general isn't a bad guy," Mona whispered to us as she led us back to the tunnel. "He just doesn't like outsiders."

I could understand that, so I didn't say anything. Besides, we would never see the man again so I couldn't have cared less whether he hated us or not.

Mona walked with us all the way to the lift station, where we showed our papers to prove that we were Provincial. She even waited in line with us at the lift dock. She tried to catch my eye a couple times, but I studiously ignored her. Actually, I was ignoring everything, but I was making a concentrated effort to ignore her in particular. She had already made it clear that she wasn't going to pretend to be family to me. I would return the favor.

When our lift finally arrived, I was the last to board. Mona grabbed my arm before I could step on. I turned back to scowl at her and yank my arm away.

"What?" I asked frostily.

Mona sighed and if I wasn't imagining things, she blushed too. "Look, kid, I'm sorry. I know I didn't handle any of this right. I didn't handle it right when you were eight and I'm not handling it right now. I just want you to know that if you need anything, I'm here."

Her words slammed into the wall I had built around my emotionally overwrought heart and slid off, harmless. I nodded and turned to go.

"You look like them," she added quietly, making me pause. "You have your dad's eyes and your mom's personality."

I faltered. The wall quavered.

"I meant what I said," Mona said, stepping towards me, apparently sensing that she had managed to worm her way into my active thoughts. "They would be *so* proud of you, Delle."

I nodded again and felt the lift lurch to life. It was time to go. The part of me that cared said I needed to say something to Mona, even if it was just for my parents' sake.

"Thanks," I said lamely. "Maybe I'll see you again."

Mona's face lit up before settling back into her amused smirk, an expression I knew well from looking in the mirror. She waved at us as I sat down beside Magely. I gave a half-hearted wave back. As far as I knew, she didn't leave until we were out of sight. She stayed there at the docking bay, watching us drift away.

***

The ride back to New Capil was long – especially since sleep was eluding me again, but we did finally arrive in New Capil. As we stepped out onto the busiest docking area in the First Province, I had the strangest sensation that I was coming home. I had never lived in the same place twice. Usually, if I ever stayed somewhere twice there were years in between.

Stepping off the lift, walking past the Micahs's star-shaped symbol on the front of their building, stepping inside their enormous home, it all felt nostalgic. As Magely commented that she couldn't believe we had only been gone a week, I felt a vague type of shock at that. Somehow, it had only been a week.

As we stepped off the lift into their living area and kitchen, the family members already present turned around instantly. I heard the surprised exclamations and joyful clapping of hands, and I think several people embraced me, but I wasn't sure if I returned the hugs. I was vaguely aware of the rest of the family pouring into the room from the hallway on the far side or coming up the lift behind us. I felt the shadow of happiness at coming back to this family, but everything was out of focus and I was suddenly so tired I just wanted to close myself in a room, fall asleep, and never get up. At least, until Steffy came in, Nanda hurrying after her.

"Steffy!" I called, the world abruptly more colorful than it had been a moment before as I dropped to my knees and caught her in my arms, hugging her tightly.

She touched my face with her hands and beamed at me voicelessly with her unseeing eyes. I clung to her like she was the last person on earth.

"I missed you so much!" I whispered, so only she could hear me.

Jag tugged on one of her many springy curls and greeted her. She instantly reached out for him and he gladly took her from me, picking her up even though at five years old she was probably too big. She signaled for Keel too, who chucked her lightly under the chin, making her giggle. I sighed and watched my family, for just a moment wanting to pull them all into a hug, to take them somewhere we would always be safe. I was pretty sure I could hear the sound of my heart tearing a bit, like a piece of worn fabric, because I knew that place didn't exist anymore.

"So," Jorge piped up, clearly envious of not having come with us. "How did the mission go? Did you find Attis?"

Fil and Lacey, the second and third oldest looked curious as well, but Nanda was watching me with a quiet expression, like she somehow already knew.

"Sort of," Keel interjected after looking at me and seeing the shadow of panic that must have crossed my face.

"They can tell us everything over dinner," Sacrif said abruptly, holding up his hands to stop the conversation from continuing. "For now, why don't you all go clean up?"

There was a communal sigh from all except me. I didn't want to tell everyone the truth, but I didn't see a way to avoid it. Steffy reached out for Nanda's hand and something became tight in my chest. She used to reach for my hand like that. The others hesitantly departed in groups, Fil accompanying Keel and Jag while Lacey and Jorge went with Magely. Nanda and Steffy simply moved to one of the couches on the far side of the room and resumed a holographic puzzle they'd been working on.

I didn't realize I hadn't moved until Appy's voice startled me into motion.

"Do you want to help me in the kitchen, Delle?"

I nodded and heard myself respond, "Sure."

"I've been practicing what I would make when you came back," Appy confided, flipping her sleek hair over a shoulder as I followed her into the kitchen with the pretense of helping her cook.

"Practicing?" I echoed, letting myself become distracted as the mother of the family coaxed me out of my silence.

"Well I didn't want to burn your first meal back," she answered with a rueful smile. "I would never hear the end of it."

I'd forgotten how much I missed Appy's unfortunate but well-intentioned cooking. I handed her ingredients for a few minutes and watched her read the recipe off the colorful screen her Tab was projecting in the air. She was mouthing the words, like she already had the recipe memorized. It was slightly amusing to realize that she hadn't been kidding. She really had practiced making this exact meal.

"So," she said, turning to me and leaning against the counter. "Do you want to talk about it?"

The sick feeling in my stomach came back and I gripped the counter behind me. I shook my head. At the same time a little voice in the back of my mind reminded me of how much I owed this woman and her husband. They had taken us in and adopted us in every sense of the word.

"There was a lot that Attis never told me," I said simply, doing my best to keep a light voice. "Like the fact that The Eye hired him to watch me because of my powers." I couldn't look at Appy's face. If there was any sympathy there, I knew it might shatter me. "Also, I have an aunt. I met her actually. She's a Rebel. Her name is Mona. She has red streaks in her hair and her eyes look like mine."

The silence stretched on for a few seconds, so I ventured to look up. Appy's eyes were shining, but she quickly looked away, saving me from an emotional implosion. When she looked back at me her eyes were clear again. I deeply appreciated her understanding.

"Sounds like an educational trip," she said lightly, and I felt relief wash over me, once again so grateful for this woman's intuition.

"It certainly was."

Appy gave me a long look. There weren't a lot of times that Appy looked her age. Usually she looked like she had to be in her twenties, but now her face seemed to age with every passing second. She was still beautiful of course. Finally, she just nodded and turned to stir the mysterious bubbling concoction that for better or worse was going to be our dinner.

"Steffy missed you," she commented warmly. "We all did, really. Jorge has been brooding all week about not getting to go."

"I don't think he would have enjoyed it," I said dryly. There was a long pause before I thought of something else that might interest her. "Magely was great, by the way," I said softly. "She told us about her gift. She really saved us."

Appy's hair shimmered as she shook her head and laughed. "Magely's always been a wild card. It seems that all of our children are destined to live on the edge at one point or another. One day I would just like all of us to be safe."

I blinked at the familiarity of her wish and caught my breath. I hadn't really thought Appy and I had anything in common, but maybe I was wrong. The dinner was just starting to burn by the time everyone arrived, which was vastly undercooked by Appy's normal standards. I braced myself for the nightmare that was to come as everyone sat down at the large table we rarely used, expecting a detailed explanation of our trip. In the back of my mind I noticed Keel sit down beside me and squeeze my hand briefly under the table. I didn't respond and it took me a moment to understand that he was trying to reassure me. Sacrif blessed the meal, like he only did when the whole family came together for a meal. No sooner had the first bite been taken then all eyes turned to me. I looked at each of them in turn, sensing the part of myself that was still able to feel retreating far back inside of me where it couldn't be reached. Although I had no doubt I would think about it every day, this was the last time I was ever going to tell this story.

CHAPTER THIRTEEN

I woke up the next day with a sense of clarity; I knew where I was, I knew who I was, and I knew exactly what I had gone through to get here. I stared at the blank white ceiling since the walls of my room changed color with my mood and I didn't want to see the empty charcoal color pressing in on me. Steffy was snuggled up beside me and as I turned on my side and gazed down at her, I could feel a little bit of warmth creep into my heart. In my peripheral vision, I could see the walls change accordingly, lightening just a tad with splotches of sunset orange. I cuddled her closer and kissed her forehead lightly enough that it wouldn't awaken her. Steffy's presence made me want to at least try and act like a human being rather than an unfeeling machine.

I tried to interact with the family because the part of me that hadn't retreated into a dark corner knew I didn't want to hurt these people. I was aware that the Micahs were concerned for me. I noticed the way they watched me when I walked into a room. It wasn't often that I walked into a room. When I started walking anywhere, even to the restroom across the hallway, I started thinking again, and when that happened I started shaking, feeling nauseated. Everything was a reminder of Attis – of betrayal. Everything he'd told me, all of the lies, pressed against the walls of the box I'd closed them in. It took all of my effort to keep them there, until I was exhausted just from the effort of trying not to think.

Steffy was the bright spot in my life. This wasn't abnormal. Whenever my caravan had gone through difficult times in the past, she was the one thing that lifted my spirits. Since returning to the Micahs, I spent hours with her every day, and although I knew Nanda was jealous of my time with her, she didn't protest. She lurked around us though, finding excuses to bring Steffy a snack or show us a new game. I probably would have minded more before, but it was clear that Steffy was just as attached to me as ever and there was no need to be territorial.

I was vaguely aware of Jag and Keel trying to interact with me whenever I made an appearance. Magely too would try at least twice a day to start up a cheerful conversation with me, but it usually ended after a few bland minutes. The rest of the Micahs did their best as well and I could feel Appy's eyes on me wherever I went, but I didn't know how to appease them.

It wasn't that I was trying to sulk. I tried to respond, but it wasn't easy. I had to think about what an acceptable response would be then struggled to form it with my words and my facial expressions. I didn't want to make people unhappy. I tried to interact in the way I knew they wanted me to.

It had been five days since our return, but it felt like only a day had passed – one long, dreary, endless day. Steffy and I were braiding ribbons together for a doll Nanda had given her. The ribbons were colorful and bright and gleamed against Steffy's dark fingers as she used her sense of touch to weave the most beautiful patterns.

"Oh good," Sacrif said upon entering the room and seeing us curled on the couch.

His eyes crinkled at the corners as he smiled at me. He smiled at me now more than he ever had before the mission. I knew it was his way of trying to show he cared, so I tried to smile back. I could tell it didn't reach my eyes though.

"We were looking for you two," Appy added, gliding into the room behind her husband and sitting down on the arm of the chair that Sacrif was lowering himself into, her long, colorful skirt pooling on the ground.

Steffy was looking attentively in their direction now, in the unnerving way she had that convinced people she could see them. I set down the misshapen braid of ribbon I had been weaving and drew my legs up onto the couch.

"Why were you looking for us?" I asked, only faintly curious.

Sacrif cleared his throat and Appy answered, "We wanted to talk to you about something for Steffy."

I looked down at the little head of curls leaning against me and heard myself reply, "Okay."

"There's a couple we know," Sacrif said seriously, leaning forward and clasping his hands. "They specialize in working with people who have genetic mutations."

He paused, waiting for some affirmation that I understood.

"They help people who are genetically screwed?" I asked, trying to show that I understood.

He nodded. "We told them about Steffy," he said, giving Appy a sidelong look. "And they believe they might be able to help her develop her speech."

I blinked and looked down at Steffy, whose head was cocked in confusion, not understanding yet.

"That would be amazing!" My own enthusiasm startled me.

Appy and Sacrif let out a mutual sigh of relief and laughed at my outburst.

"We think so too," Appy said affectionately, coming to sit beside me. She took one of Steffy's hands and one of mine. "There is one unfortunate aspect to the arrangement though."

I could feel my enthusiasm fading. "Unfortunate?"

"It's not bad," Sacrif assured me. "She would have to stay with them though. The therapy they want to try with her requires constant attention and learning."

I frowned and leaned closer to Steffy, wanting to pull her into my arms and hold her jealously there. "Alone?"

Sacrif nodded and Appy squeezed our hands.

"They need to isolate the form of communication she uses now from the one she needs to learn if she's going to develop her speech. With any of us there to encourage the old form of communication, it could hinder the learning process," Appy explained softly. "That's the simplest way they could put it for us. It's a form of immersion learning. Not to mention, their work with genetic mutants isn't entirely legal so the fewer people involved, the better."

I withdrew my hand from Appy's and took Steffy's other hand in both of mine, looking back and forth between Appy and Sacrif – trying to fathom why they would try to take Steffy from me.

"For how long?" I asked hollowly.

Appy looked to Sacrif and he cleared his throat. "They said it could be anywhere from six months to a year. No more."

I felt like someone had punched me in the stomach. I hoped it didn't show.

"They're both trained doctors and good people," Sacrif continued, his voice less gruff than usual in his attempt to sound reassuring. "We've known them for years. The work they do is illegal, but it's helped many people who suffer from debilitating genetic mutations."

"Where are they located?" I asked, managing to sound somewhat calm even while my heart pounded erratically in my chest and I had to fight to keep my breathing normal.

"They live in Flor," Appy responded, keeping her crystal blue eyes trained on me, like she could see right into my head.

"It's just East of Tac," Sacrif elaborated. "There are enough Rebels in the area to keep the government out but not so many that the fighting ever reaches past its borders."

"It's safe," Appy simplified, watching me knowingly. "And we can still visit Steffy while she's there."

There was a long silence as it became clear that the couple had spoken their piece and the decision was being left to me. Except it wasn't. It was really up to Steffy.

"Well Steffy," I said lightly, hoping my voice would fool her into thinking it sounded like a wonderful idea – something I was eager for her to try. "What a good surprise. How does that sound to you? Would you like to meet them? They could help you learn to talk."

Steffy pulled away from Appy and crawled into my lap, wrapping her arms around my waist and clinging to me. I sighed and put my arms around her, holding her close to my heart. Forcing away the dramatic thoughts that screamed this could be one of the last times I got to hold her for a long time. Appy had already pointed out that we could visit her.

"Well, Steff?" I asked gently, leaning back enough that I could look down into her face and push the bushy black cloud of curls away from her face. "What do you think?"

I didn't want to push her to go to these doctors, but how could I deny an opportunity that would give her something I had never been able to give her before? We didn't know why she couldn't speak. We didn't know if it was a physical problem or a mental block. Either way, if these people could help her learn to communicate, her entire life would be different, better even. I couldn't even imagine what her voice would sound like.

Steffy appeared to be contemplating my face even though I knew she couldn't actually see me. Her unruly eyebrows were drawn together and her little lips were puckered in serious, distressed thought. She released her tight hold on me and settled for leaning against me, staring into space as she touched her throat.

"Six months to a year isn't all that long," I said optimistically, feeling the last functioning part of my heart start to shrivel up and die with the rest of me.

We had talked about trying to find someone to help Steffy learn to speak once. Attis and I had talked about it, but it was never feasible. It was an unattainable dream – just like the rest of the life Attis promised us. I swallowed and blinked, closing my thoughts on the subject of the traitor.

Steffy signed a question and waited in silence for one of us to answer.

"It's not far," I said smoothly, looking up at Appy and Sacrif, hoping they would jump in with more answers.

"It's just a day and a half to get there by the lift system," Sacrif added.

Steffy remained motionless for a few moments before signing again.

"You could leave as early as tomorrow evening," Appy said. Although she was using the voice people generally talk to children with, she was looking at me, knowing that this was killing me. "The couple is currently here in New Capil on business, but they'll be leaving for Flor tomorrow. If you both agree, they would like to take you with them, Steffy."

"We could meet them first?" I asked, feeling just a glimmer of hope. At least I would get to approve of the people who would be caring for my Steffy for the next six months to a year.

"Of course," Appy said solemnly. "And you can change your mind about going whenever you want, Steffy. You can even change your mind once you get there – and they promise to bring you right back here if you ask."

"That doesn't sound so scary," I said, entirely for Steffy's benefit since I was still petrified with the fear of losing her. "It's up to you, of course."

Steffy's little fingers stroked my forearm and hand, like she was reassuring herself I was still there. Finally, she nodded and signed a yes for us. I wanted to both laugh and cry at the same time. Steffy was going to be able to speak – one of my biggest dreams for her. But I was going to lose her for a time.

Just six months to a year, I reminded myself somewhat frantically as I swallowed again and forced myself to remain outwardly calm.

***

Like every other major event in my life, it seemed to come suddenly and without warning. I was constantly biting the inside of my cheek to distract myself as I dressed Steffy in her nicest little white dress and tied her hair into bows with the ribbons we had braided together – originally intended for the doll tucked away in the small bag with the rest of her belongings. The entire family made the rounds, saying goodbye. I vaguely noticed tears on some of their faces, but it was agreed that only Jag and I would go with Appy and Sacrif to avoid attracting attention.

My mouth was sour with the taste of blood from biting my cheek. I held Steffy's hand in the indoor lift and down to the street, walking with Appy and Sacrif to the lift station where we would meet the doctor couple. I had done my best to dress in a way I felt looked respectable to hand off Steffy to the doctors. Nanda had left me one of her old dresses in my closet. It had hardly been worn and the shifting blue colors all over the long, trailing fabric looked like shifting water. The dress felt like a silent peace offering and I had accepted it, feeling an echo of gratitude. In the back of my mind I knew losing Steffy would be especially hard on her too. Nanda had lost her little brother once and now she was losing Steffy too.

Not losing, I corrected myself. *She's just going away for six months to a year. She'll be safer there. This is what's best for her.*

I wondered if the separation would have been easier if I had been given more warning. If I had been preparing for it, maybe it would have been easier by this point. Or maybe it would have been immeasurably harder. I tightened my grip on Steffy's hand as we followed silently behind Appy and Sacrif, Jag trailing silently behind us. It felt like we were going to a funeral.

We met the doctor couple outside the lift station. They seemed nice enough. The woman had long, straight hair that flowed down her back in a waterfall so black it almost looked blue when the light hit it. Her husband had trustworthy eyes. Then again, I had been fooled before. I was obviously the worst person to try and judge people's characters. My past was proof enough that I was easily fooled. I clutched the blue bullet on my necklace and tried to look less suspicious than I felt as Sacrif and Appy introduced us.

As soon as Sacrif and Appy fell into a conversation with the doctors that didn't involve me, I knelt down in front of Steffy and grasped her arms.

"Well, Steff?" I asked in a near-whisper. "What do you think? Do you like them?"

Steffy cocked her head and a brief smile flashed across her face as she nodded. Since I couldn't trust my judgment, I was left with no judgment to rely on but hers – and Appy and Sacrif's, of course.

We walked them all the way to the lifts and waited in line with them, like Mona had done with us in Laylen. Putting Steffy on the ground and peeling her arms off my neck was the hardest thing I had ever done. I knew it was hard for Jag too as he kissed her on the top of the head and gave her a gentle nudge away from us. I felt like a cold hand was squeezing my heart, trying to crush it over and over as I watched the doctors each take one of Steffy's hands and guide her into the lift. The three of them looked like a little family. My Steffy and two strangers.

I'm supposed to be her family, my inner thoughts raged as the lift lurched away from the ground and began climbing up the first of many tracks that would take it to Flor.

I didn't speak on the walk back, but Jag held my hand. I wondered if his hand hurt – I was aware of holding it too tightly. Appy and Sacrif each gave me a brief hug before we reentered their building, but they didn't speak to me. I tried to thank them like I knew I should, but I didn't know if my voice was working. That was okay though, because Jag thanked them for us both, watching me go with worried eyes.

I passed each member of the family on the way to my room. They were strategically placed in positions beside the lift and on the couch in the lobby before my hallway. They were waiting, trying to seem casual, but really wanting to see if my sanity had finally cracked. I got to my door and Keel was there, waiting like the rest of them, although the others were finally out of eyesight.

"Delle," he started, stepping towards me, starting to offer a hand.

I flinched. I wanted to take his hand, but I just couldn't do it. That would be trusting him – relying on him. I couldn't rely on anyone again after what happened. I was still recovering from the first time I was wrong. I couldn't handle being wrong again. My heart couldn't take it.

"Thanks," I said, doing my best to smile as if I was going to be okay, so he wouldn't worry – so he wouldn't tempt me to rely on him like I almost had.

He shook his head and stepped forward, but I was already inside the room so I pretended not to see as I shut the door. Maybe I could have trusted him once – before I knew how deceptive the world was and how destructive people could be. I couldn't do it anymore. If I dared to care about him, I would become attached. When the time came to lose him, it would hurt that much worse – and the time to lose him would come. If life had taught me anything by this point, it was that you couldn't hold on to anyone, because they could leave you at any time – and they could take your heart with them, whether they meant to or not.

CHAPTER FOURTEEN

I wanted to stay shut inside my room forever, but there were two reasons I couldn't do that. The first was that I knew the family was worrying about me. My dramatic behavior had concerned all of them and I knew they were likely to break down the door if I didn't come out. The second was that every time I looked over at the second bed in my room, I thought of Steffy who used to sleep there even though she technically had her own room. Now she was sleeping in her own room somewhere else.

I carried on conversations with the family and joked with Fil, even though I could never figure out how to fake laughter. I tried to insert myself into conversations with Jag and Magely, but it was awkward and uneasy, like I wasn't really wanted there. I didn't blame them. I was surprised the family was still trying to talk with me at all. Lacey and Jorge gave up quicker than the others. They were prone to quick bursts of energy and cheer, so again I didn't blame them. Nanda spent a lot of time with me though. We rarely talked, but sometimes we would clean together or organize the contraband medical supplies in the medical floor of the Micahs' building. I helped Appy make dinner and listened to Sacrif and Jag discuss the Rebel progress. Keel was the only one I couldn't figure out how to interact with on any level. I knew I was being contradictive. I was allowing myself to get closer to some of the others, but for some reason I still couldn't justify putting my emotional state into such a risky position by trusting Keel. Maybe it was because in some ways he still did remind me so much of the one person I never wanted to think about again. Who was to say he wasn't capable of betraying me in the same way?

Still, he didn't leave me alone. That only made me feel worse. He didn't try to talk to me, but I could feel his eyes on me. He was always there, no more than a shout away. He didn't try to touch me anymore and I didn't blame him. There were some times though when I would watch him from across the room, when I was sure he wasn't looking at me, and I would remember how he had hugged me once and held my hand. He had been there. Unfortunately, every time I would follow this train of thought and consider going over to talk to Keel – to apologize to him for my cruel behavior – the little voice would pop up in my mind and remind me of what could happen if it was all a lie.

It had been a week and a half since I saw Attis and learned the truth. I mostly succeeded in keeping him off my mind, and that was when I was able to pretend I was capable of interacting normally with the Micahs. Still, I could always feel him – rather his memory – like a ghost at my shoulder, haunting me, ready to point out everything that reminded me of him, everything that was a potential threat.

I dropped my eyes as Keel turned around, briefly interrupting his conversation with Appy and Sacrif in order to check on me. I continued to pretend to listen to Lacey chatter away about the party that had been blasting off the rooftop next door only the night before, as if I hadn't seen and heard it myself. I pretended to be amused by Jorge and Fil topping each other's jokes. Nanda was laughing genuinely at their antics. I was forcing myself to smile. Jag and Magely were sitting off to the side, murmuring to each other in low voices like they always did.

Simply *being* wasn't as painful now as it had been even the day before. I was satisfied in my imaginings that one day I might not feel a constant aching in my lungs at all. I couldn't envision myself fully participating in any sort of social interaction, but I was getting better. I could picture myself living without the gnawing anxiety in my stomach like something was about to go wrong.

I startled myself by genuinely laughing at one of Fil's jokes I hadn't even realized I'd been listening to. It was funny enough to distract me and everyone seemed pleased to hear my laugh. I couldn't recreate the sound, but I paid more attention now than I had a moment before, hoping desperately that they might say something to produce the same unexpected reaction from me as they had a moment before.

I was vaguely aware when Appy's Tab made a light, metallic sound as it received a message of some sort. The laughter from our little comedy show continued, until Appy interrupted. Her posture stiff and her lithe arms frozen at her sides as she addressed us.

"We have a visitor," she said coolly. "He'll be up in a moment. I don't imagine any of you will be thrilled to see him, but he says he has some important information for us."

My gaze traveled over the expressions of each of my adopted siblings as I watched them interpret her announcement in their own way. Finally, my eyes locked with Keel for the first time in days. I imagined my eyes widened as did his when we read the same conclusion in each other's eyes. I was on my feet even before the door of the lift slid open. Sacrif was already standing in front of us, blocking both Keel and I who were on our toes, practically growling at the little weasel of a human being that stepped into our living room.

I snarled and was moving forward before I knew it, only stopped when Fil grabbed me around the waist and pulled me backwards at a signal from our adopted father.

"Stole." It was only one word, but coming out of Keel's mouth, in that voice, it sounded like a threat – an icy threat that he probably would have acted upon if Appy hadn't placed a hand on his shoulder.

"You!" I shouted, only managing to free one arm. "You sold us out!" I accused.

I was teeming with energy all of a sudden, awake and interactive like I hadn't been in days. Gerrit Stole at east had the decency to look slightly abashed – or maybe he was afraid. My powers were right at my fingertips again and as I clenched my fist I didn't have to look to know they were glowing, dying to release the tendrils of blue light that could easily strangle the life out of the little rat in front of me.

He held up his hands and kept his eyes trained solely on Sacrif. I looked back and forth between Sacrif and Gerrit, wondering why I wasn't allowed to mangle the traitor – just a little. I jerked out of Fil's grip and gave him a withering glare.

"I only came here out of courtesy," Gerrit Stole said, in a tone that was probably supposed to pass for sincere. His eyes flicked over to me and I flexed my fingers, glowering at him. He quickly averted his gaze.

"Brave," Keel snorted.

"Thank you," Gerrit responded with a smirk, his eyes snapping over to Keel.

Keel's mouth twitched. The air crackled with tension.

"Why did you come here, Gerrit?" Sacrif asked tersely, crossing his arms.

"And without any body guards?" I observed out loud. "You really must be brave."

Gerrit Stole answered without taking his eyes of Sacrif's intimidating figure. "I really am, thank you, dear."

I heard Sacrif's fingers crack as he flexed his hand and a disgusted sound tore out of Keel's throat.

"Like I said, I'm here as a courtesy," Gerrit said quickly, his jacket flickering with electricity as he smoothed it down. "No guards required."

"What is this courtesy you're here for?" Appy asked coolly, releasing Keel and walking forward to stand beside her husband, her shoes clipping across the hard floor. She was easily as intimidating as her husband.

Gerrit reached into his pocket and everyone tensed. I lifted my hand and the blue lights flowed from my fingertips, swirling around my hand as I waited to see if I was going to need to defend or attack. He withdrew his hand and held up a Tab.

"Out of the goodness of my heart," he said, tossing the small device to Keel. "There is a recording on this you'll want to watch. It will be broadcasted sometime within the next twenty-four hours. I only came to warn you."

"Why would you do anything helpful for us?" I snapped.

Gerrit shrugged and winked at me. "What happened in Laylen wasn't personal, Claudelle. I'm an informant and I work for whoever has the deepest pockets. I would still prefer to see you alive than dead."

The Tab in Keel's hand was trying to draw my attention, but I resisted. I was intensely curious about what was on the recording. I couldn't imagine something terrible enough to make Gerrit Stole feel guilty.

"Sweet," I said with a snort.

"Is that all?" Sacrif asked.

Gerrit looked up at Sacrif and I didn't miss his swallow. He nodded and stepped back onto the lift.

"That's everything," he said with false lightness. "Good luck, Claudelle."

I scowled and watched him go, only breathing again when the lift door closed, taking the spineless little man away from us. I whirled around to face Keel and he looked up and met my eyes.

He held out the Tab to me and said, "Do you want to do the honors?"

I hesitated for a fraction of a second before swiping the Tab out of his hand and pressing the button. There was only one thing saved on the device – the video that Gerrit had been referring to. The holographic screen hovered in the air in front of us and Magely stepped forward to expand it so we could all watch.

The images that started moving across the holographic screen were all too familiar, but it still took me a moment to recognize it: a video of Keel and I approaching the security workers at the ORC.

A strangled sound come out of my throat as I tried to process what I was seeing.

"The camera-killer." Keel's voice was shaking – he didn't even try to hide it. "It didn't work."

I watched in horror as my blue lights made their appearance and the two workers fell to the ground unconscious. The video continued only long enough to show Keel and I dragging the workers inside. Then it repeated, looping back from the beginning, zooming in on me – on my powers. I looked like a killer. Then the voice began.

"Many of us think we have never seen a genetically altered person before. Many of us are wrong. The Tainted population is hidden among us, masquerading as civil people of the provinces. They have been biding their time, waiting for the right opportunity to destroy us. This Taint is just the beginning. The power she used to kill these two valued security workers in a civilian facility in Laylen is just one example of the atrocities these beings are capable of committing. They do not think we know about them. Fortunately, we have been gathering data on them for years by placing our own people in positions to observe these genetically Tainted individuals. What you're watching now is merely a small fraction of what this specific Taint is capable of. And she is not the only one – not by far. You may wonder how these creatures have managed to hide among us for so long, unnoticed and unchecked. The answer is simple. The Gypsies have been hiding them, sheltering them. Most Gypsies are themselves Tainted. The time for tolerating threats like these is over. If you have any information on suspicious Gypsy activity among the provinces, contact your local law enforcement immediately. It is up to all of us to keep our provinces safe."

"This is going to be broadcasted?" Lacey gasped.

I stepped away from the video as it started to repeat, on the loop. I wasn't aware that my hands were clapped over my mouth until I realized I couldn't breathe. I dropped my hands quickly and inhaled what I had intended to be a deep breath, but ended up being short and harsh.

"If Gerrit was telling the truth," Sacrif confirmed grimly. "It will be all over the province in the next twenty-four hours."

"What are we going to do?" Jorge asked, imitating Sacrif's grim tone, acting unafraid because he clearly didn't understand the repercussions this video would bring.

"We'll be the first to be reported," Fil observed.

Sacrif held up a hand and the trembling voices stopped. We all looked to him for an answer – for something that would save us.

"We're going to leave," Sacrif announced, looking around at all of us. "Tonight."

"Where are we going?" Jag asked.

"We're going to leave the provinces for now," Sacrif responded. "We won't return until it's safe."

There was a moment of silence and stillness. I realized I was shaking. Nobody was moving.

"Everyone pack a bag – just one – with only your necessities," Appy instructed, clapping her hands, jolting everyone into motion.

The family scattered, all except for me, Keel, Sacrif and Appy. I stared at them, trying to form words, knowing I needed to say something.

"I'm sorry," I finally managed. "I'm so sorry. We used a camera-killer, but it must have been broken."

Appy put her hands on my shoulders and looked me in the eyes. "This isn't your fault, Delle. No one blames you. Chances are after you used the camera-killer in New Capil they updated their technology so it couldn't happen again. We should've thought of it. Besides, this is nothing we haven't done before. We've all been on the run at one time or another."

I nodded because I knew that's what she wanted me to do.

She released me and sighed, saying, "Now go pack."

***

I stared at my clothes where I had rolled them up and set them beside my bag. The bag was already a quarter full with what few smaller items I owned. It was a small bag too. Two pairs of pants and three shirts. That was all I had left to pack besides the skips and our gun. I opened my closet and stared at the two dresses I owned. I didn't particularly like dresses, so I wasn't going to take them. I was just checking for anything else useful. In the corner of the closet my eyes stuck on something I had tossed there when we first moved in. It was the musty sack I used to carry around in the old days, which wasn't actually that long ago. I dragged it out and dumped the contents on Steffy's bed.

The only items worth anything were some of the medicines I had purchased at a Gypsy camp and a few knickknacks we could have traded out in the bomb lands. There was a disc light too, which would be useful to stick to the ceiling if we were going to sneak into any storage lifts in the near future. These items I tossed onto the other bed beside my clothes. I felt something left in the bottom of the sack, so I turned it over again, but the object didn't fall out. I reached inside the bag and felt the sharp edges of something flat that must have cut the sack and gotten caught in the fraying threads. I disentangled it and drew out the broken shard of a mirror I used to keep with us. All the edges but one were wrapped in medical tape to keep from cutting us or tearing a hole in the sack, like the now bare edge had done.

I stared at myself in the shard of mirror. My reflection was no different than any other time I had looked in it. The same blue eyes looked back at me with dark circles underneath. If anything I looked a little older – and meaner. I looked like the murderous Taint the Provincial from the video talked about. I hesitated with the mirror, unsure whether I wanted to bring it with me. I exhaled heavily and reached over to grab the half-roll of medical tape I had tossed onto my bed. I fixed the open edge of the mirror shard before tossing it into my bag, not wanting to look at it again.

I stood in front of the bed, looking down at what little I owned. Now that my packing was basically done, I couldn't distract myself anymore. I couldn't stop myself from thinking about the video.

It made me look like a monster. Maybe I was. That was basically what Attis had been telling me since the first day I met him. That was why I needed to control them. Also because the scientists Attis was working for wanted to see if I even could. Attis said I needed to hide the powers because they were dangerous and volatile. They were destructive and they would only hurt people. I couldn't control them. Even when I thought I had used them in a controlled manner to knock out those guards in Laylen, people had still gotten hurt. The Micahs, who had already sacrificed so much in taking us in, were being forced to flee their home. The powers were terrible. They really weren't good for anything. What had they ever done to make anyone's life better?

"Delle?"

I turned around slowly, still too wrapped up in my bleak realizations to be alert. Keel was standing at my door, which I had left wide open. There was no telling how long he had been watching me stare at my clothes, frozen.

"I shouldn't go with them," I surprised myself by saying.

Keel's eyes narrowed. "What?"

I shook my head. "Being connected to me is dangerous. They could be killed just for knowing my name. I shouldn't go."

Keel crossed his arms and leaned against my doorframe, shaking his head as well. "Stop it, Delle. That's not true."

I glared at him, feeling a crazy mixture of emotions – all of them extremely intense. The walls did nothing to help my case, because they were listening to my mood and were shooting fireworks of random colors in all directions.

"It *is* true, Keel," I snapped. "Name one person whose life hasn't been negatively affected by knowing me!"

Keel stepped forward, his skeptical look dropping away, replaced by concern. He was probably right to be concerned. Clearly, I was losing my mind.

"Whether I control the powers or not doesn't matter – they're always there," I heard myself continue. "They're always a risk. You saw what happened to those security workers in Laylen. That was easy! If there is ever even one time I slip up and don't control them, people could *die*. Not just because the powers could kill them – but because The Eye will murder anyone associated with me. Do you know what that's like? And now the only people I ever put myself through that for, who I controlled the powers for because I was terrified they would be implicated, had ulterior motives. Attis gave them that information on me – he's been giving them information on me ever since he met me."

My brain told me I needed to leave it there, but my mouth decided it wasn't done yet and I heard myself continue, nearly shouting now. "I keep losing everything that matters to me, Keel.

First Attis, now Steffy, and then Attis again and even Jag is distancing himself from me. I'm losing everything and it's awful because I know that's the way it should be. It's safer for everyone if no one has anything to do with me. Besides, if I get close to anything, the universe is sure to just take them away again, because apparently that's my punishment for being born Tainted!"

Suddenly Keel's arms were around me and he was holding my shaking, hyper-tense body tightly against his solid, unwavering one. His hand on the back of my head forced me to drop my face onto his shoulder. He didn't say anything for several moments and I was once again aware of my brain telling me this wasn't safe – that this was exactly what I was talking about, but my body was slowly relaxing, and my breath was coming easier. I wasn't gasping to get oxygen into my lungs. My body had decided it was safe, which was probably why I was clinging to Keel so tightly there was a good chance he would have bruises from my fingers. My face felt wet and took me a long moment to realize I was crying. I buried my face in his shoulder at this realization and told myself to stop, to get control of myself and calm down, to push Keel away and tell him I was fine. But then his voice stopped me from doing any of those things.

"First," he said softly. "I can name a person whose life hasn't been negatively affected by your presence in it. That would be mine."

I started to protest on instinct, but he interrupted me, guiding me over to Steffy's bed and sitting me down on it, kneeling in front of me.

"Second, you do have excellent control of your powers and I know you won't hurt anyone by accident. Those security workers are fine," he reminded me. "They were already waking up when we left them, remember? Don't believe everything The Eye tells you."

"I don't," I said defensively.

"Oh, really?" Keel asked dryly, raising his eyebrows, doubt in his grey eyes that were storming full force. "The things you keep saying about yourself didn't come from your own mind. I know that because it's stuff that I've heard before. It's what The Eye tells Taints and Gypsies about themselves. It's what they tell the world about you. The Eye wants you to believe that you're just a threat, that you can't have anything good because you'll ruin it or lose it. It's not true though. You need to stop believing that."

I was silent. I didn't know what to think about that.

He stood up and sighed, turning around to face my bed. He started packing my clothes and the last few items I had into my bag.

"The Micahs would be heart-broken if you left them," he observed, and as he reached over to pick up the disc light, I noticed his eyebrows coming together like he was really bothered about something. "They all love you, Delle. Appy was right. No one blames you for this. Besides, with the way the Micahs blatantly disregard social and legal rules, this was bound to happen eventually whether you were here or not."

"Maybe," I said with a sigh, knowing he was probably right.

I felt a bit like I was floating. I had just experienced all of the emotions I had been trying to ignore for the past two weeks. Now that they were all out of my system, I felt immeasurably light.

Keel yanked on the drawstring of my bag harder than necessary and turned around to sit on my bed, facing me. The suddenness of his actions pulled me back down to earth and I was able to start piecing together a shaky version of composure.

"Can I ask you something?" Keel said, looking at his shoes, his face working like he was trying to solve one of Steffy's confusing puzzles.

"Sure," I said, glad to hear my voice stronger than before – much more *me* than it had been in days.

"Is that why you've been avoiding me?"

"What?"

He let out a heavy breath and wiped a hand over his face, still not looking at me. "Have you been avoiding me because you don't want us to be close? Because it would hurt more if I turned out to be like him?"

I stared at Keel, his beautiful dark hair and pensive eyes, immeasurably deep. I knew I needed to say something – or at least blink – but I didn't want to tell him that he was right. Instead, I dropped my eyes as soon as he lifted his head.

"That's it, isn't it?" he asked perceptively, and I could feel his eyes on me, reading me like a book.

I finally sighed and stood up, taking what felt like a huge chance and sitting beside him on the other bed. I pulled the bag into my lap when it tipped over as my added weight tilted the mattress, stalling for time.

"I just don't think I can handle it," I began slowly, trying to figure out a way to explain my behavior – why I had done it even though I knew it was hurting him. "I don't think I can handle losing one more person I care about."

"So the solution is to not care about anyone?" he asked skeptically.

I frowned. "Well yes, actually. Can you think of another solution?"

He surprised me by snorting and rolling his eyes. "Of course not, because there isn't a solution at all. You can't stop yourself from getting attached to people – and you're only going to make yourself miserable trying. You just have to accept and enjoy the people around you for as long as you have them."

"I understand that concept," I said carefully. "But sometimes losing someone is so painful that I almost wish I had never met them."

"What happened with Attis was a freak thing," Keel said firmly, seeing straight into my real meaning. "That's extremely unlikely to happen again."

"Says who?" I challenged. "Who's to say it won't happen again?"

"Look at me, Delle."

I looked at him.

"You're right," he said unexpectedly. "It could happen again. But the chances of it happening are extremely low. And even if they weren't, you still wouldn't be able to go through life blocking everyone out. We're human, Delle. Making attachments is what we do – and even though it can feel like death when someone breaks one, it doesn't dissolve all of the other good things that come from all of the other attachments."

I sighed and was silent for a long time.

"Is that something else your mom told you?" I asked eventually.

Keel cocked an eyebrow at me. "Why would you think that?"

I shrugged. "Every time you say something sentimental that makes a lot of sense you usually follow up by telling me it's something your mom told you."

Keel laughed, an unexpected and pleasant sound. I felt the beginning of a smile at the corners of my mouth.

"I guess she taught me the concept, but I applied it to you on my own," he said, nudging me.

"Oh."

I looked down at the bag in my lap and the silence between us stretched on for a few moments. It was a comfortable silence though. I was putting off the thought of having to leave New Capil and was ignoring the guilt that was still lurking around the edges of my mind, but for a moment I was calm. It was like the feeling you get when you stand in the very middle of a storm. You think it's over, but it's really just a break before all hell breaks loose again.

"So does this mean we're friends again?" Keel asked eventually.

I laughed, it was a harsh sound, but it was a step closer to sounding human again. "Yeah, we're friends."

"Good," he said, smiling at me pleasantly. He stood up and briefly touched my cheek with the back of his fingers. "I'm going to finish packing."

I nodded and he left. I sat there in silence for a few more minutes, trying to decide if the change Keel had inspired in me was something that could last through the next time I lost someone.

CHAPTER FIFTEEN

We waited until dark to leave. The Micahs were one of the wealthiest families in the country – also one of the largest – so travelling was going to be hard if we wanted to remain inconspicuous. For that reason, Sacrif and Jorge came with my caravan and Appy, Nanda, Fil, and Lacey travelled separately. We left at different times from the same lift station, planning to meet in Juta, which was the first stop on the way to Flor. If all went as planned, we would be in Flor with Steffy in just under two days. The only issue with the plan was that it required none of us be caught in the process. As soon as the video Gerrit had given us became viral, that was going to become much, much harder.

My caravan and I plus Sacrif and Jorge were the first to arrive in Juta. Appy and the others followed. We stayed in a hotel that night, which I thought was a terribly dangerous idea, but Sacrif assured us that we would leave as early in the morning as possible – as soon as the province's lift station opened. From that point forward, we only had one more stop to make in Cadom and we would have to travel the rest of the way in secret. Neither Appy nor Sacrif would tell me how they planned to get from Cadom to Flor without being caught, since the video would definitely be aired by then. Every time I asked them they would reply with the same mantra, saying "trust us, we've done this before". Clearly they didn't know me very well, considering trust was probably my weakest quality.

Everyone was understandably tense. We had all been on the run at one point or another, but this situation was something entirely new. There was going to be a public announcement made about the threat that Taints and Gypsies posed to society – especially Taints. It's not as if the general public didn't already hate us, but the majority was satisfied with ignoring us or viewing us as urban legends. The Eye was stirring the pot – and someone else too. I had no doubt that Presid was behind the campaign against my kind. That included Magely now too, so to show I hadn't forgotten about the affect this had to be having on her, I put a hand on her head for a second. I planned to pass by her, but she lifted her eyes hopefully so I sighed and stopped, turning back to her and cross my arms.

"How are you doing?" I asked.

She heaved a sigh and admitted, "I feel like everyone else is handling this really well, but I'm terrified. I've heard stories of what they do to Taints who get arrested."

I nodded and affirmed, "Yeah, it's pretty terrifying."

Jag shot me a dirty look over Magely's head as he approached, apparently trying to discreetly inform me that I wasn't being encouraging.

"But it won't come to that," I added. "I've come this far without being caught. We're going to get out of this and be just fine."

Magely nodded, appearing at least mildly assured. I gave her what I hoped was a convincing smile and continued to the sofa that was going to be my bed for the night. It was much softer than anywhere I used to sleep when travelling with my caravan, but I had the sinking feeling this might be the last time for a long time that I slept somewhere so comfortable.

"That was nice," Keel commented, sitting down beside me without hesitation.

I raised an eyebrow at him and replied "Of course it was. I'm a nice person, aren't I?"

Keel grinned at my renewed attitude and shook his head. "Of course you are, Delle."

I drew my feet up onto the sofa and leaned against the arm of the couch. Appy and Sacrif were still quietly discussing something as they scrolled over some screen on their Tab, sitting at the table that dominated the center of the hotel room.

"You can lean on me," Keel offered, watching me squirm around as I tried to find a comfortable position.

I hesitated and observed his innocent expression for a moment, before shifting my position so that I was leaning against him. He tried to move his arm, but it was trapped under my body so I instantly sat up.

"No, you're fine," he murmured, encouraging me to settle back down. "I just wanted my arm. Go to sleep."

I shook my head. "I can't go to sleep when I feel like there's something I should be doing to help."

He draped his now-free arm around me and brushed his fingertips across my upper arm, making goosebumps break out all the way to my wrist. He followed my gaze to Sacrif and Appy, deep in concentration.

"There's nothing you can do right now," he said, considering them with a slight frown. "They adopted you into their family, and now they're going to do everything they can do to take care of you. That's what parents are supposed to do."

I didn't miss the edge of bitterness that had crept into his voice. I knew why it was there.

"I'm sorry about your father, Keel," I said quietly, watching Sacrif lean closer to the floating screen. "I mean, I'm sorry he wasn't the father he should've been."

"Me too," he answered wryly. That was the end of the conversation.

***

We had just touched down in Cadom, on our way to the friends Sacrif and Appy claimed were going to help us reach Flor, when the video reached us.

We were walking in three separate groups, trying not to attract attention to our mob-like family. Keel was walking in front of me, but the minute the hologram screens on the buildings around us flickered to life, he dropped back to my side. Even though I was waiting for it, it still took me a moment to realize what was happening. Then the speakers blasted into the stillness with the beginning of the monologue from the video.

"Many of us think we have never seen a genetically altered person before…"

There I was, larger than life, savagely attacking and allegedly killing two security workers. I hadn't realized how much more terrible it was going to be, watching the secret I had hidden from the world broadcasted all across Cadom, knowing it was broadcasting in every province in the country.

I must have slowed down to watch the traitorous video, because Keel put an arm around me to grip my shoulder and held my other arm against his side. He never moved more than an inch away from me as we hurried through the streets, keeping our heads down as the first round of gasps and horrified shrieks filled the air. The Provincials around us were practically fainting from the shock of the atrocity The Eye had up until this point shielded them from.

We were walking so fast we were nearly at a run by the time we made it into the power district, where the video hadn't quite reached yet thanks to the poverty of the area. Keel had finally let me go, except for my hand, which he kept a firm hold on. The rest of the family was waiting for us on the corner of the third alley from the main street.

"Where are we going now?" I asked breathlessly, doing my best to seem unaffected by the video.

"We're going to see a friend," Appy said, looking sideways at her husband and then at me. "I believe you know him."

I raised an eyebrow at Jag, because if we were going to see someone I knew, chances were he knew this person too. He shrugged, clearly just as bothered by having no idea what the parents were hiding.

"This friend is going to help us get to Flor?" I asked skeptically, slipping away from Keel to follow Appy as she began leading the way down the alley again.

The other Micahs were silent, walking along as if they were on their way to a funeral.

"That's the plan," Appy said calmly.

"How?"

"You'll have to wait and find out."

I frowned and fell back to Keel, who took my hand again and gave me a consoling glance. Jag walked on my other side and even though I knew the situation didn't call for it, I felt somewhat whole for a moment. It felt a little like the old days, but different – and this time I didn't miss Attis. I was too furious to even imagine missing him.

We approached a building that looked like it used to be important, but had clearly fallen into disrepair. It probably had twenty stories, so it was a relatively average sized structure for the provinces. Appy led us around the back of the building, Sacrif following at the rear of our group. She approached a piece of scrap metal leaning against the wall that looked like it had fallen off a piece of machinery. She shoved it out of the way with surprising strength. Sometimes I forgot that she was a Gypsy for most of her life. Underneath the piece of metal was the emblem of a fish carved crudely into the side of the building. She touched it and smiled in a way that I could only assume was nostalgic.

"This is the place," she announced, pulling the metal piece back into place and guiding us to the door, which she didn't knock at before opening.

We trailed after her and Sacrif closed the door behind us. The light was dim. There were no windows, just some florescent lights that were flickering weakly in the ceiling.

"Is this a Caretaker's place?" Jorge piped up.

"It used to be."

It took me a moment to realize the answer hadn't come from any of us. I whirled around. From toe to head, a man appeared, seemingly out of thin air.

"Richy?" I gasped, blinking and staring at him.

I turned to look at Jag, making sure he was seeing who I was seeing. His jaw was dropped in uncomprehending shock.

"What are you doing here?" I asked, launching myself into his arms without thinking.

He laughed and ruffled my hair like I was a kid again before gently pushing me back in order to greet Jag and offer Keel a friendly nod. His hair was graying at the temples and he seemed to have lost some of the energy that usually kept his posture upright, but he was still the same Richy I remembered, scruffy but never without smiling eyes.

"Appy contacted me yesterday and I was already in the area," Richy said with a broad smile. "I knew of this place from the old days so I suggested it could be a good place to meet."

"Hello Richard," Appy said warmly. "It's been a long time. I don't believe you've met my husband or my other children."

Introductions followed, and we were soon scattered around the room, some of us chancing the rusty chairs and others of us sitting on the ground. I sat on the ground with Keel on my left and Nanda and Lacey on my right.

"So, what's the plan?" Fil asked.

Everyone seemed to be holding their breath as we waited for an answer.

Richy gestured to Sacrif and said, "Perhaps you'd prefer to explain it?"

Sacrif nodded and cleared his throat, standing up. "A group of Rebels are going to be hijacking a train today. Richy has negotiated with them on our behalf, and we're going to be playing the part of passengers who happen to be in the wrong place at the wrong time and are taken hostage by the Rebels."

"Great," Jag said, although I couldn't tell if he was being sarcastic or not.

"That could work," I said, not entirely sure if I believed it or not. "The chaos of it all could get us to a safe place before anyone has the chance to recognize us or stop us."

Sacrif nodded. "We're hoping it will. Delle, you'll be staying with Richy at all times."

"What?" I said on instinct, before turning to my old mentor and raising an eyebrow. "You're coming with us?"

He nodded.

"But what about Maricket?" Keel asked suspiciously. "That place can't function without you – aren't you the mayor?"

Richy shook his head and sighed, looking like an old man for the first time. "Something like that. The Eye sent in a league of troops and cleared the place out two weeks ago. No one was hurt because we had advance warning, but there's nothing left."

"Oh no," Magely said, just above a whisper. "That's terrible."

I scowled. It was just like the Provincials to ruin something good. Maricket used to be a safe haven for new Gypsies; it had been that for me and Attis – or maybe just for me.

"Yes," Richy agreed. "It was. But we can all be grateful that no one was hurt. And besides, without the responsibility of the camp, I'm free to help you on your way."

Magely blushed and nodded, obviously not sure whether to express sympathy again or gratitude.

"Thank you, Richy," I supplied for her.

"Don't thank me yet," he admonished. "There are quite a few ways this plan could go wrong. So many, in fact, that no contingency plan could cover all of them."

"If something goes wrong we'll just have to improvise," Jag said grimly.

"Exactly," Richy said, meeting Jag's serious stare with a disturbingly sober one of his own.

I hate improvisation.

Improvisation has its place of course, but it didn't belong in an escape plan. There weren't a lot of things I knew for certain, but this was one of them.

CHAPTER SIXTEEN

The plan began simply enough. The entire province was in mid-hysteria thanks to the panic The Eye had induced in its unsuspecting and unaware citizens. I imagined by this point all of the provinces were experiencing similar levels of chaos. In a way it was good, because nothing makes sneaking around easier than mass panic. Unfortunately, it also tends to make people paranoid. If we had enough time and weren't so recognizable, we might have been able to try the disguise trick Mona had taught us, but we didn't have either. We were relying completely on our ability to move unseen towards the train station. The last time I had ridden a train was when Jag and I jumped the tracks with Steffy. It was extremely dangerous, and while I wasn't comfortable with the idea of getting on a train, being inside one seemed much safer than clinging to the top of one.

Nanda and Lacey stayed close by my side, shielding me from suspicious eyes on the short way to the train station. We managed to stay among the back alleys for the most part, so there weren't too many Provincials to avoid. However, we were going to have to make our way through the train station without being caught. That was going to be the most challenging part. As we crossed the threshold into the extra air-conditioned station and Nanda reached up to move her hair from behind her ear, I noticed her hand shaking.

"Nanda," I said under my breath, knowing she heard me even though she didn't look at me. "Are you okay?"

She nodded, but now I noticed that her whole body was shaking. She seemed to be on the verge of some sort of breakdown.

"Nanda, what's wrong?" I asked urgently. I felt Lacey press closer to my side as she peered over at her older sister, also concerned.

"I don't like trains," Nanda replied shortly, stiffly.

I was about to ask why, when I remembered.

Bo.

Her little brother had died jumping the tracks. Of course she would never want to see another train in her life.

"It will be fine," I said, trying to sound confident. "The only danger anyone is going to be in will be the danger of being arrested before we get on the train. The Rebels are already on board, so once we're inside and the train starts moving, we're going to be on the winning side."

I didn't know if my words were doing anything to soothe her. She was still shaking, but she didn't protest. She just nodded and her tight lips relaxed just a bit.

We boarded the train together and my breath caught as I felt the hard stare of a Provincial man passing by. I made sure to turn my face away and Lacey, seemingly absentmindedly, shielded me from view with her body. We made our way to the back of the train where the rest of the family would be meeting us. Even though the hardest part was over, I was more nervous than ever. Nanda at least seemed to have relaxed quite a bit since stepping on board.

Magely didn't look up as I sat down beside her and I saw her hands wringing nervously in her lap.

"What's wrong?" I asked under my breath, leaning towards her and letting my hair make a curtain in front of my face to stop any other passengers from seeing me clearly.

"What if they're right?" Magely asked back, still not looking at me, her voice almost below a whisper. "What if we're just unnatural threats? Our being different puts everyone in danger."

I reached up to hold the nostalgic and lonely charm on my necklace. Magely's words were scarily similar to my rant from the day before. Again, I had the sense that much more than a day had passed since everything had changed again. I rubbed the old bullet between my fingers and reflected on why Richy ever gave it to me to begin with.

As if summoned by my thoughts, Richy sat down in the seat across from us, acting as if we were complete strangers. This was part of the plan.

When he'd first given me the bullet, I knew he was trying to inspire me to do something. He had wanted me to see the powers for the gifts he thought they were. He didn't want me to be afraid to use them because he knew I could do good with them. Apparently I already had when I stopped that very bullet from killing him. That was why he'd kept it for me all that time. I understood that now – at least a little bit. Anyways I certainly wasn't the one in need of that reassurance at the moment. Keel had managed to reassure me enough – at least for the time being.

"Here," I said, slipping the leather cord over my head and placing it over Magely's sleek blonde head. "I ask myself the same thing about my gifts all the time." I had never referred to the powers as gifts until that moment. "And this is what reminds me that even though our gifts create risks for us, they can do a lot of good things too."

"But this is yours," she whispered, glancing sideways at me.

"It was," I confirmed. "I saved a friend from that bullet once by using my gifts. You can think of it when you start to doubt your goodness."

Magely rubbed the bullet between her fingers and stared at it hard for a moment before tucking it into her shirt, out of sight. Neither of us had looked directly in each other's direction yet, not wanting to attract even a little bit of attention to what could be a minor scene. She did look at me now though, for just a second, her enormous dark eyes gleaming as she looked back into my own, which felt far less spectacular in comparison.

"Thank you."

I turned my head away, pretending to find something fascinating to look at on the windowless wall of the train.

"You're welcome."

Ten slow minutes later, I could feel the vibration of the train coming to life under my feet. There was no sudden jolt of movement as the train began moving forward, picking up speed. The trains were too sleek for that. I sighed and leaned back in my seat. I made eye contact with Magely and Richy, relieved. Surely the hardest was over now.

Suddenly, the train lurched to a stop and I nearly flew out of my seat. The train designed to never make any unexpected or jerky movements had *lurched*. My gaze whipped back to Richy and he instantly stood up, reaching for my hand.

"Plan B," he said shortly, helping me out of my seat and then pushing me down the aisle.

We passed all of the family on the way, who did their best to act like they didn't know me as I hurried to escape the vehicle that had, in all likelihood, just become a death trap for me – the psycho Taint girl from the video. Someone must have recognized me. Sacrif was holding tightly to Jag's wrist and Appy was holding Keel's, physically keeping them in place even though it was clear they were in agony over not coming with me.

I wanted to tell them I would be fine – that Richy and I would catch up with them – but I couldn't because I didn't want anyone else on the train to realize we knew each other. Not until the train started moving again and the Rebels eventually put their plan into action and took over the train. So I didn't say anything. I clenched my fists and didn't even look in their direction as I passed inches from them. Richy was on my heels as I raced towards the exit, not even bothering to try and look like I fit in. I stopped at the door to the train. It was shut tightly and I could hear commotion coming from the other side of it, probably Runners organizing themselves.

"It's locked," I gasped, hitting the door with my palm, wishing that was enough to make the door move.

I could feel the pinch of panic in my stomach. As I whirled around, expecting Richy to have an answer.

"Claudelle," Richy snapped – surprising me since I had rarely heard him snap. "Open the door."

"I can't, it's locked," I insisted, kicking the door ineffectually as the Provincials around us just stared uncomprehendingly, or fearfully at us.

"Don't be ridiculous! Open it – hurry!"

The panic in my stomach grew a hundred times stronger at hearing the urgency in Richy's usually unflappable voice. I glanced up at the square window set into the door, looking out at the crowd of Provincials clamoring to see what was going on. My distraught reflection caught my eye. I stared back at myself and knew what to do.

I looked from Richy to the door and hesitated for just a second before stepping back and lifting my hands, feeling my fingers tingle and watching the blue swirling lights appear. I appraised the door for a moment, trying to figure out what the quickest way to force it open would be. I shifted my attention to the control panel on the wall beside and instantly directed the blue lights into the panel. I had never done this before. I was acting on pure instinct, not letting the light harden yet, not until I twirled my fingers around and was sure the lights were inside the device – the entire wall, really. I clenched my fists and knew the lights were solidifying, turning into their dark blue glass like substance, sharp edged like the shard of my mirror, slicing through the wires and disrupting the electricity powering the lock. I dropped my hands and the door of the train moved swiftly away, up into the roof of the train.

I was right to assume there were Runners outside the train, but they weren't organized yet. Richy and I leapt to the ground, making sure to not touch the tracks, which were still flickering with what looked like purple lightning. The electricity dancing around the tracks was the only reason the crowd of confused Provincials hadn't pressed forward to see what was going on yet. The Runners were just closing in, but they weren't close enough to block us yet. I lifted my arm and the lights appeared, spinning away from my hand in a tornado of luminescent blue smoke. This was enough to forge us a quick path through the terrified Provincials. The Runners weren't intimidated though – clearly they'd been warned about me. Their weapons were already drawn. I could imagine the sound of the switches flipping as they released the electrobullets into the barrels of their guns.

We were almost clear of the train station by the time the Runners were close enough to take a clear shot. I could hear Richy behind me, but I didn't turn around to check on him. I hoped he was taking advantage of his gift, staying invisible.

I used the lights as extensions of my fingers, grabbing the gun out of the nearest Runner's hands, tossing it away into the crowd behind me. I didn't bother to try anything so intricate on the next nearest Runner. I simply caught her up in a sphere of blue light and let it harden into glass around her, then threw her into the Runner behind her. Unfortunately, they were only two of many. It looked like there were three entire troops closing in.

"We have to run," Richy said gravely, stepping up beside me. "Even your gifts aren't a match for this many."

"Run where?" I asked, not daring to take my eyes off our approaching attackers long enough to look at him.

"This way," Richy advised, grabbing my elbow and pulling me after him, back towards the now shrieking, fainting crowd of neon colored Provincials.

He let go of my arm so I could run unhindered after him. He was much taller than me. I had never realized just how tall Richy actually was. I had to take three steps to match one of his. I raced after him, looking over my shoulder with every other step. To discourage anyone from getting in our way, I shot streams of light out into the crowd at periodic intervals. Richy grabbed my arm and yanked me into the crowd and past them into one of the alleys leading off the main street.

"Richy," I gasped. "Where are we going?"

"The sewers," Richy said, whirling around to look behind us, his jacket flapping at the top of his boots.

I didn't like what I saw in his face. He was uncertain – and afraid. I'd never seen him look afraid before. I knew the plan was that he would stay beside me just in case something exactly like this happened, but the danger had come too late. By the time we made it onto the train, everything that could have been a feasible escape was useless to us. Maybe if the Runners had shown up before we boarded the train – but now they were too close.

"How far is that?" I asked, satisfied in a cold way that my voice didn't shake at all.

"Far," Richy said, confirming my worst fears.

The mere fact that he was no longer moving was a clear enough sign that he didn't think we could make it to the sewer in time to escape.

"You have to go," I said, realizing how true that was as the words came out of my mouth.

"Absolutely not," Richy snapped. "That is out of the question."

"Then what do you suggest?" I hissed, waving an arm around at the other alleyways each just as hopeless as this one. "I don't see any other escape route nearby."

"You can stand behind me," Richy said, his brow furrowed, because he was thinking hard. "I'll use my gift and stand in front of you."

"No offense, Richy," I said sincerely. "But that's a terrible idea."

Richy might be tall, but he was skinny. He couldn't shield me from that many Runners. Besides, even if he did, I would only be invisible from one angle – as long as neither of us moved.

"You have to go," I repeated, firmly. "There is no reason for both of us to get arrested when you can use your gift to get away."

"I will *not* leave you here, Claudelle," he said passionately, but I saw the tired resignation of weakness in his eyes.

"You can come find me later," I assured him, not bothering to evaluate whether that was even plausible. "But for now, you have to go."

I heard a shout and voices responding, coming in our direction. In a second more, Runners would round the corner with their guns leveled at us.

"Now!" I shouted, stomping my foot like a child as he hesitated.

I could see he was thinking about it. He knew it was the only logical thing to do at this point. But he hated himself for considering. I understood. I could imagine being in those shoes. I had been once – when Attis sent me away. But I went, because I knew it was the only thing I could do to protect the rest of my caravan. I knew Richy well enough to know that he would go.

"I will come for you," he promised, stepping away from me and dropping his eyes.

In a few moments I had become the adult – the experienced Gypsy who knew what they were doing – sacrificing myself for the sake of the caravan – in this case my mentor.

"Go!"

I watched him disappear, from his toes to head as the Runners came racing around the bend in the road, already lifting their weapons on straightened arms. I spun on my heel to face them, the wind blowing my hair into my eyes and mouth as I lifted my hands, fingers spread wide. I was only able to stretch the lights into half of a glass-like shield before I heard the click and saw a flash of red. Then I was on the ground.

I was frozen. I wasn't unconscious though. They had used a red bullet. That much was clear as I tried to force my limbs to move but had no control – as if my brain wasn't connected to my body anymore. I saw the agents holstering their weapons as they approached me, looking down at me. One of them kicked me lightly with their foot, like they thought I might be faking. I was awake when the transport came to take me to the lift station, strapped to a sort of table on wheels. I remembered being loaded onto the lift, with an escort of agents surrounding me. They knew I was paralyzed – they knew I couldn't do anything to them. As I lay there frozen, able to see and think, but not to react, I knew why they were doing this. They wanted the Provincials to fear me. They wanted the ignorant people to believe I – a single Taint – was enough cause for this mass panic and high security.

They wanted the people to fear me because if they could do that, they could make the people hate me too. It wasn't a new idea. I'd always been aware of it. I just never thought I would be experiencing it in such a direct way. If The Eye could make their people hate me then no Provincial's moral state would feel even mildly tickled when I was disposed of.

It was probably only twenty minutes that I was frozen like this, but it felt like an eternity. I could see the sky changing and passing overhead in the lift. We were speeding off in a direction I quickly lost track of. I shut my eyes as the feeling started to make its way back into my limbs. I squirmed around and flexed my fingers. One of the Runners looked over at me and raised an eyebrow. Our gaze met only briefly, but I didn't miss the look of contempt there. She turned to one of her partners and said something under her breath. He responded by nodding and pulling something out from under his seat, a case of some sort. Inside was a box. My stomach churned at the sight of the box and I had a feeling that everything was about to become much worse.

The man stood up and straightened his jacket. I could tell the other three were watching him – waiting for something impressive to happen. He pressed a button on the box and it opened with a soft hiss. He lifted a syringe out of the box. I didn't think people still used those anymore, not with penshots around. He set the box down on my makeshift bed and as I strained to look down I caught a glimpse of what looked like a symbol for radiation elevated on of the top of the box.

"What is that?"

My voice sounded hoarse. I wasn't intending to say anything at all, but as the Runners exchanged uncertain glances and the needle approached my arm I couldn't help it.

"What are you doing?"

I sounded obviously panicked, and perhaps in response to that one of the other Runners stood up.

"Get that away from me!" I yelled, trying to kick the Runner aside out of instinct, even though my legs were strapped down and it made no difference. I struggled violently against the restraints on my body and my fingertips tingled as my lights started to appear – a last ditch attempt to keep the needle no-doubt filled with radioactive poison away from me.

"Stop!" I screamed.

Just as the needle touched my skin, the other Runners jumped forward, grabbing my hands and holding them flat against the table. I couldn't control where I wanted the lights to go; they were swirling around in chaotic patterns as I twitched and strained under the Runners' grip.

"Don't – please don't!"

The lights were building up in my fingertips and my arms were practically vibrating with the energy. My vision was clear and crisp – I could see the pores of the nervous man about to put the needle in my arm. Suddenly everything was washed in blue light. I knew it was me – I knew I was doing it somehow. I felt the prick of the needle entering my arm – but that was nothing compared to the pure liquid fire that was screaming through my veins. I think I screamed – there was so much confusion though – both internal and external that I wasn't exactly sure what was happening. Something made a sharp crackling sound – like electricity. I smelled burning. Then I felt coolness on my face, like fresh air and rain – but it was probably just a hallucination my mind invented in order to distract me from the all-consuming pain lighting through my limbs as I thrashed, trying to escape the scorching pain inside of me. I heard shouts that I was dimly aware didn't belong to me, but the crispness of my vision had turned into blurry images all around me instead. I counted only three Runners. Another wave of pain wracked my body and I cried out again – this time I recognized my own voice.

When the wave of pain dissipated for a few moments I realized one of the Runners was holding a penshot against my arm – just like the one Keel had once used to inject anesthetic into my arm before stitching up my hand. I looked drowsily around, still in pain, but able to see more than just spotty outlines. I blinked again and realized it was raining. Two of the Runners were peering over the edge of our lift at the ground below. And I was wet. I was still inside the lift though – I could see the thick cable above us that kept us suspended on the track, swaying lightly. The weather shield was gone. Something had broken it. That's why the rain was falling on us. Had I done that? I didn't know it was possible to break a weather shield. It took me another moment to realize that we weren't moving forward anymore, we were just swinging gently in the air.

I turned my head and saw the Runners standing up, gaining their balance. I looked down at my wrists and saw that the restraints were broken – snapped in half. If only I didn't feel so heavy, I could have stood up – and then what? We were swaying on a rope, a thousand feet in the air over the deserted bomb lands between one province and the next. The mixing chemicals racing through my system were attacking my consciousness, forcing me under a dark blanket, blocking out my senses, encouraging me to sleep. I soon did just that, still unsure what had broken the weather shield and where the last Runner had gone.

CHAPTER SEVENTEEN

I didn't know how much time had passed. At first I tried to count the days, but it was soon obvious that what seemed like a day to me was multiple days in the outside world. They kept me strapped down at first, but at some point the straps became unnecessary. It was clear I didn't have the strength to get farther than the edge of the bed – some days I couldn't sit up.

I didn't know what they were doing to me, but every twisted story Attis had ever told me about the Tinkers came to mind. I couldn't clearly remember what they had done to me even hours before, but there were a lot of syringes – and sometimes penshots. Sometimes I would go under for days at a time – at least I could only assume it was days. I tried to make out the faces of the doctors working on me – the Tinkers – but everything was fuzzy. As soon as I thought I had memorized one of them, they would move away and I wouldn't know if hours or days had passed again. I would forget what they looked like. It was a terrible, twisting feeling to understand so little of what was happening to me. I tried to listen to their conversations, but as soon as I would understand something and feel shock at what they were saying, I would forget again. I think I tried to speak to them, but I couldn't remember if they ever answered me. They were destroying my mind along with my body.

I don't know when the headaches started, but they were intolerable. I think they only happened every couple days, but sometimes the Tinkers would ignore me for hours at a time when I was in that state. I started to fear the headaches, which only made them worse. Eventually I would feel a prick in my arm and the headache would fade away and I would sleep if I was lucky. It was an endless cycle. When I floated closer to the surface of awareness, I tried to use the powers, but I never could. It made the headaches too painful to stand. Despite this, I once dreamed that I managed to summon a few little blue streaks of light, but it couldn't have been real. I was too drugged to concentrate on the powers.

I woke with a start, more alert than I could remember since the Tinkers first took me. Something was changing. I was strapped down again and it took me a few moments to realize that my bed was being moved. They hadn't ever moved my bed – at least to my knowledge. The large monitors and screens I was connected to disappeared and were replaced with smaller, older monitors. I winced as a Tinker knelt over my arm and pulled one of the tubes out of my skin. I tried to ask what was happening, but I didn't know if the sounds I was hearing even resembled words. Honestly I didn't know if the sounds were coming from me at all.

Daylight flashed into my eyes and I gasped, turning my head away before the daylight disappeared again. I blinked the spots out my eyes and realized I was inside some sort of vehicle. I was vaguely aware of a vibrating sensation as the vehicle warmed up. I didn't know where we were going or how long it took, but we were moving. Time was slipping away faster at some times and slower at others. I tried to think back to a time before the Tinkers and the needles and the headaches. I could picture my caravan and the Micahs – but not all at once. I had to concentrate all of my efforts on remembering little details about them. Attis kept coming to mind and I didn't know why. I was confused. I felt like I needed to be upset with him, but I couldn't remember what for.

Daylight flashed into my eyes again and I was vaguely aware of being rolled into a large, black snake. I had the feeling we were moving again, even though there was hardly a hum to indicate it. It took me a moment to realize that it felt familiar. I knew where I was – I was on a train. Or maybe I was hallucinating. How long had I been on the train? Had I already fallen asleep and woken up? I couldn't remember. Maybe this was all just my imagination. Maybe this train was going to take me somewhere the headaches couldn't find me. I stretched my fingers and felt for my powers, thinking that perhaps they would return with the coming transition. Instead I felt the warning twinge of pain spearing through my temples. I gasped and turned my head away from the fuzzy outline of the Tinker adjusting a monitor. I quickly relaxed my hand, thinking it might encourage the throbbing in my skull to go away. My whole body was tingling. I needed to use the powers. The energy was building up inside of me. A Tinker approached me, although I didn't know how long after my almost-headache, and administered a penshot that made me sleepy.

I woke up later with a lurch. Or maybe it wasn't a lurch. Maybe I was hallucinating an earthquake. Trains didn't lurch. The sounds around me that had seemed muffled for as long as I could remember were becoming clearer in my ears with their increased volume. Was that an alarm? Surely not. Where were the Tinkers? I didn't see any, but then again my scope of vision was limited and I could hardly lift my head to look around. If there were no Tinkers around, this had to be a dream. I was asleep. No Tinkers and no headache couldn't be real.

I dreamed that the door to my compartment of the train slid open and a group of shabbily dressed Provincials came storming inside, holding weapons at ready. They were angels. They must have been the ones who took away the pain in my head. I dreamed that Keel was holding my hand again. It was more of a feeling than anything else. I heard sounds that I vaguely remembered were my name. *Delle.* Yeah, that was my name. Delle. I had almost forgotten.

"Delle, can you hear me?"

The voice was serious, but I wanted to enjoy the peace I was finally experiencing. I think I nodded. I tried to at least. I felt a few tugs on my arm, probably the last of the wires and tubes coming out. I had become numb to the pain of needles at this point. I think I finally understood what was happening. The train had crashed. I was dead – dead or dying – and these people were going to take me away to the safe horizon.

"Delle, wake up."

The voice was measured, controlled, no more and no less urgent than the last time it had spoken. How long had it been since it first spoke to me? It could have been an hour or it could have been a second.

I tried to focus my vision, but I knew what I was seeing couldn't actually be real. It was just one more sign that this was the end I'd been wishing for during the worst of the headaches. Keel's face was looming in my vision, his black hair mangy and hanging nearly over his eyes.

He needs a haircut, I thought dreamily.

His hands were on my face, slapping my cheeks lightly, trying to convince me to wake up. I focused in on his mouth and vaguely recalled that he had once kissed me. At least I think that's what I was remembering. No, it was twice. He kissed me twice. Once in New Capil and once in Laylen.

"We can't wait."

This was a different voice. This voice was more urgent than Keel's – shriller.

"We're ready," Keel said, looking at something over my head then glancing back at the other angels who had stormed in behind him. "I'll have to carry her out."

Then I was in someone's arms, being carried like a child. Daylight hit me in the eyes and I gasped again, my eyes feeling bruised as I was jarred to the bone. It took me several moments to realize that we weren't in the train anymore. We were leaving the train behind us, flames waving goodbye to me as my dream rescuer deposited me in the trunk of a car. This was just one more sign that what I was experiencing wasn't reality. Cars had been outlawed over a hundred years ago. Somehow, my muddled brain managed to hold onto that fact. Someone climbed into the trunk after me and I felt another jolt as someone closed the door. I blinked and the arms that had carried me out of the death train were around me again, holding me tightly against his chest, shielding me from the questions that I could feel creeping up on me as my more aware brain wondered if any of this hallucination might be real.

***

I woke up – *really* woke up – for the first time in longer than I could remember. There was noise coming at me from all directions and the entire room including the bed I was lying on was colored with dingy shades of white that might have been grey at some point. I turned my head and saw people rushing – nearly running – through the hallway outside my room. Something was happening. I didn't know what. Where was I?

I tried to sit up, remembering the train crash the way someone might remember a hazy dream and not know for sure if it was real or not. I tried to remember what events led up to the crash, trying to find context, but the last thing I could remember clearly was being detained in the lift after first being captured by the Runners. I winced as mild pain speared through my temples. I put my head to my hand as if I could physically stop the pain from coming back.

I looked down at my arm and saw little white disks stuck to it, releasing their chemicals into my body little by little. Something snapped inside of me then and I could almost hear a physical *click*. In a flood, the few moments I had been awake during my stay with the Tinkers came rushing back. I instantly leaned over the side of the bed and put my feet on the ground, frantically ripping the discs off my skin. I needed to throw up, but there was nothing in my stomach to go.

I stood up and dizziness took over, darkness overwhelming my vision. I gasped and sat back down. It wasn't the idea of fainting that was terrifying. It was the idea of fainting *again*. I had no idea how much time I'd spent unconscious as of late, but I had a terrible feeling it was a lot. I took several deep breaths and put my hand on the wall. Once I was sure the ground was firmly situated under my feet, I stood up again and staggered towards the door. Why did walking feel so foreign?

I looked down at my hand as I reached for the wall again and saw it shaking. My entire body was vibrating with the effort of moving. I vaguely noticed there was no door on the mismatched hinges of the doorframe as I passed out of my room and into the hallway. Nobody looked at me twice, even though a lot of people passed by. They all looked important and were clearly off to do important things.

I wobbled a few more steps down the hallway before I thought I heard someone call my name. I hesitated a moment before turning to look over my shoulder. Keel was rushing towards me and it hit me that he was the one who pulled me out of the train and carried me to wherever this place was. *Not a dream.*

"Keel?" I asked, not even startled when he reached me and pulled me into a desperate hug, holding me tight and close. I could feel his fingers curling into the tangled hair at the back of my neck, smoothing it down as he held me. He was shaking too.

"What happened?" I asked, my voice croaking from disuse.

I didn't resist the embrace, but I was reacting too slowly to respond to it. Keel looked up and glanced towards the stream of people still hurrying by us. I thought for a moment there was something familiar about their ordered pandemonium.

"I'll explain," he promised, and I didn't miss how tense his voice was. "But let's get you out of here first."

I nodded dumbly as he put a strong arm around my waist, never letting me drift more than an inch from his side. He hurried me down the hallway and into an older model lift. I looked down at my bare feet and then at the feet of the other people who crowded in around us. They were all wearing similar shoes – boots. When the lift squealed to a stop he practically carried me out.

"Keel, where are we going?" I asked as he guided me out of the building and onto a sidewalk.

Again I looked down at my feet and realized the pavement was crumbling underneath us. Then it hit me. Provinces didn't have sidewalks, because there was no reason to stay out of the streets if cars were banned and, I had assumed, destroyed – except in my almost-dream of being rescued, we were in a car that smelled like mold. I looked up and sucked in a breath of surprise. I pulled away from Keel and turned in a circle, taking in everything around me.

"Are we in the bomb lands?" I asked, turning back to Keel.

He nodded. "It's an old province right outside Tac. This is where the Rebels send their injured to recover. They started rebuilding here a couple years ago."

"Injured?" I echoed, turning to look down the street, where the concrete was cracked and weeds were starting to crop up. I could feel Keel watching me. He was anxious.

"Where are Steffy and Jag?" I asked, whirling back around so quickly I nearly lost my precarious balance again. I could feel all the blood rush out of my face as my body threatened to shut down. "Where's the family?" I asked, ignoring Keel's attempts to make me keep still as he grabbed my elbows. "Where's Richy?"

"All safe," he assured me. "Please, Delle. Just take it easy until we get to our quarters, then I'll tell you what happened."

I nodded, knowing I wasn't in any condition to argue about it but still wishing I was. There was a surprising hiss of hot, foul-smelling smoke at my ankles and what looked like a section of a train pulled up beside the sidewalk.

"Is that –?"

"A bus," Keel finished for me as the doors opened and he ushered me up the steps, which felt rubbery and sticky under my feet.

"Where are we going?" I whispered.

"You'll see," he responded mysteriously.

It couldn't have been more than five minutes later that we stopped and Keel led me off the bus. I was tired of being dragged around without any explanation, unsure of where I was or even where the rest of my family was. Keel took my hand and pulled me through the swinging doors – not even automatic doors – and nodded at the man standing behind the desk with a security card around his neck. The man waved him on and Keel guided me about halfway down a hallway before knocking on a door and listening for a moment before opening it.

"These are our quarters," he explained, opening the door and nodding me inside.

I frowned at the brown carpet, which was completely torn out in some places. There was a sheet hung across the room just beyond the kitchen area.

"Our quarters?" I echoed.

"Well, this half is ours. There was a guy on the half behind the sheet, but he left yesterday. They'll be moving someone else in soon. I'll get you something to eat," he offered. "You can sit down over there."

"Thanks," I mumbled, crossing the room and sitting down on the grungy sofa with stuffing coming out the seams. I could have laid down and slept for hours on that sofa, except that part of me was afraid if I went to sleep I would wake up to find myself back in the Tinkers' lab.

"Can you tell me," I began slowly, "How I got here?"

"Do you remember anything?" he asked, crossing over to me and handing me a bowl with a piece of bread and a couple skips in it.

I frowned and looked down at the food. What had I been eating for the past who-knows-how-long? I didn't remember. Keel sat beside me and I could tell he was waiting for me to answer, watching me closely. I winced as my skull pounded with the headache I thought had gone away but had really just gone into hiding for a short time.

"I remember being taken," I said, shutting my eyes and trying to remember back as far as I could. "I was in a room somewhere. There were Tinkers. They were testing some sort of chemical on me. Then I was in that train and it crashed and you were there."

"That's all you remember?" he asked quietly.

"Basically," I muttered, realizing for the first time that I was wearing new clothes – well, clearly not *new* but new to me. I fingered the course material of the tank top and picked at a fraying tear in the pants. "How long was it?"

I looked up after the silence stretched on for several moments too long. Keel wasn't looking at me. His eyes were hidden from me and his mouth was set in a dull line.

"Keel, if I don't start getting some answers soon I'm going to lose my mind," I snapped, feeling fear pinch my gut. "You have to talk to me and tell me what's been going on because I have no idea what's been happening to me or anyone else."

"About a month," he said wearily. "They had you for about a month. We didn't know where you were until they decided to move you to the First Province. Everyone except for Fil, Nanda, and Jag went to Flor to be with Steffy. They're all safe, by the way. Fil, Nanda, and Jag are in Tac. Before we knew where you were, I was in Tac too. I asked around and found Mona. I told her what happened and she dropped everything to find you. She's the one who found out about the train you were on and organized the attack."

"A month?"

I knew my voice broke, but it wasn't because I was crying. I had no desire to cry. I was just amazed – amazed and horrified. I couldn't even remember an entire day clearly since I'd been taken.

"Please eat something," Keel said, pressing the bowl closer to me as I stared at him uncomprehendingly.

"Right," I responded, blinking and reaching into the bowl to tear a piece off the bread. I shook my head to clear it of the news I couldn't process yet. "Is Mona here?"

"She's in Tac."

"Everyone's in Tac," I said slowly.

Keel nodded and there was silence for a few moments. I chewed on the dry bread and swallowed it before looking over at him and watching him brush his hair out of his face.

"You need a haircut," I commented, surprised to feel myself smile when he laughed at my change of subject. "You're starting to look like a real Gypsy."

He rolled his eyes.

"So," I said with a sigh. "What next?"

"You should probably rest for a couple days, Delle," he said, raising an eyebrow at me. "Then we can talk about what to do next."

"I've been 'resting' for a month, Keel," I responded, probably sharper than I needed to. "I'm not going to take a nap and wait until I feel better to get out of here."

Keel brushed the loose hair away from my face and looked me in the eyes. "A lot has changed in the month you were gone. Your well-being is just one of several reasons we're going to have to stick around here for a few days."

"What are you talking about?" I asked, annoyed that I still didn't understand the situation. I wanted back in the loop as soon as possible, wanted to pretend that I hadn't lost a month of my life.

"The Eye," he started, then hesitated, searching my face. "The Eye started a campaign against genetically altered people – Taints, I mean." He paused, apparently waiting for my reaction.

I couldn't think of how to respond, so I didn't. I didn't fully believe it yet.

"They've been rounding them up – killing those who don't cooperate and imprisoning the others."

"How many?"

"What?" he asked uneasily, even though he knew what I meant.

"How many have been killed?" I clarified, trapping him in my gaze.

He was silent for a moment. When he spoke, his voice was soft – barely more than a whisper.

"Four hundred and counting."

I sucked in a sharp breath, like I'd just been punched in the stomach.

"That video started all of this, didn't it?" I asked hollowly.

Keel shrugged uncomfortably. "It might have contributed to Provincial support of all this, but the Rebels have been expecting this for some time."

"Mona never mentioned it," I growled, thinking bitterly about my unattached aunt. An ominous idea began creeping into my heart. "What are they doing with the people they're imprisoning?"

"No one knows," he admitted, watching me carefully, clearly confused by the expression on my face. "All we know is that when the Runners take the Taints who come willingly, they promise to make them 'clean'. Even the Rebels don't know what that means yet."

I suddenly remembered bits of conversations that had happened around me as the Tinkers took my blood and replaced it with their own chemicals, over and over again, always trying new mixtures with the same purpose in mind. I suddenly thought I might throw up.

I dropped my head into my hands to cover my face and the bowl fell off my lap and onto the ground, cracking from one half to the other.

Keel instantly moved closer, putting a hand on my back and trying to pull my hands away from my face with the other. "Delle, what is it? What's wrong? Are you in pain?"

"I know," I breathed shakily. "I know what it means."

CHAPTER EIGHTEEN

"I want to walk," I said suddenly, standing up and moving towards the door, already reaching out to steady myself against the wall for the dizziness I knew was coming.

"What?" Keel asked worriedly, standing up. "Why?"

"I need to walk," I said.

I threw open the door and only paused a moment to look down at my borrowed pants, which were pulled up almost to my waist and cinched with a belt – clearly much too big for me. I pulled them up again and continued my escape from the building, Keel taking long strides to keep up with me.

"What do you mean?" Keel persisted as we stepped out into the cool, damp breeze blowing through the destroyed city. "Where are you going?"

I crossed my arms against the breeze and shook my head, hoping I was wrong about what The Eye intended to do to my kind.

"I don't know, Keel. I just need to think," I snapped.

He stopped me and spun me around, gripping my upper arms firmly, refusing to let me look anywhere but at him.

"Delle, you have to talk to me. Please."

I looked into his confused and tortured eyes and let out the breath I had been about to use to reject him.

"They took a whole month from me," I whispered, looking at him earnestly, trying to communicate just how sincere my need to figure this out was. "And I hardly remember any of it."

"I'm so sorry, Delle," he said softly.

I shook my head again, stopping him. "That's not the worst part. I remember just enough to feel like I *almost* know something important."

"'Almost'?"

"They were talking about chemicals," I stammered. "They were trying to find the right balance, to suppress something."

"Your powers?" he asked, not sounding surprised, just grim.

I shrugged. "I don't know. I know every time they gave me an injection I wouldn't be fully awake for days afterwards. I don't know if they ever got it to work."

"Well have you tried to use the powers since then?"

"No."

I pulled away from Keel and he let me go. I turned around and looked down at my hands. I turned them over and realized for the first time that there were new scars on my palms and my fingers. The scars were clean and thin. They were surgical. They didn't come from an accident – although I still had the scars from the ladder accident on one hand. I wondered at how I hadn't felt them cutting apart my hands. I felt the familiar tingle of energy run down my arms and into my fingertips as I tried to summon the powers. I waited for the energy to burst from my fingertips in tendrils of blue light, for the growing tension in my fingers and arms to dissolve – but it didn't. I rubbed my hands together and clenched my fists. I shook out my hands one more time and looked down at my arms, inspecting them. I had been given so many injections and penshots that in the daylight I could see the marks on my skin more clearly. My arms looked freckled now. I could feel Keel's eyes on my back as I again tried to produce the glowing blue lights that both destroyed and protected so much of my life.

"I can't," I stammered, feeling tears sting in my eyes for the first time since I'd really woken up. "They're gone."

"What?" Keel asked, disbelief in his voice.

I whirled back around, holding out my hands to him desperately. I could still feel the energy filling my body, swirling around uselessly with nowhere to go, ever expanding.

"They won't come!" I didn't know if I was crying. "The powers are there – I can feel them, Keel! But they won't come!"

Keel's mouth was hanging open. He didn't know what to say. I didn't blame him.

"That's what they meant by 'clean'," I continued my raving. "They were using me to experiment, to find the right mixture of some chemical that can suppress a Taint's powers."

I flexed my fingers again and tried to find the powers, shaking with the energy building up inside. Suddenly I staggered under the pain that struck me right in the temples, like I'd been hit with a hammer. I cried out and fell forward. Keel caught me. I was aware that he was talking to me, but for a few moments I couldn't make out his words because of the sheer force of the pain.

"Delle," Keel said, holding me against his chest to keep me from crumpling to the ground. "Delle, are you okay? What's wrong?"

"My head," I gasped, shutting my eyes tightly and clutching my head like I could keep it from splitting apart.

"What's wrong?"

"It *hurts*."

"Do I need to take you back to the hospital?" he asked, trying to hold me far enough away from him that he could see my face.

"*No.*" I heard myself grind out the words. "No, we need to tell someone what The Eye is planning."

"You can hardly stand," he argued, and somewhere in my mind I knew he was probably giving me his signature exasperated expression. "Now isn't the time to tell anyone anything. It's time to find a doctor." He caught me around the waist and tried to guide me in a new direction.

"No! No, it's going away," I said desperately, relieved to find that it really was. I put my hands on his chest and tried to push him away, trying to collect myself.

"Has that happened before?" he asked quietly, one hand still held out to me, like he thought I might relapse at any moment.

"I think so," I muttered. "I don't remember clearly, but I think so." I took Keel's hand and stepped closer, looking up at him. "We need to get to Tac. They're going to do this to all of us."

"We still won't be able to leave for a few more days," he said, his eyebrows coming together. "I'm sorry, Delle, but there are Runners everywhere and The Eye is watching. The Rebels are tightly regulating transportation to and from Tac. The next group is leaving two days from now."

"Keel, they could be doing this to people right now!" I protested. "We have to leave now!"

I didn't mention that the ground seemed to be shifting beneath my feet again, or that I just realized I hadn't stood up or moved around in the month that the Tinkers had me. Keel raised an eyebrow at me, apparently noticing more than I thought.

"You're not going anywhere," he said, crossing his arms and giving me a skeptical look when I glared at him. "We'll talk once you get some sleep. And finish eating."

***

The two days passed slowly, but Keel was right. I couldn't seem to be active for more than a few hours at a time before falling into a deep exhaustion. I tried two other times to try and produce the blue lights, but every time my constantly present headache would erupt into the most painful migraine I'd ever experienced. Keel was gone the first time I had the headaches and I never told him what happened.

That day, a pair of twins moved into the part of the room behind the sheet. I had never met twins before so it was hard not to stare. They didn't even bother to hide the fact that they were staring at me too. Every time they came or went, passing by Keel and I sitting on the couch, they would look at us shrewdly and whisper to each other as they pulled the curtain closed, dividing us.

I think the second time I tried to use the powers terrified Keel even more than it pained me. It was so painful that I couldn't pretend I was okay. He ran his hand anxiously through his hair so much that I thought he might tear it out. He begged me not to use the powers again until we found someone who knew how to reverse whatever the Tinkers had done to me. He didn't make me promise though, like Attis had done so many years ago. I noticed this and for some reason it reassured me. I told him I would try and not to worry.

I tried to convince Keel to help me find someone who had some way to communicate with Tac. He tried for my sake, but everyone he spoke to refused to lend him a Tab, saying that none but the most important messages could be sent because, although their line was secure, they were concerned it wouldn't stay that way for long. They wanted to stay off the radar as much as possible.

I was practically vibrating with tension – not with energy exactly, because I was constantly exhausted and the constant pounding in my skull did nothing to help. However, I was getting better at hiding the discomfort – I was almost used to it now. On the morning of the third day in the old city, Keel and I walked side by side towards the electric bus that was humming and trembling at the side of the crumbling curb. As we piled into the monstrous machine behind other ragged and weary looking Rebels, I overheard some of them talking about the shortage of food the Gypsies were experiencing. Apparently the Brokers were no longer trading for the seeds our Farmers needed in order to grow food out in the farthest bomb lands. There was too much general paranoia for them to barter safely with the hunt for Taints going on and the suspicion of Gypsies in general. I swallowed at the thought of a mass food shortage. There wasn't that much to go around in the first place. This war was more serious than I ever imagined.

Keel touched my arm and I sat down beside him. He took my hand and turned it over, tracing the new scars on my palms where the Tinkers had opened my hands up over and over again – trying to figure out how I produced the blue light. It briefly occurred to me that Presid Bertley would appreciate the irony of my new marks. The scars reminded me of something else too – and because of that reminder I now had a plan. It was more of a hope really. It wasn't detailed and it relied solely upon the cooperation of one specific Provincial, but I wasn't about to dismiss it as impossible.

We would be in Tac within a few hours and once we were there I knew what I needed to do. First I needed to find Mona. The last time I had seen her I got the impression that she had some pull with the higher-ups of the Rebel army. If she could convince them that my purpose was important enough, they might let me use a secure line to get a message out to the one person I was sure had answers that we needed. Of course Jag, Fil, Nanda, and Richy would be there too and I was desperately eager to see them – to see with my own eyes that they were all alive and well.

Keel stuck close to me as I stepped off the bus. If I thought the underground base in Laylen was bustling with activity, Tac was practically swarming with Rebels. This place was different in other ways too. It was a province, but it was full of all kinds of people. Some people appeared to be Rebels while others looked like they could still be wandering Gypsies. Still others looked like purebred Provincials, all conversing with serious expressions.

Keel took my hand and pulled me along. Clearly he had been here before – some time during the month the Tinkers had stolen no doubt.

"They were there, you know," he commented abruptly as we paused to let a group of armed Rebels hurry past us.

"Who?"

"Jag, Fil, and Nanda," he responded, picking up the pace and heading towards a slightly outdated building sitting across the street. "Mona and Richy too. They all had a hand in your rescue. The only reason they weren't in the old city was because the officials wouldn't allow more than one of us to stay with you since it's already so crowded over there."

"Oh." I was suddenly overwhelmed with a rush of gratitude again, thinking about my friends and all they had risked for me. "Where are they?"

"Jag will probably be here," Keel said with a shrug as the doors to the building slid open with a rusty squeal. "Mona too. They spend most of their time here."

"Where is 'here'?" I echoed, looking up at the massive skylight far overhead. The balconies of what looked like endless floors jutted out over the silent but busy lobby we stood in the center of. "What is this place?"

Keel smirked a little. "Basically, this is headquarters. This is where the decision making and strategy happens."

"Perfect," I muttered, thinking immediately back to my own desperate strategy.

We took a lift up to the thirteenth floor and stepped off. It felt strange, not instantly seeing my little family like I was so used to. I felt a sharp twinge in my stomach as I thought about Steffy who I wouldn't be able to see again for quite some time. I said a silent prayer for her safety and clutched Keel's hand even tighter. He looked over at me, obviously trying to discern what was wrong. I carefully avoided his gaze.

"This way," Keel murmured, tugging me lightly down a hallway and pausing outside a plain metallic door, knocking on it twice before it slid open to let us through.

I stepped inside after Keel and looked around. The room was stark and sparsely furnished. There were eight people inside, all standing around a table, looking at a holographic map projected between them. They barely glanced up as we entered and didn't even bother to pause their conversation.

We came further into the room before a voice from behind us said, "Well it took you long enough."

I whirled around to see Jag raising an eyebrow at Keel's hand and my own tightly joined.

"Jag!" I cried, stumbling forward and throwing my arms around him.

He hugged me back tightly – nearly a head taller than me. It seemed like much longer than a month since I'd last seen him.

"Delle," he said, relief gushing from his voice. "It's so good to see you awake and moving. We didn't know what they had done to you or if the damage was even reparable."

"Some of it was," I said quickly, not wanting to mention that my powers were essentially long gone.

Jag pulled back and frowned at my mysterious statement. I was saved by the appearance of Mona, who stopped in her tracks when she saw me. We looked at each other for a moment, silent.

Finally, Mona's voice came out in a breathy question. "Delle?"

"Mona," I greeted her, not sure whether to smile or keep a straight face.

Even though she was my aunt she had made it clear she chose her duty to the Rebels over her family a long time ago. I wasn't going to resent her for it. At this point that would be a waste of valuable energy. Besides, I'd managed this long without blood relatives.

"Thank you for rescuing me," I said seriously, sounding much less flustered than I felt. "I heard about what you did, convincing the general to let you come after me." She didn't say anything for a moment, just watched me like she was waiting for me to follow up my thanks with a rude remark. "I'm really grateful," I finished.

She blinked and seemed taken aback for just a moment before she managed to recover and offered me an uncertain smile. "You're welcome. It's good to see you functioning again – even if you look like you hit the tracks."

I raised both eyebrows at her observation and in response her too-familiar smirk turned up the corner of her mouth.

"I know it's probably a bad time," I said, looking between Jag and Mona, uncomfortably realizing that both were holding themselves like soldiers, while I felt completely clueless. "But I need a favor."

Mona was busy and even though it was beyond frustrating, I understood that I would have to wait to explain my whole idea to her. She suggested we meet up with Fil and in the meantime she would come over as soon as she was available. Jag came with us, even though I could tell he really wanted to stay behind and join in the meeting taking place.

"You can stay, Jag, really," I said, trying to sound like I meant it as we walked back out the sliding doors from the lobby into the pulsing street. "Go back to your meeting and I'll see you later. I don't want to take you away from something you want to do."

"No," he said stubbornly. "I want to spend time with you before the real hustle kicks in. Besides, I'm still not completely convinced you're okay and now that you and Keel seem to be a new thing someone has to chaperone you two."

I rolled my eyes and felt my cheeks grow warm even as Jag laughed and Keel grinned, taking my hand again.

"You're both children," I snapped grumpily, although I think it was obvious I wasn't really mad. I was too relieved at seeing my family again to be mad at any of them.

When we arrived at the apartment the Rebels had given us to stay in, Fil was the only one there. Nanda was away doing some kind of work for the Rebels and wouldn't be back until the next day. I tried not to show my surprise at Nanda's philanthropic efforts to save the world. When I first met her she was grim and cold – so wrapped up in her own grief that she barely ventured to speak to another person. Then Steffy had befriended her and now they were practically sisters – not that Nanda wasn't still painfully quiet and a little unfriendly. It was hard to imagine her choosing to be anywhere except where Steffy was. I know I wouldn't if I had a choice.

I barely made it through the door of the apartment before Fil hugged me and lifted me off my feet, proclaiming that he was glad to see me and never doubted I would pull through. As usual, after only a minute or so with him I felt like he could read my thoughts. Unlike Lacey and Jorge, he was more of a thinker than a doer. He seemed amused by my poorly concealed surprise about Nanda's new spirit of heroism.

"I know," he said with a wink. "I didn't think she would be into this sort of thing either, but she's really taken to it. She's good too. Mostly she works infiltration. We've only been here for a few weeks and she's already made a name for herself. Her troop should be getting back later today."

"Infiltration?" I echoed, shocked. "Wow."

Fil grinned. "I know."

"She's in a troop?" I asked, thinking he might tell me it was just a joke or that I had misunderstood.

"Yup."

"She has to work with other people?" I asked skeptically, raising an eyebrow. "Like, teamwork?"

Nanda was the only person I knew who seemed less capable of teamwork than myself.

"She's good too," Fil repeated, laughing at my dumbfounded expression and guiding me farther into the little apartment.

Keel convinced me to sit down and rest while we waited for Mona, but the whole time I was fighting the urge to get up and run. I wanted to go out into the streets and demand that someone listen to me. I don't think anyone understood the urgency of the matter – not even Keel.

Taints were being killed and cruelly experimented on even as we sat there, smiling at each other and talking about the family. Every time the throbbing ache in my head worsened, I thought of the countless other people like me who were going to have to live with the same thing – if they survived the experiments. I was starting to get used to the constant pain in my skull, but it wasn't pleasant. It left me constantly exhausted and unable to fully engage in anything, no matter how slight the ache.

Thanks to my stupid promise to Attis all those years ago, I could control the powers. Currently, I didn't dare touch them – not if I didn't want to be throwing up on the ground with the excruciating sensation of my skull being cracked open. But most Taints weren't like me – I knew that. Most Taints couldn't control the powers like I had learned to. I had practice suppressing and controlling them for the majority of my life. Magely though, she couldn't control the powers at all – she told me so. The splitting headaches would tear her apart with no reprieve if she couldn't learn to control it. And she was just one of the many. Someone had to stop it.

Mona's knock at the door startled me out of my dismal thoughts. She didn't even wait for someone to answer the door, letting herself in, already greeting us. "Hey guys. The meeting finished earlier than I expected."

I stopped scratching my hand and lurched to my feet, waiting for her attention. She noted this with an uncertain expression.

"What did you need to ask me?" she said, her tone both concerned and hesitant.

"First," I replied, taking a deep breath. "I know what The Eye is doing with the Taints they aren't killing."

Mona didn't look at all surprised. Her expression just darkened.

I had almost forgotten she was a Taint too.

One more person at risk.

"The Tinkers are using a chemical to suppress the powers. I don't know how long they've been developing it, but I'm definitely not the first Taint they tested it on," I said, hearing the unexpected bite in my voice, realizing that even as much as I had always thought I wanted to be rid of the powers, it wasn't true. I relied on them – they were my safeguard.

"But I think I am the first one it worked on," I finished grimly.

Mona didn't say anything at first. I glanced around the room, gauging everyone's reactions.

"I don't remember much," I continued when nobody spoke up. "But I think something about my powers in particular helped them figure it out. And this chemical doesn't only take away the powers – there are side effects too." I was frustrated to find that no one was answering me.

I glanced back at Keel and he shrugged. He also looked slightly confused.

"They're planning to inject this chemical into every Taint they don't kill straight out," I persisted. "They're probably already doing it!"

Still, no one answered. I suddenly had the horrible feeling that I was giving them old news. Mona finally shook her head and sucked in a breath. She didn't look stunned, which bothered me more than a little.

"We thought it might come to that," she finally admitted, sitting back onto one of the stools in the kitchen. "We didn't realize they'd fully developed it, but we always knew they might."

"And you didn't try to stop them?" I snapped, horrified for more than a few reasons. "Or at least warn people about it?"

"Of course we tried to stop them," she snapped back, glaring at me. "Some of us. But we didn't think they were anywhere close enough to fully developing something like that."

"Well thanks to me, they are," I growled.

The room fell silent again. I could feel the faintest tingling in my fingers and up my arms and the faint throbbing in my head turned into a steady pounding. I shut my eyes and for a second I wasn't aware of anything besides the pain. Then the pounding receded and I realized Keel's hands were on my arms – he was standing in front of me, trying to get my attention.

"I'm fine," I said, shaking my head and opening my eyes. I looked up at Keel whose expression made it clear that he didn't believe me. "I'm *fine*," I repeated, taking Keel's wrists and removing his hands.

"What just happened?" Fil asked, stepping forward, his eyebrows furrowed.

"Nothing," I muttered, looking away from Keel's searching gaze.

Keel snorted and turned back to Mona. "It wasn't nothing. It was the side effect Delle was talking about."

"*Keel,*" I hissed furiously, trying to stop him without bringing back the headache.

"They need to know," he argued sharply.

I frowned and after I didn't answer for a moment he looked back at me, questioning. Finally, I broke eye contact and sighed, crossing my arms and shifting my feet. He took that as a positive signal.

"What do we need to know?" Mona asked, speaking in measured tones, her eyes flicking over to me every few moments like I might burst into flames.

"The side effects," Keel said, sounding much calmer now than a moment ago. "Anytime a Taint is agitated or tries to use their powers, they experience crippling pain as a deterrent that forces them to stop."

Mona's jaw tightened. I knew she was probably imagining what that would be like, since she was, after all, Tainted.

Fil looked over at me, his expression mingled horror and sadness. I quickly looked away, putting a hand on Keel's arm so that he would step to the side, allowing me to face Mona again. I cleared my throat and shook my head, focusing on sounding confident.

"But," I said firmly, staring back into Mona's blue-green eyes, about to find out if she was my ally or opponent. "I think I know someone who can help."

CHAPTER NINETEEN

"I don't want you to get your hopes up," Mona warned me. "The general doesn't have anything against Taints, but he has no interest in picking up our cause."

"Not wanting to be murdered or sadistically altered isn't really a cause," I said, hurrying to keep up with her.

Mona rolled her eyes. "If you go in there like this he's not going to listen to a word you say. You know we're lucky he even agreed to meet with us."

"I feel honored," I replied dryly.

Mona laughed and the sound surprised me. I looked over at her suspiciously to see her shaking her head as she reached towards the door pad.

"You're just like your mom," she muttered.

I didn't have time to respond before the door slid open and Mona entered the room. I was right on her heels, approaching the general. He was currently in the middle of a conversation with two other men and didn't acknowledge us at first. The woman that had accompanied him at the base in Laylen stood at his shoulder. It wasn't clear whether she was paying attention to their conversation or not, she was so busy with a screen she had open on her Tab. From her serious expression, I assumed she was doing something important – not watching one of the ridiculously repetitive shows the Provincials love so much.

When I shifted my feet and sighed impatiently, the general held up a hand in Mona's direction, signaling her to wait. I frowned.

"The codes on every computer in the capital were changed last night," one of the men reported. "We had to pull two of our teams when the alarms were tripped."

The general turned to address the other man. "How long until we get the new codes?"

"An infiltration team is returning tomorrow," the man replied. "We can brief them and send them out again as soon as possible."

The general nodded then lifted a hand dismissively. "Make it happen. Let me know the second the situation changes so we can continue preparations."

"General," Mona addressed him as soon as the men left the room.

"I don't have long," he answered, turning to power down a Tab that had been projecting a series of numbers a moment before. "What is it you wanted to talk about?"

"It's the Taint situation, sir," she began, her expression resolved. "It's advanced quicker than we anticipated. They've finished developing a chemical that can block a Taint's powers by producing extreme amounts of pain."

The general raised an eyebrow. "This is why you're here?"

"Taints are being killed," I broke in, capturing his attention for the first time since we entered the room. "Those of us who aren't killed are being tortured with this chemical, not to mention the Tinkers' other experiments. Something has to be done to stop them."

The general's lips pursed. Clearly, there was something about me that he didn't appreciate – whether it was my tone or my Taintness, I didn't know.

"While that's unfortunate, there are more pressing matters I have to attend to right now, so if this is all –"

"*More pressing matters?*" I interrupted, even as Mona hissed my name, a warning to stop. "You don't find it *pressing* that every person with powers is now being –"

"My obligation is to the greater percentage of the population," he cut me off, his voice cold. "I can't expend valuable resources to protect people who don't want to be found."

"And why do you think we don't want to be found?" I snapped. "Because we're being *hunted* and *no one* is doing anything about it – no one has *ever* done anything about it!" The tingling in my fingers was now more than enough warning to stop.

The general considered me for a moment, calculating, before he turned to Mona. "Well, Mona? What do you think?"

"I think there are definite pros to stopping the production of this chemical or at least finding a cure for it. It would be a sign to the Taints that we're defending them just like we are everyone else," she said firmly, giving me a hard look when I opened my mouth to interrupt. She continued glaring at me until I rolled my eyes and shut my mouth so hard my teeth clicked together. "Imagine working with Taints rather than disregarding them. Their powers can be impressive to say the least. If we gain the faith of the Taints, we can convince them to work with us. We'd be gaining valuable assets the First Province could never match."

The general considered this for a moment. He appeared to be thinking, but maybe that was giving him too much credit. I had to admit that Mona had stated our case better than I had. It just seemed stupid that none of this had occurred to them before – that Taints hadn't been considered important enough to protect until now.

"I assume you have a plan to stop the production of this chemical – or something of the sort?" he finally said, raising an eyebrow at me.

I nodded, steeling my nerves so I wouldn't let my annoyance with his pompous manner get the best of me again.

"There's a doctor I met once," I said evenly. "For the right price, I think she'd be willing to help."

***

"Dr. Reece," Nanda said slowly, holding a cup of tea and giving me an uncertain look. "You think she'll be willing to help us?"

"I think she'll be willing to do groundbreaking research into what turns a Taint's powers on and off," I said with a sigh. "If the general will give her a place to study and will put out the message that he'll protect any Taints who join the cause or agree to work with

187

her, I don't see why she wouldn't do it. She already told us she doesn't like the restrictions The Eye forces on her research."

"So now we just have to contact her," Nanda mused. "On a secure line, without it being traced back to us. Rebel tech blocks all frequencies except the ones they specifically approve."

"Sounds problematic," Fil commented helpfully.

"The general said he would send the message last night," I said with a frown. "Not that I trust him, but he's our best chance."

"Unfortunately," Keel added, sitting beside me on the couch. "Now we can't do anything but wait to see if Dr. Reece responds."

"I guess so," Nanda said, not looking too hopeful. "Well, I have to go to a briefing. I'll see you guys later, okay?"

"Later Nanda."

"Bye."

I thought about the computer codes the general wanted. I hoped the mission wasn't too dangerous. Although if Nanda was anywhere near as good as people kept saying, she would have no problem.

"I have a meeting to get to as well," Fil said, standing up and stretching as the door shut behind her. "They want to open another hospital, but we're still trying to acquire the necessary supplies."

"Sounds like a ton of fun," I said dryly.

He smiled easily and shrugged into his jacket. "Not fun, but probably a good idea."

We watched him go and then it was just me, sitting in between Jag and Keel. I leaned back against the lumpy sofa cushions and closed my eyes. If only Steffy was there, I would have felt a million times better, I was sure. But at least she was safe where she was. I wouldn't take her away from that just because I missed her.

"Do you really think other Taints will be willing to join the fight?" Jag asked doubtfully.

I opened my eyes and gave him a curious look. "I don't see why not."

"You don't?" He gave me a doubtful look. "Really?"

I raised an eyebrow at his tone and he rolled his eyes.

"You never let anyone see your powers unless it was a life and death situation," he pointed out. "Why would anyone else willingly join a fight where their powers are going to be exposed?"

"First off," I said, narrowing my eyes. "Thanks to Attis, I'm not like most Taints. I learned how to suppress my powers a long time ago and not all Taints can do that. Secondly, what else do we have to lose? We'll either be hunted down and killed if we resist arrest, or cut apart then put back together the wrong way if we cooperate. At this point, running away isn't a feasible way of survival anymore. We have to fight."

"So you're joining us then?" Jag asked, watching me closely, like he was fishing for something.

"*Us?*" I echoed, frowning, my heartbeat picking up as I tried to decide who he was referring to.

"No – I mean – the Rebels, Delle. Are you going to fight with them?" Jag said, his hair falling over his intense, dark eyes, gleaming with the importance of his question.

I hesitated, looking over at Keel who had been listening quietly to the conversation. I wondered if he sensed it too – the anticipation – like Jag wasn't telling us something. I looked down at my hands and swallowed. I couldn't think of a time when Jag had kept a secret from me.

"I don't know," I finally admitted. "It's a pointless question anyways since I can't use my powers. I'm useless like this – I can't even argue with Mona without feeling like my head's about to split open."

"But if you still had your powers," Jag insisted, flipping his hair over one shoulder. "Would you fight with the Rebels?"

I glanced over at Keel, hoping to find some sort of help. However, he appeared to be waiting for my answer as well, his silvery eyes considering me, thoughtful.

"I guess so," I hedged. "I mean, probably." Jag continued looking at me as if waiting for something more. "Look, if they could use me, then yes, sure, I would try to help out here," I finally surrendered. "But I can't do anything until Dr. Reece fixes me – if she can."

"Okay," Jag said, leaning back. "I was just curious."

I grunted. His curiosity sounded more like interrogation. And he had referred to himself as one of the Rebels. He took it back, but it disturbed me that he said it at all. I didn't want him to stay with these people. I didn't want him to fight. Instead of saying any of these things, I searched for something less polarizing to talk about.

"You need a haircut."

Keel snorted with laughter and Jag looked hurt, picking up a strand of his shoulder-length hair to examine it closer.

***

I had just prepared to start cutting Jag's hair when the door burst open. I whirled around, dropping the scissors. Jag stood up instantly, whether to escape the haircut or because he was as eager for news as I was, I didn't know.

"Mona said to come get you," Fil said, not even bothering to step fully inside the apartment.

I could see Nanda peering over his shoulder at us. When I caught her eye she nodded.

"Dr. Reece made contact," she explained. "She wants to speak with you personally, Delle."

I practically flew out the door, pounding down the stairs after Fil with the others behind me. I wasn't sure what I was going to say to try and convince Dr. Reece, but at least she was intrigued enough to respond. I had no idea why she would rather talk to me than the general – he was the one in charge – but I was willing to do whatever it took. I was harboring a desperate hope that Dr. Reece might be able to figure out an antidote to whatever the Tinkers had given me. I wanted to stop being afraid of the headaches and I wanted to use the lights again.

Mona met us in the hallway and ushered us towards a room where a Tab was open, a screen flickering in front of us with the words "Accept Transmission?" scrawled across it. I stopped just short of it and caught my breath. Mona nodded and motioned to the screen.

"The general doesn't even want to be here?" Keel asked skeptically.

Mona looked over at him and rolled her eyes. "He's trusting us to handle this one on our own."

"How generous of him," Keel muttered, crossing his arms.

I swallowed and redirected my attention to the hovering screen in front of me. I squared my shoulders and glanced back at Keel, who was watching me with a steady expression. He nodded encouragingly and I half-smiled at him, knowing that no matter how this turned out at least Keel wouldn't blame me. I turned back around resolutely and tapped the screen, not letting myself hesitate a moment more.

The blank screen flickered then produced the image of Dr. Reece, her yellow eyes so vividly bright that they practically beamed through the screen at us.

"Delle!" she exclaimed happily, tossing her purple hair over a bare shoulder. "My, I must say I'm surprised to hear from you, dear. Especially after all that nasty business with your love – Attis, wasn't it? I assume you found him, didn't you? That must have been an awful shock. I just didn't have the heart to tell you myself."

"Didn't have the heart is right," I snapped, my stomach tightening at the mention of Attis – and the fact that she had known the truth about him the entire time.

"Oh, now don't be cross," she said with a noisy sigh. "As I understand it, you want something from me?"

"I have a proposition," I stated, working hard to remain calm. "If you're open to hearing me out."

"Why, Delle, of course," she said, clapping her hands together and laughing lightly, like I'd told a marvelous joke. "Anything that might give me a chance to research your powers further would be intriguing to say the least. Although I must admit that I'm curious why you assumed it was safe to contact me considering your current position – we all saw the video, dear."

"Not 'safe'," I corrected, raising an eyebrow. "But worth your while."

Dr. Reece considered me for a moment, her head turned slightly to the side. "Alright, let's hear your proposition, dear."

"We need your help," I began, thinking she would like to hear that. "The Tinkers – your researcher friends – have been developing a chemical."

"Exterophine?"

I blinked and glanced over at Mona, who shrugged, clearly just as clueless as I was.

"What was that?" I asked warily.

"Exterophine is the name of the drug you're referring to," Dr. Reece supplied, a smile twitching around her ridiculously painted lips. "I must admit that I'm not terribly familiar with it. It's become a sensitive topic between me and my 'researcher friends'."

That's interesting.

"Well they've finished developing it," I stated coolly.

I was mildly satisfied to see Dr. Reece's eyes open a bit wider. I was happy in a cold sort of way to see that I knew something she didn't. For a moment she didn't say anything.

"And how do you know this?" she finally responded, her voice stronger than usual – almost sounding like a normal person.

"They kidnapped me just over a month ago," I explained, clenching my fists at my sides where the purple woman couldn't see me. "Somehow I was the key to their breakthrough." I halted again, grinding my teeth together at the flashing memories of being trapped on the Tinkers' table skipping over my mind. I could feel Keel's attention sharpening on my back, his concern palpable. I relaxed my fists and forced myself to relax. "I was the first Taint this 'Exterophine' worked successfully on," I continued, working hard to make my voice sound unaffected. "But the side effects are bad."

"Bad?" she echoed, raising an eyebrow. "Can you describe them?"

"If you agree to my proposition," I countered, feeling Mona's approval.

Dr. Reece pursed her colorful lips but waited for me to continue.

"This drug is being used on any Taints that The Eye isn't outright killing. We want to know how to reverse the effects."

Dr. Reece glanced at someone who must have been outside the range of her Tab. Her expression darkened for a moment. I leaned closer to the screen instinctually, as if I could look around her room and see who she was looking at. She quickly reverted her attention to me then and flipped her hair over a shoulder.

"You want an antidote?" she guessed.

"Yes."

"If I attempt to do this for you, what will you do for me?" Her voice was thin and light again, like a breeze coming over the Tab's speaker. "You do understand, dear, that a proposition generally benefits both parties in some way. And since I will have to put myself at great risk to obtain a sample of this drug in the first place, it really had better be a good deal."

I was about to roll my eyes but stopped myself. If Magely was there, I probably would have requested she handle the conversation at this point. But Magely wasn't there, so I had to be the polite and reasonable one.

"In return for finding an antidote, the Rebel forces are offering you a place to work and Taints to work with – providing you don't harm them. No other restrictions apply," I said, glancing at Mona again to make sure I had repeated exactly what she told me the general agreed to.

Dr. Reece laughed delightedly. "My, what an offer! Well, Delle, I must say I'm more than a bit intrigued. I would like to agree to your proposition, but only on one condition."

I could see Mona stepping forward in my peripheral vision, already shaking her head, but Keel caught her arm, stopping her. He looked at me and nodded.

"What condition?" I asked suspiciously, ignoring Mona's lethal expression.

"You, my dear," she replied breathily, smiling at me just slightly.

"Me?"

"Yes. I would like to be permitted to study you specifically – it could be important to understanding the way Exterophine works – since it wasn't successful until you, my dear. Also, I want you to answer those questions I mentioned after our first little meeting," she added this last part thoughtfully, as if it had only just occurred to her.

"The data I took requires further clarification for me to fully understand it and I believe only you can answer my questions."

I didn't have to look over at Mona to see that she thought this was a terrible idea. I didn't look at Keel either, not wanting his guaranteed disapproval to turn me off of an idea that might save every Taint currently being power-blocked. I looked at Jag instead. Jag's expression was grim, but I didn't see a *no* in his expression. He was a realist. He knew as well as I did that we couldn't afford to sacrifice an opportunity like Dr. Reece just because I was squeamish.

"Fine," I agreed, turning back to Dr. Reece, who was already flashing her blinding smile at me. "You'll be sent further instructions soon," I continued with a frown.

"I look forward to seeing you again, Delle," Dr. Reece said in her wispy voice. "And you do remember my body guard, don't you?"

I nodded hesitantly.

"He'll be coming too, of course," she said, waving a hand through the air as if this couldn't possibly matter.

"Fine," I responded, ignoring Mona's hissing.

"I do look forward to seeing you children again," she replied. "Where is that attractive young man? Presid's boy?"

I opened my mouth to tell her that wasn't any of her business, but then Keel stepped in front of the screen and I sighed. Keel raised an eyebrow at me and greeted Dr. Reece relatively politely.

"My, those eyes," she commented, clearly admiring, practically purring. "It's no wonder Delle has fallen for you now that she knows the truth about her first love."

I snorted furiously, but to my surprise, Keel just took my hand below Dr. Reece's range of vision and replied, "We look forward to seeing you Dr. Reece."

Dr. Reece smiled dreamily at him and waggled her fingers at the screen. "I'm sure you do, dear. Goodbye now."

I just scowled, finally allowed to express my irritation with her now that the deal was made.

"And don't forget to send me those instructions, dear," she reminded me with a wink. "I'm really quite eager to begin my research."

With that the screen flickered again and Dr. Reece's colorful image disappeared, leaving the screen blank.

"I'll bet she is," I growled.

Everyone in the room seemed to let out a pent up breath.

"I really don't like her," I complained.

Keel squeezed my hand sympathetically and replied, "Let's get something to eat."

CHAPTER TWENTY

Nanda was waiting for us on our return to the apartment. Keel lifted the broken door enough that it would slide into place, then came to stand beside me as Nanda cleared her throat.

"My commanding officer saw the video from the ORC in Laylen," she began, her eyes only briefly meeting mine before dropping to her shoes.

I inwardly groaned. Not that I was surprised; everyone had probably seen the video by now. It made me look like a danger – wild-eyed and irresponsible. I was symbolic for the war on Taints.

"Does he want me to leave?" I asked glumly, thinking that if I was in his shoes I wouldn't want the face of the war to be hanging around my covert Rebel camp either.

Nanda looked confused for a moment, looking over at Fil like maybe he would understand my question. "No," she said slowly, turning back to face me. "He wants your help."

I blinked. "My help?"

"Yes," she said, clasping her hands behind her back like she was preparing for a negative response. "You and Keel snuck into the ORC virtually undetected. My commander wants to know how you did it and if you're willing to do it again."

I looked down at my feet, trying to understand what she was saying without her hopeful expression wavering in front of me.

They want us?

"I can't," I replied, looking back up at her, pained to know that I truly couldn't. "Things have changed since then."

I didn't miss the slumped shoulders as her spirits fell.

"It's not that I don't want to," I tried to amend, wondering if I actually did want to or not. "I just *can't*." I looked to Keel for help.

"One of the major benefits we had last time was Delle's power," Keel continued for me. "Without that, the plan would look different."

"We would give you weapons instead," Nanda said hurriedly. "Instead of personally knocking out anyone in your way, you could stun them."

"I'm also wanted all over the country," I persisted. "Everyone knows what I look like."

"That's a good point," Keel agreed, as he paced across the room towards the couch.

"Right, about that," Nanda hedged, gesturing towards the living room and waiting for me to fully enter and sit down before continuing. "The main reason he wants your help is because he's hoping if the Runners spot you, they'll be distracted enough that we can get a team in and out."

It took me a moment to understand the implications of what she was saying.

"Like bait," I clarified. "What you're saying is that your commander wants to use me as bait?"

"We would assign people to protect you, of course," Nanda said hurriedly. "It should be perfectly safe."

Keel snorted and continued pacing.

"Alright, not *perfectly* safe, but safe-ish," she corrected herself with a sigh. "There are some codes that we can only obtain from the inside and, although we already have our covers in place, someone is sure to notice something odd going on if there's nothing to distract them."

"The codes," I realized, remembering where I had heard about them before. "The general was talking about some sort of codes earlier too."

"Probably the same ones," Fil commented.

He was sitting on a stool and turning an old, leathery looking apple over in his hands. I watched him regard it thoughtfully before setting it back down and giving his full attention to us.

"What are they planning to do with these codes?" Keel asked.

Nanda shifted uneasily under his concentrated attention. "I'm not sure. I just know they're important."

Jag was oddly quiet. I was getting the feeling that he knew much more about the codes than he was letting on. I swallowed and forced myself not to think about the fact that I was growing to know less and less about Jag.

"Where is this place you're busting into?" I asked with a frown, snagging Keel's hand as he paced by, tugging on his arm to make him sit down. "Your pacing is making me anxious," I explained briefly.

"It's in Calio," she replied, apparently relieved to have an answer to something. "The codes are held in the InterLine Complex."

I sighed and pulled a few tangles out of my hair, thinking. "I've never travelled that far before. Besides, you've all made it this far without me."

Nanda didn't reply, she just exchanged pleading looks with Fil who was calmly waiting for someone else to speak.

"If I'm not here when Dr. Reece arrives, she might leave," I added weakly, already feeling myself give in to this plan even though I really didn't have any reason to.

"The general could make her stay," Jag suggested.

I rolled my eyes and leaned back against the torn cushions. "I don't think she'll cooperate if we try to force her into anything."

"Probably not," Keel agreed. "And there are other factors that need to be taken into account."

"Like?" I asked hopefully, thinking that perhaps he had found a rock-solid reason why I couldn't participate.

"Like your health," he said pointedly.

I felt my hopes shatter. "My health is fine."

"Sure," he said, narrowing his eyes at me. "When a troop of Runners is barreling towards you and you get a headache strong enough to make you pass out that will be *fine*."

"If I stay *calm* that won't *happen*," I snapped, letting my anger make me sound more convinced than I actually felt.

I looked over when I realized that Fil and Nanda were having a quiet conversation, purposely excluding us. I tapped Keel's knee and nodded towards them. Unfortunately, we didn't get to eavesdrop for more than a second because Fil looked up and caught my eye, ending his sentence abruptly.

"What are you arguing about?" Keel asked, right to the point.

"I was just telling Nanda," Fil began, ignoring the death-glare Nanda was shooting at him. "That it's only fair for you to understand what's at stake."

"What is at stake?" I snapped, feeling the beginnings of the electric tingles in my fingers. I clenched my hands into fists then pressed my fingertips together, trying to relieve the pressure. I wish I could say that Keel didn't notice, but I was fairly certain he did. He was kind enough not to win the argument in that particular moment though and just shook his head.

"If you do this for us," Nanda began with a sigh, shooting another piercing glare at Fil who was busy inspecting a slightly less withered apple. "The Rebels are willing to compensate you."

"Compensate," I said dully. "What does that mean?"

"There's a possibility that one of our scientists has invented a piece of technology that could allow someone who is blind to see in a manner of speaking," Nanda explained, dropping her eyes, probably so I couldn't read in them what I knew was probably in mine.

"In a manner of speaking?" I echoed.

"Shapes, mostly," she murmured, still not looking at me.

"For Steffy?" I asked eagerly, feeling the tension build in my fingertips and travel up my arms. "If I do this they'll help her see?"

My stomach was a jumble of knots. I was practically vibrating with the possibility that Steffy could learn how to see. Jag had gone visibly pale across the room. This was a miracle if such things existed.

"Yes," Fil answered for her. "But only if you help. Otherwise Nanda says they won't give it to her."

"Sounds more like blackmail than compensation," Keel said dryly, but I could hear the undercurrents of anxiety and hope in his voice as well.

"I'll help," I said instantly, standing up and pacing, shaking my hands to try and let out some of the energy that was trying to fry me from the inside out as my head started pounding.

"Wait a minute, Delle," Nanda said, reaching out as if she could physically pull me back from my exhilaration.

"What?" I snapped, whirling. "Of all people, Nanda, I would think that you understand why this is so important."

"I *do* understand," she snapped back.

I blinked, startled. I don't think I had ever heard her snap before.

"But I don't want you to do this unless you think that you actually can," she continued, her voice tinged with worry. "Steffy wouldn't want you to sacrifice yourself even if it meant she was able to see. She would rather have you in her life. She misses you enough as it is."

I was surprised by the unexpected drop in my energy. The buzzing feeling disappeared and I had to catch my breath.

"She misses me?" I asked, mostly because I wanted to hear someone confirm that for me one more time, to know that Steffy missed me back.

"Of course she misses you," Fil said as Nanda gave me an incredulous expression. "You're her best friend."

Keel took my hand and I remembered to breathe again. I could feel myself smiling despite the fact that nothing had been resolved. Frankly, I had been fairly convinced that Nanda had taken my position as Steffy's best friend.

"She relies on you," Nanda continued, clearly trying to drill her point in. "So if you don't feel like you can handle this, don't do it."

My instinct was to bristle at her remark about whether or not I could "handle" this mission, but she had a point. However, if there was an opportunity to give Steffy sight, I wanted that even more than my safety.

"Killing yourself isn't worth it," Keel said gently, nudging me as if he could read my mind.

"I know," I sighed, rubbing my temples, still feeling light at the thought of Steffy being able to see. "But I think I can do it."

I wasn't sure if I was lying or not at this point.

"Don't say that unless you're sure," Nanda said abruptly.

I flashed my eyes open and looked at her intently. "If there are going to be armed people around to protect me, I'll manage. I'll try to stay calm so the headaches don't hit me as hard."

"And if you can't stay calm?" Jag asked quietly.

I shifted uncomfortably as everyone fell into an expectant moment of silence. "Then someone will have to carry me out," I said with a scowl. "Or leave me behind if it comes to that. I mean, what else can they do to me, right?"

Nanda sighed and Fil rolled his eyes. Keel stiffened beside me and I felt his fingers flex around my hand.

"It's a good point," I persisted, frowning at their reactions.

"It's a *point*," Fil corrected.

"Besides it's probably not going to happen," I continued, acting much more flippant than the situation called for in an attempt to make them relax. "I have years of practice controlling my powers. If I can't do it, I don't think anyone will be able to."

No one seemed convinced yet. It was like I was talking to myself.

"Guys, please," I insisted. "I'll cover my ears or something. I can do this." Still no response. "I can do this and help Steffy see and help the Rebels get the codes."

"And be back in time to let Dr. Reece poke and prod you," Jag reminded me cheerfully.

I scowled at him, then pointedly ignored him, turning to Nanda.

"Nanda, you can tell your commander that I'll do whatever I can to help."

"Me too," Keel said, although I didn't miss the grudging tone or the slight roll of his eyes.

"Hey, you don't have to come," I pointed out, then instantly felt guilty. "I mean, I appreciate it," I amended. "But if you don't think this is a good idea, you don't have to come along."

"Oh, I think it's a bad idea," he confirmed, looking me in the eyes. "But I think letting you go alone is an even worse idea."

I could've kept the argument going, but I could tell it was circular. Arguing would be pointless. I had the feeling that Keel would follow me into whatever danger I chose to throw myself into. It was both reassuring and more than a little worrying considering my track record.

"If the love birds are going, I'm coming too," Jag piped up.

I felt heat rise to my cheeks, but I didn't contradict him. Again, it wouldn't have gotten us anywhere.

"We don't need to put anyone else in danger," I tried weakly, knowing that I wouldn't be able to stop him anyways. I probably could've stopped the Jag from a few years ago, but he was confident now – grown up. I couldn't protect him anymore and it was a terrible feeling.

Keel cleared his throat and asked the question I had just been about to ask myself. "When do we leave?"

Nanda squared her shoulders and for a moment she reminded me so much of Appy that I almost smiled. "Tomorrow morning."

CHAPTER TWENTY-ONE

The trip to Calio was long and boring. Despite that, my body still seemed to have enough nervous energy to keep my knees bouncing up and down at a constant speed that was driving Keel insane. He periodically reached over and pressed a hand on my knee, halting my tapping. I couldn't help it. I had never volunteered to be bait before. Frankly I wasn't even sure how we were going to get close enough to this InterLine Complex to do anything effective without being recognized until a convenient moment.

We mostly travelled through the bomb lands, but I knew to reach Calio we would have to either take a lift or a train. Either way, my chances of not being recognized as a national threat seemed slim. Whenever we stopped I trudged towards Nanda's car and pestered her about it, but she wasn't at all concerned. When we finally reached the edge of Calio, one of the officers in the front seat of the car turned around and shoved a Tab full of digitalized travel papers into my hands, complete with false name and picture. Then when they finally let me get out of the car, another officer came up and handed me an orange wig and fake eye colors. I stared in horror at the little rubbery lenses that I was supposed to put on my eyeballs. I tried to catch Nanda's eye and signal for her help, but she was too busy directing different people around to notice me. I turned in a full circle, looking for some sort of help when I noticed the car mirrors. I hurried over and bent down by one of the side mirrors, balancing one of the eye colors on my fingertip and clumsily trying to put it where it needed to go. I gasped as I nearly dropped it on the ground and only caught it at the last second.

"Do you want some help?" Keel asked wryly, appearing at my elbow as I straightened up.

"Don't laugh," I groaned. "I've never had to put anything in my eye before, alright? These colors are ridiculous."

He grinned and shook his head. "Magely likes them."

I made a face at him and turned back to the mirror. "Well good for her. If you're not going to help me then go find somewhere else to snicker. You're distracting me."

"Didn't I just offer to help?" he asked, leaning against the side of the car, his arms crossed.

"Was that a serious offer?" I asked, turning to him and raising an eyebrow.

He nodded and smiled at me, his dark hair flopping over his warm eyes. "Sure."

"Do you know how?" I asked nervously.

"Not really."

"*Keel*," I complained. "Please."

"I'm kidding, Delle," he reassured me, catching my wrists and holding my hands steady, still balancing the ridiculous purple lens on my finger. "I understand the procedure."

"Procedure makes it sound so serious," I whined.

He raised an eyebrow. "Do you want my help or not?"

I sighed and looked up into his waiting eyes. Then I nodded and he wordlessly turned me back towards the mirror. The next five minutes involved him teaching me how to hold one eye open with my free hand while balancing the lens on my other finger then gently placing it on my eye. The result was lots of poking myself in the eye, but in the end brilliant purple eyes gleamed back at me, red-rimmed and watery.

"I look so weird," I observed, thinking that I truly would be unrecognizable after I put on the orange wig.

"Yup," Keel agreed.

I rolled my now purple eyes and blinked back more tears. Then I turned back to Keel.

"Thank you," I said.

I tried to smile even though my nerves were coming back now that I was past the purple-eye challenge. In response he put his hands on either side of my face and gently swiped some of the tears from underneath my lower lashes. Then he kissed my forehead and pulled back enough to smile at me.

"You're still beautiful," he assured me, smiling as the heat rushed into my cheeks, probably laughing at the color in my face.

A noise from behind made us both turn around to see Jag watching us, his arms crossed.

"You're disgusting," he stated calmly, although it looked suspiciously like he was hiding a smile. "Also, we're about to leave, so Delle, you have to put on the wig."

I scowled and handed the wig to Keel as I started piling my hair on top of my head in order to fit the wig over it. He handed the wig back to me and I fit it over my hair, pulling it down, feeling the cheap plastic hairs scratch my forehead.

"Still beautiful?" I asked dryly as Jag led us towards Nanda and her team.

Keel shrugged noncommittally and made a face. I punched his arm lightly but smiled despite myself.

We walked in silence for a few moments before he replied, "Of course you are."

It took me a moment to realize that he was responding to the question I'd asked jokingly. I was saved from having to respond because at that moment we reached the troop and Nanda turned to me with a questioning look, like she was wondering if I had decided to bail. For a second I felt the strong urge to do just that, but then I thought about Steffy. If I could do anything to help her regain her sight – at least a little bit – I owed that to her. After all it was my fault that bullet hit her eye in the first place.

"Ready?" she asked.

I nodded, orange hair swaying around the edges of my vision. "Just tell me where to be."

***

The trip to the InterLine Complex was less stressful than I imagined. After following Nanda and her company, also decked out in convincing Provincial clothing, through the milling crowds without being recognized or even noticed, I started to relax. Clearly, I looked nothing like the Tainted monster who had terrorized the screens of the nation with my blue death lights.

The InterLine Complex itself also defied my expectations. I had expected some huge, elaborate building, but aside from the curved glass front and the word *InterLine* in enormous metallic letters, it actually looked fairly neglected. The sides of the building were made from concrete and were stained with rain where the weather shield must have failed. I also didn't get the sense that there was much going on inside the building. I wondered how many people actually worked there. For a place that held such important codes, I was surprised it didn't look more important. Not that The Eye had ever developed a foolproof security system. I'd busted in and out of two of their major facilities now without being caught.

"Now don't approach the building until we give the signal," Nanda advised me at the meet-up point, a place just outside the electric fence surrounding the complex that she assured me was currently not electrified. We were hidden in the narrow alley between the fence and an obnoxiously colorful clothing shop.

"The signal," I echoed, raising my eyebrow to let her know I didn't know what that meant.

"Your security detail knows," she assured me. "We've been working on our covers here for a while, so the people inside shouldn't realize anything is going on at first. Once we download the codes though there will be a system wide alarm – there's no way around it. That's when we'll need you to make an appearance – make them believe that *you* have the codes."

I could tell she didn't like what she was saying to me. She kept fidgeting and almost wincing as she detailed the plan for me again, as if I didn't understand it the first time. I stopped her as she was about to elaborate even further on what was actually an extremely simple plan.

"Nanda, I get it," I promised. "Go on already."

She sighed and gave me a searching look, as if I was about to burst with whatever questions she hadn't managed to answer yet. I didn't say anything though. I just continued crossing my arms and raising an eyebrow at her.

"Okay," she finally conceded, turning to give Keel an imploring look, probably in regards to him making sure I didn't die.

Keel and I were given weapons and as I wrapped my fingers around mine I realized that it was heavier than any other gun I had used before. I briefly remembered how a trader had once tried to buy my necklace – the one I'd given to Magely – because the Rebels down in Tac were repurposing them. I checked my weapon and sure enough in place of the soft-cased gel bullets, these were hard-shelled, flickering electrobullets. These were much more dangerous. Even the stun bullets didn't just shock people. They punctured too. I had heard about bad bullets that could be buried in a wound for days before the shell finally broke and the electricity charged out.

Keel caught my eye and I glanced down at the gun. He nodded. He noticed it too. I paced while we waited for Nanda's mysterious signal. I couldn't imagine what Nanda and her team were taking so long to do inside the complex. I was doing my best to stay calm, ignoring the tingling in my fingertips and thinking about what it must be like to see for the first time.

I startled when the signal finally came. It was unmistakable. The alarms inside the InterLine Complex were blaring so loudly that even from the outside I wanted to clap my hands over my ears. My heart was beating as fast as the alarm as I waited for my security team to let me approach the building and begin the distraction. The tingling in my fingertips grew so strong that it stung and my head was already pounding so much that I was seeing little spots of light everywhere. I felt a cool, strong hand take mine and I looked over at Keel to see him watching me.

"Alright?" he asked.

I took a deep breath and focused on Keel's face and the feeling of his hand over mine.

"Alright," I agreed, grimacing as some of the pain receded but the dull throbbing in my skull remained.

My team moved at once and I hurried after them, keeping my gun pointed towards the ground as I ran. We stopped a couple hundred yards away from the front door and my detail backed off, giving me room. Soon the only person standing within any helpful distance was Keel, who remained stubbornly beside me.

"Here we go," I muttered, my fingers tingling as I tore the orange wig off my head and tossed it away, stepping on it just for good measure. "No need for that anymore," I said, trying my best to smile at Keel even though I could feel my blood pounding painfully through my temples.

"But that color suited you so well," he replied, his voice too tense to sound sarcastic, although I appreciated the effort.

One of my security team nodded at me then at the front door. I nodded back and faced the building, taking a deep breath.

"Hey!" I shouted at the building, waving my gun in the air like a maniac. "I'm out here! You want your stupid codes? Come get them!"

I couldn't see the cameras, but I had to assume they were there. Even if there weren't cameras, I was pretty certain my shouting could attract enough attention – that and the fact that I happened to be the crazy monster girl from the anti-Taint video and I was waving a gun recklessly around in the air. I guess I had expected more of an immediate reaction from the InterLine Complex. I shouted some other nonsense about the codes that I most definitely didn't have and felt my stomach trying to crawl into my throat as my shout fell with no more response than a slight echo. There was no movement and no sound besides the blaring of the alarms for several long seconds.

"Do you think they can hear me over the alarms?" I finally asked, only loud enough for Keel to hear.

Keel's brow was furrowed as he considered this. "I think so. Even if not, the entire front of that building is a window. Surely they can see the crazy girl pointing a gun at the sky surrounded by armed Rebel guards."

I ignored his crazy comment and took a breath, dropping my gun to my side and stepping forward.

"Hey!" I yelled at the building as the Rebel guards readjusted their positions around me. The silence that followed couldn't have been more than half a second long, but it felt like an eternity. I had the undeniable feeling that something had gone wrong. Keel must have felt it too, because he grabbed my hand as our guards turned around, responding to a noise that had come from behind us instead of in front.

"They knew we were coming."

My breath caught in my throat as I realized that Runners were practically flooding past the fence, guns already raised, trapping us inside the gates of the Complex. I knew my security team was talking to each other, snapping out commands and alternate plans of action, but as much as I tried I couldn't understand what they were saying. One of them grabbed my arm and started pulling me away from the oncoming Runners, also away from Keel who was resolutely facing someone down when I glanced back.

It took major effort, but I managed to focus through the splitting pain and neon spots in my vision to recognize the formerly-smooth and arrogant Presid Bertley, now glowering at Keel, practically trembling with rage – or fear. I couldn't tell from this distance, but it looked like Keel was saying something to him. Or spitting. And Presid looked unhinged. He wasn't the self-assured, in-control troop lead that had been chasing me all my life. He was more dangerous now, more volatile. Another yank on my arm redirected my attention and I hurried to keep up with the guard who had now effectively separated me from the standoff occurring between Keel and the other guards.

"Where are we going?" I gasped, focusing on my breathing, relieved that I could now hear other things besides my pulse throbbing against my skull, my splitting headache subsiding to a dull growl.

"We have to get you to the ground transport," the man replied stiffly, barely glancing at me as I yanked my arm away, running to keep up with him as we rounded the building. "They're here for you."

It wasn't that I hadn't expected people to come after me once they recognized who I was – that was the entire point of having me act as the bait. I just didn't expect it to happen so fast. It was like they already knew I would be here.

"Did they know?" I huffed, ducking under the large piece of fence the man was holding out of the way for me, clearly cut beforehand as a prepared escape route.

"Seems like it," he grunted, glancing around before moving towards the alley behind the clothing shop.

I followed, shaking my head. "Where are the others meeting us?"

"My directions are to get you out," he stated, approaching a black transport like the one the Tinkers had used to move me around when I was comatose.

I stopped abruptly as he slid the back of the transport into the roof of the vehicle and gestured for me to get inside.

"We're not leaving without them," I protested, stepping back.

"No choice," he replied, but I could see the regret at the corners of his mouth and hear it in his voice.

"Yes there is," I snapped, stepping farther away and looking back the way we had come. "We can fight with them."

He hesitated. I didn't imagine it. The man hesitated. I took the moment of weakness and jumped on it.

"You have friends back there," I said, now stepping forward. "I have a friend back there too. I'd rather die than leave knowing I left them behind to fight for me."

He shook his head and stepped up into the back of the transport. "This was my assignment."

"Scrap your assignment," I pleaded, my voice sharper than I intended. He paused again. It was a pause I knew none of us had time for. I suddenly remembered something Magely had done once – when we first met Dr. Reece.

"What's your name?" I asked, trying not to sound as desperate as I felt, ignoring the confused pause that followed.

The man scowled and shifted.

"Tam," he finally replied, stepping back down from the transport, apparently intending to forcibly make me leave.

"Tam," I repeated. "Tam, we have friends back there and if you try to make me leave without them I'm going to have to do something drastic." To prove my point, I raised my gun and pointed it at his leg.

Okay, so I wasn't Magely.

Tam's hand immediately moved to his weapon but I snapped, "Don't do it. Go for your gun and I will shoot you."

I couldn't tell if Tam was angry or conflicted at this point. Both responses seemed appropriate.

"Unless," I continued, shaky, knowing that I would have to follow through on what I said. "Unless you promise that we're going to do the right thing and go back there to try and help our friends."

I could see his desire to go back warring with his sense of duty to stick to his assignment. He glanced up at me briefly, like I might change my mind. Finally, he nodded and sucked in a breath of air.

"We'll take the transport around the front, load them in, and make a break for it," he said, jumping up into the transport and heading towards the driver's chair, not even looking back to see if I was following.

"This isn't a trick?" I asked, following hesitantly. "Because if you try to drive off without them, my promise to shoot you still stands."

"We're going to help them," he promised, jerking his head at the transport, indicating that it was time to go

I hesitated for one last second and put my gun back in its belt, hopping up into the transport and turning back to pull the door down – before I could though, I heard a startled yell from the front and whirled around, already going for my gun as someone boarded the transport through one of the front doors.

"Tam!" I shouted, standing upright, my hair not even brushing the roof of the transport. The intruder came farther inside, but their face was turned away. It was a woman with dark hair. "Put your hands up or I'll shoot!" I threatened, my voice ricocheting off the walls of the transport.

The woman turned around and I froze. My fingers suddenly felt numb where they gripped the gun, finger on the trigger. No headache pounded through my skull, dropping me to my knees. I stood still, unwavering, unfeeling. I knew this intruder.

CHAPTER TWENTY-TWO

"What are you doing?" I asked, my reasonable side telling me to lower my gun while my instincts whispered to leave it raised.

"Delle," she said, her voice pleading as she stepped farther into the transport. "You have to understand."

"Why did you shoot Tam?" I asked, my voice sounding hollow and confused, like a kid who didn't want to believe that the terrible thing their older sibling had told them was true.

"Tam is alive," she promised, putting a hand over her heart, apparently trying to prove her sincerity. "You need to come with me."

"Come where?" I asked, my mind flashing back to Keel, facing off with his father where I left him.

"Away from here," she said evasively, stepping closer.

I readjusted my grip on the gun and levelled it at her. "What's going on?"

"Tam was trying to sell you to The Eye," she replied. "I didn't want him to."

I shook my head, wanting it to be that simple, but knowing that it couldn't be. Something was missing.

"How did the Runners get here?" I asked, my finger tightening on the trigger, my head subtly throbbing as my mind began to function again.

"He must have tipped them off," she replied instantly, her expression still regretful.

"No he couldn't have," I whispered, my voice not wanting to come out of my mouth, not wanting to vocalize what I was starting to understand. "I know how hard it is to contact anyone outside the Rebel camps without the permission of the general. Tam was just a guard. He couldn't have done it. It had to be someone higher up."

"The Eye could have given him a secure line when they planted him," she replied, but the conviction in her statement didn't reach her eyes.

"'Rebel tech blocks all frequencies except the ones they specifically approve'," I quoted glumly.

She didn't respond. She just frowned. The silence stretched on for several seconds. I finally had to ask it.

"What are you doing, Nanda?"

Nanda shook her head and, for a moment, I thought I saw tears glimmering in her eyes, making them look bluer than usual. Then they were gone.

"Look, Delle, if you come with me, The Eye is going to give us that tech for Steffy's eyes," she said, lifting her head, tossing her hair in the proud way I'd seen Appy do so many times when she was defending her family.

"I thought that tech belonged to the Rebels," I said bleakly, knowing even as I said it there was no way the Rebels would be spending their energy on tech like that when they had a war to fight. I should have thought of it before.

"Unfortunately not," she said, her voice tense, the look in her eyes truly sorry.

"You don't want to do this, Nanda," I reasoned, wanting to step towards her but thinking better of it when her eyes flickered to her weapon. "We can get that tech for her another way. I know it."

She shook her head. "But what if we can't? It's not worth the risk. I have to get this for Steffy while I can."

"Steffy wouldn't want this," I exploded, surprising myself. "She wants us in her life, Nanda, even if she has to wait a little longer to see again. Do you really think she would want you to do this?"

"Steffy's just a kid," Nanda snapped suddenly. "She doesn't know what she wants yet, but I know she'll want to see."

"Well, she's just going to have to wait," I growled. "You know I'm the first person who would be willing to do anything to give Steff her sight back, but right now I have to go save Keel and you should help me save your team."

Nanda shook her head wordlessly as a tear overflowed and slid down her cheek. She was at war with herself. I felt like maybe I could tip her back over the line she was balancing on, back into a safe place. I knew in that moment that the practical thing to do would be to stun her before the situation got out of hand. But I didn't want to shoot her. If I could just get through to her everything would be okay.

"*Nanda*," I persisted, my finger tightening on the trigger as I started to form a plan. "Nanda, think about what you're doing. Think about Appy and Sacrif."

I couldn't chance her cooperation. I would just have to stun her and dump her body here. Hopefully she would be safe while I took the transport to pick up the team. Not that I had ever driven a transport before, but hopefully necessity would make up for talent.

"Don't you think I have?" she asked softly, although I would have preferred that she yell at me because it would be easier to justify shooting her, which was clearly my only reliable course of action. "But I have to do this for Steffy."

"No, you don't," I said evenly. "Nanda –"

The next part of my sentence was cut off by the sudden force of my body being slammed back into the wall of the transport. I gasped in surprise and looked down at my thigh where Nanda's gun was still aimed, as if she expected me to fight back. I watched in confusion as blood started to seep through the material of my pants. *Hard-shells.* Of course I would bleed. Nanda's gun came from the Rebels armory. I had never imagined an electrobullet would make me bleed. I touched the bloodstain quickly growing on my thigh and looked at my fingers, slick with blood. My blood was much warmer than I expected. Then the pain hit me and I gave a strangled shriek, collapsing to the ground. It wasn't electric pain like the bullets I was used to – it was a burning, searing pain.

I think Nanda was talking to me, but I couldn't understand a word of it. Between the feeling of my leg being set on fire and the feeling of my skull wanting to explode out of my head as my powers bounced around inside of me, growing in strength but unable to find a release, I was dealing with a lot. There were sounds, but I couldn't tell if I was making them or Nanda or maybe Tam. I was blind to everything except the pain. Honestly, I think the pain in my head was worse than my leg, but it was all so intense I really didn't care about comparing. I was about to pass out. I could feel myself approaching it as darkness started creeping into my vision, some of the fire mercifully drifting away the darker it became.

Then something jerked my shoulders and I slammed my head into the wall of the transport, fully awake again and aware of the feeling of my skull trying to crack into pieces and my leg trying to burn off. I must have had my eyes closed and my chin tucked against my shoulder in an attempt to be as small as possible, trying to hide from the pain, because someone was trying to pry my chin out from where I had dug it into my shoulder.

"*Della*," the voice pleaded.

I gasped and my eyes flew open. That voice had managed to pierce through everything else and still manage to make it to the part of my brain that was functioning.

"*Della*, I want to help your friends but I can't do that until I know you're alright."

Between the spots of light that were currently occupying most of my vision, I recognized the fair hair, crystal blue eyes, and pronounced jawline.

"*Attis*?"

With all the pounding in my head, I couldn't tell if I whispered his name or shouted it.

"It's me," he confirmed, his voice sounding tense. "I need you to calm down. I can try to take care of your leg but I can't do anything for your head. You have to do that yourself by calming down."

I don't know how long it took me to process what he was saying, but by the set of his eyebrows, he would've liked me to process faster.

Attis, my hazy thoughts repeated. *What is he doing here? He sold me out.*

His betrayal came rushing back to me along with Nanda's recent behavior and I cried out, rocking forward as pain exploded in my head again.

"Delle, *you have to calm down,*" he pleaded, his hands on my face, trying to hold my attention.

"What are you *doing* here?" I intended to sound furious, even in my haze of pain I knew that much, but I think I sounded more pitiful than anything else, like I was sobbing.

I couldn't tell if he answered or not. To be honest I wasn't even sure if I had actually spoken out loud. The pain hit me again and I reeled forward, my face connecting with Attis's collarbone. I didn't bother to move away because the darkness was starting to take over my vision again, that is, until I became aware of a hand on the back of my neck, tangled in my hair and holding me firmly against Attis's chest. I wanted to be furious – I should've been furious, but the pounding in my head was going away and my vision was clearing. I focused on my breathing, shoving away my thoughts about Nanda, Attis, Keel and every other crazy thing that was driving me to anxiety – anxiety that my body couldn't handle thanks to the Tinkers. For several long seconds I was only aware of my lungs inflating and deflating and my pulse pounding in my temples. After a few more moments, the only major pain I had to deal with was the scalding pain in my thigh. I took a deep breath. My headache was receding to a dull throb and all I could feel was a faint pins and needles sensation in my hands. I realized that Attis had his other hand pressed firmly over the wound on my leg.

"Better?" he asked hopefully.

Hearing his voice was like being punched in the stomach. All the air whooshed out of my chest and I felt sick. I forced myself to suck in a difficult breath and blink away everything that came to mind when I thought of Attis – of what he'd done – of who he was.

"Sure," I mumbled, my breath hitching as I gritted my teeth through the pain in my leg. "If you count being shot in the leg as better."

Attis laughed. It was a ridiculous laugh, like he knew he shouldn't be laughing but he was so relieved that he had to. I felt a pang of nostalgia and instantly shoved it away.

"We have to get to Keel!" I cried, sitting up straight, nearly hitting my head on Attis's chin. "He and the team are facing off with Scars and his creeps right now."

I only caught myself after I spoke. I had reverted to calling Presid what Attis and I used to call him. Attis pretended not to notice. I was conveniently distracted with the gushing wound in my leg, no pretending necessary.

"We can't go anywhere until we stop the bleeding," he said firmly.

"Forget about that," I growled, trying to shove him away. "We have to go *now.*"

"We will," he promised gently, his brilliant eyes flashing up to meet mine, making me forget for a second that I hated his guts. "Just let me wrap something around this."

"There's no time!" I snarled, grabbing the railing above the transport bench and trying to haul myself onto my feet.

"No time to save your life?" he clarified, turning away from me to reach for the medical kit that was strapped to the shelf above the bench "Come on, Delle. There's always time for that."

"Is there?" I snapped, purposely looking away from Nanda who was lying inert on the floor of the transport. "This must be a new idea of yours, because I distinctly remember that last time we spoke –"

"Not now, Delle," he cut me off, narrowing his eyes at me as he held up a roll of gauze. "We'll have that conversation, but not right now."

"Why not now?" I asked, only mildly hysterical, my voice taut with pain. "It's not as if we have anything better to do. If we're going to waste a bunch of time bandaging up my leg, we might as well waste even more time on that conversation."

"Geez Delle," he responded, rolling his eyes. "You really haven't changed."

"At least one of us hasn't," I retorted, really committing to my scathing attack on his character now that I realized it was distracting me from my leg, which was heavy with the blood-soaked fabric of my pants. Gravity had made my blood trail out the back of the transport, dripping onto the ground.

"I'm here now, aren't I?" he snapped, turning me so that I could put my leg up on the bench.

"Great timing, by the way," I spat. "You couldn't have showed up *before* she shot me?"

Attis rolled his eyes again as he put a hand under my knee, bending my leg so that he had room to start winding the gauze around my wound.

"Well at least I showed up," he muttered.

"Yes, at *least* you showed up, Attis. It really was the least you could do after –"

"Not having this conversation right now, remember?" he interrupted, giving me a smirk when I glared at him.

"How about this conversation then?" I suggested. "What did you do to Nanda? You didn't kill her, did you?"

"Who?" he asked, actually managing to sound like he didn't know who I was talking about. "You mean the girl that shot you?"

"Yes," I replied, fuming, gripping the railing by the bench so hard that my knuckles turned white and my fingers ached.

"She's fine, I just stunned her," Attis assured me, tying off the gauze. "Why do you care? She shot you."

"None of your business," I replied, not at all interested in sharing any of my life with the guy who had lied to me since we were kids in order to hand me over to the people I hated most. "We need to get to Keel," I repeated stubbornly. "Can you drive this thing?"

Attis sat back on his heels and examined his work. "Yeah," he said distractedly. "Of course. Should we dump the girl?"

"*Nanda,*" I repeated. "And no. Just pass me a pair of the cuffs up there and then move the guard in the front seat back here and get us to the front of the InterLine Complex."

Attis shrugged and reached above me to retrieve a pair of the cuffs. He tossed them at me and I fumbled to catch them as he slid the backdoor of the transport closed then turned and stepped over Nanda's body to move to the front. I took a deep breath and lifted myself off the bench on my good leg. I managed to bend down and hook an arm under Nanda, dragging her close enough to the bench that I could cuff her to the railing by extending the metal cord between the cuffs. Attis dragged Tam out of the driver's chair and into the back. I sat on the ground beside the large man to try and hold him steady as the transport lurched out of the back alley, towards the InterLine Complex.

"You okay?" Attis called.

He took a sharp turn, causing Tam and I to both slide across the floor of the transport, ramming into the bench on the other side.

"Are you sure you know how to drive this?" I asked critically, sweating with the pain in my leg, carefully not thinking about any of the things that would inspire my powers to ineffectually attempt an appearance and make my skull explode.

Attis didn't respond, but I imagined he was probably rolling his eyes again. I tried to protect Tam's head from slamming into the ground as Attis drove over something that clearly wasn't meant to be driven over. I was fooling myself if I thought I was strong enough to hold onto Tam when I could barely sit up. I'd lost so much blood that I was woozy. Not only that, but the pain in my leg hadn't receded. If anything, it had gotten stronger.

The transport lurched to a halt and I blinked. I had almost fallen asleep. Attis turned around just long enough to give me a searching look, then said, "Stay here. I'll get your friend."

If the circumstances were different I would've kicked and screamed and forced him to let me come along. But I couldn't do any of that. So I just nodded. Before I realized I was going to say them, I heard words start to roll off my tongue.

"Be careful."

I bit my tongue after I said it and glared down at my bandage.

"Have a little faith, Della," he called in a much more cheerful tone than was appropriate. He then exited the transport and slammed the door behind him, leaving me alone with Nanda and Tam, both unconscious.

I hadn't cried – not once. Not even when I'd been shot in the leg by Nanda – Nanda who I now realized I had considered a sister. But I almost cried now. Seeing Attis here – Attis saving my life – it was too familiar, too wrong after everything he'd done.

I don't know how much time passed before the back of the transport slid open and the team piled in. Again, I had essentially fallen asleep. I didn't even realize what was happening until the door was halfway slid away. I hazily counted the security team, but I only counted two guards. We started out with seven. I glanced down at Tam and pushed him away in an attempt to get to the door.

"Where's Keel?" I asked, or at least tried to ask, grabbing the torn sleeve of one of the guards.

The man's eyebrows came together slightly when he noted the bloody bandage on my leg and my hand placed protectively on Tam's chest. He opened his mouth to respond, but then a commotion at the back of the transport made us both look. One of the other guards and a man from the infiltration team were dragging a fourth limp guard into the transport. The panic was starting to rise in me when I saw a tall, dark-haired figure clamber in behind them, directing them to place the limp guard in the back. Relief flooded over me for a moment as Keel turned to shut the transport. Then I realized someone else was missing. I shouldn't have cared. I shouldn't have asked but my voice slurred out loudly anyways as the first guard to enter started the transport and we tore away from the InterLine Complex.

"Attis?" I asked clumsily, trying to snatch at the jacket sleeves of the guards who were settling in on the benches, hands tense on their knees. "Where is he?"

"Delle," Keel said, his voice full of horror as he instantly came to me, kneeling down and touching my face then the bandage on my leg. "Oh gosh, what happened?"

"Attis," I repeated, grabbing his collar, hating that it was so important to me to know where he was. "Where is he? What happened?"

"He went back with them," Keel said, putting his hands on my upper arms, firmly holding me still.

"They took him?" I muttered. "Did they take him?"

Keel shook his head, hurrying to explain, "He went with them willingly. He told us where you were then found a different direction to approach the Runners from, shouting something about how he'd lost you."

I shook my head and found myself cradled against Keel's chest, my head tucked under his chin.

"Why did he do that?" I asked, clinging to Keel in a desperate attempt to cling to consciousness.

"I don't know," Keel responded, his voice tight, although I was too confused to read into it.

"I hate him," I said vehemently.

"Delle," Keel said urgently, leaning away enough to put a hand on my face and look into my eyes. "Delle, this is important. What were you shot with?"

"What?"

"What kind of bullet, Delle?" he asked slowly, carefully.

"The recycled bullets," I said hesitantly, not entirely sure I understood his question.

"And you didn't pass out?" he pressed, brushing my matted hair away from my face.

"I don't think so." I honestly wasn't sure at this point.

He nodded and dropped his forehead against mine. "Try not to worry, Delle, but you need to stay as still as possible until we get the bullet out of your leg. If it ruptures, it could be really bad."

I probably would have been more concerned if I was fully aware, but instead I just felt slightly anxious. "Really bad?"

"Don't worry about it," Keel tried to assure me. "There's nothing we can do about it in here. We'll remove it as soon as we can, just *don't move.*"

I swallowed and nodded. "Okay."

"Okay?"

I nodded again and he kissed my forehead. Again, I probably would've cared more about him kissing me in front of all the Rebels if I wasn't drunk with blood loss. I remembered something important that I was shocked he hadn't already asked me.

"Don't you want to know why is Nanda handcuffed?" I asked, my voice breaking as I asked it, no plan about how I was going to explain this to him.

Thinking through everything that had happened brought the spearing pain in my head back, but I shut my eyes and took a few deep breaths.

"*Delle*," Keel insisted, sounding truly alarmed. "Delle, don't go to sleep."

I opened my eyes and told myself to open my mouth, hoping the words would come. A first nothing did.

"It was Nanda," I finally managed, forcing myself not to look at her where she lay with her arm limply extended above her, chained to the railing. "She stunned Tam and shot me. It was a set up."

I chanced looking up into Keel's eyes which were stormier than ever, dark grey beneath his black hair, red-rimmed and watery.

"She set us up," I repeated, surprised when my voice hitched again and the pressure behind my eyes began noticeably building up.

Keel disentangled himself from me and stood up.

"I'm sorry," I muttered, reaching for him, suddenly afraid in my disoriented state that he was going to disappear, that this was my fault.

Keel didn't respond and I was about to turn around and start looking for him when arms encircled me from behind and I was pulled back against someone's chest. I inhaled deeply and Keel's familiar scent surrounded me. My mind wandered, content to assume that Keel didn't blame me. I don't know how long the quiet stretched on, but I remembered Keel told me not to sleep. I was uncomfortable too and I wanted to shift around, but he also told me not to move.

"My leg is bleeding," I told him pointedly, trying to look up into his eyes even though I couldn't turn around.

"I can see that," he responded, looking down at me and raising an eyebrow. "We'll take care of it as soon as we reach the nearest camp."

I nodded and leaned back against his chest, settling in for the ride.

CHAPTER TWENTY-THREE

No one spoke for a long time. I don't know how long exactly, but it was definitely more than an hour. Even when the Rebel guard driving the transport finally broke the silence by informing us we had just made it into the bomb lands, no one mentioned what had happened to the other guards or the rest of the infiltration team. We were leaving with fewer than we came with though. I couldn't bring myself to count.

The Rebel guards looked like statues. I probably moved more than they did, despite my bum leg and Keel's constant warnings not to shift too much in case the electrobullet decided to detonate. Tam stirred by my feet, but Nanda remained motionless. I knew they would both wake up soon, but I didn't know what to say to Nanda when she did. It wasn't that I didn't understand why she did what she did, I just wasn't sure if I would have done it myself. I always said I would do anything for Steffy, but I wondered if I would have crossed the same line. Who's to say I wouldn't have? If more than one person's safety hadn't been at risk, maybe I would have. But it wasn't just one person. Nanda risked my life, and Keel's, and the infiltration team, and the security team. I'm not sure I would have done that.

I drifted in and out of sleep. Keel woke me up every now and then and checked on my leg, adjusting and applying more bandages to the wound, careful not to move me too much. Keel told me that we were making a break for the bomb lands. We would have to take the long way back to Tac instead of cutting through the provinces like last time. Every time I woke up I expected us to be stopped, but it never happened. We'd gotten away clean – well, not clean exactly. We'd lost too many people and we hadn't even gotten the codes. Maybe if we had gotten the codes we would have been pursued more. As it was, I was the only object in this transport even mildly interesting to them, and that was for revenge purposes rather than practical. I wasn't high priority anymore. In fact, I wasn't even a threat.

I guess they won.

***

I woke up on an operation table. For a moment I panicked, thinking that my rescue had just been a dream – that I was still trapped with the Tinkers. I tried to lurch upright, but hands quickly stopped me.

"It's okay!" Keel said hurriedly, his face appearing in my vision, hovering over me. "You're safe. We're just going to remove the bullet now and we need you not to move."

"Oh," I said dumbly, blinking. It took me a moment to process before I realized I was safe, that at least some of us had made it out of the mission alive, and relief flooded through me. I strained to look down at my leg without lifting my head. Someone was leaning over it, holding a pair of shiny, blood-slicked tweezers. They were rubber, of course, to avoid getting electrocuted if the bullet decided to rupture. I should have felt pain, but I didn't. I then noticed the spots on my skin, the little numbing discs they had shot all over my leg.

"Try to think of something to distract yourself," Keel advised, giving me a rueful smile when I frowned.

"Where's Nanda?" I asked.

"Really?" he asked dryly, stepping around to stand by my head. "That's what you want to think about to make yourself feel better?"

"*Keel*," I pleaded. "Where is she?"

Keel sighed and brushed some hair out of my face, cupping my chin with his other hand. He looked almost comical from this angle, looking straight down at me.

"She's locked up. The general is going to decide what to do with her."

"What to do with her," I echoed. "If it was anyone else I would want them locked up for life."

"But it's not just anyone," Keel finished for me. "It's Nanda."

I observed his features as he looked away, seemingly just wanting to look away from me. I was watching him pretty intensely, so that wasn't surprising. His eyes landed on the doctor and followed the man's motions as he worked to carefully remove the bullet from my thigh.

"I'm sorry," I said, very carefully lifting one of my arms to wrap my hand around his wrist. "I know she was like family to you."

"Yes," he responded with a sigh, still not looking at me. "I've had interesting luck with my family, haven't I?"

It didn't occur to me until that moment that Nanda turning on us was similar to Keel's father turning on him and his mom.

"You still have the rest of us," I replied, referring to the rest of the Micahs plus Jag and Steffy.

"I know," he replied. His eyebrows were furrowed, so he was either deep in thought or disturbed by something. I watched him for a few moments before letting go of his wrist. As soon as I let go of him he returned his attention to me. "I know," he repeated, smiling at me then bending down to kiss me.

This time I was aware enough to feel the blush burning in my cheeks, knowing there were other people in the room, although mercifully it seemed they were pretending not to notice.

"And good news," Keel said, his voice surprisingly cheerful.

I frowned doubtfully. "What's that?"

"The bullet's out," he replied, winking at me.

I let out a breath I'd been holding and hurried to sit up, not wanting to lay on an operation table any longer than I had to. I had spent far too much time like that in the last few months. I watched as the doctor carefully placed the bullet in an opaque rubber sack before standing up and exiting the room. Keel took his place and began cleaning and bandaging my leg. As I watched him I wondered what kind of doctor he would have been if he had stayed in the provinces.

He probably would've been a good one – a necessary one – not like the doctors who performed the ridiculous trending surgeries. I never would've met him if he'd become a real doctor. That much was certain.

It took another day and a half to reach Tac. We were surprised to find Sacrif, Appy, Jorge, and Steffy on arrival. Apparently news had travelled fast over our oh-so-secure frequency. They already knew about Nanda – really I think that's why they came at all. Although they were happy to see us, there was an undeniable cloud hovering over the family. It was understandable. I mean, one adopted daughter shoots another adopted daughter in an attempt to get technology that could cure yet another adopted daughter of her blindness. That was upsetting stuff. After hugging Appy and quickly reassuring everyone that I was fine – I didn't want to answer any questions about Nanda – I went off to find Mona. I knew they would want to see Nanda and if I had stayed they would have asked me if I wanted to come, but I didn't – not yet. I wasn't sure if I ever would. It wasn't that I was mad at her. I probably should have been, but I understood her motives. I just couldn't really think of any appropriate conversation topics. *"Hey, remember that time you shot me in the leg?"* didn't seem appropriate.

I was surprised by how much concern Mona voiced over my leg, which was actually doing pretty good. Well, all things considered it was doing good. The bullet hadn't gone deep. The real risk had been the fact that it was unstable and could electrocute me at any moment.

"Have you heard from Dr. Reece?" I asked curiously, sitting down on a stool in her sparsely furnished apartment.

"She won't be here for a few more days," Mona said with a sigh, sitting down across from me. The red streaks in her hair were the only vibrant color in the place. They literally glowed.

I pulled a few tangles out of my own mangy hair and sighed. "I'm glad she's helping us, but I really don't like that woman."

Mona grunted in agreement and handed me a bruised banana. There was a moment of silence between us, but it wasn't uncomfortable. It actually felt nice. For the first time I felt relaxed around Mona. I kind of wanted to take a nap, something I'd been way too high-strung to even consider before.

"How's Keel doing?" she asked suddenly.

I startled and looked up at her to find her watching me with a sly expression, eyes glinting as she smirked. My feeling of comfort vanished instantly.

"He's okay," I replied, frowning. "Obviously what happened with Nanda is upsetting, but he's handling it well."

"He bandaged your leg, didn't he?" Mona asked, winking at me and leaning on her elbow, giving me a significant look.

"Yes," I answered slowly, setting down the banana and glaring at her. "He did bandage my leg, to keep me from dying of blood-loss, you know?"

"And he kissed you?" she asked, grinning wickedly. "More than once."

I was dumbstruck. I didn't know how to respond. The only person who had ever teased me about boys was Jag, but that was on extremely rare occasions and in a boyish way, not this prodding, persistent coercion.

"I –" I struggled for a sharp reply. "Who told you that?"

Not your best denial, Delle.

"Tam did," she replied, crossing her arms.

Clearly I need to have words with Tam. Who knew he was such a gossip.

"He also said that he was impressed with the way you handled the situation. You went back for your team even though in all likelihood it meant death for you," she said, abruptly serious.

I scoffed in an effort to lighten the mood. "Probably not death," I corrected. "Experimentation maybe, but not death – at least not straightaway."

"Regardless, Delle," she stopped me, putting an awkward hand on my shoulder. "I'm proud of you. And your parents would be too."

I knew I was unnecessarily stiff, but I didn't know how else to respond to Mona's uncharacteristic affection. Neither of us were the warmest people. So I nodded and wondered when she would remove her hand from my arm.

"You look just like your dad," she continued with a sigh. "And you act just like your mom. They loved you so much."

I nodded and looked down at my knees. I never missed my parents very much, not like I probably should have. I always had Attis, and while he wasn't a parent, he used to be a role model. Clearly, my discernment skills were poor at that point in my life, but still he had filled a hole. In that moment I felt something I hadn't before – I *wanted* something I hadn't before. I was actually kind of surprised to find that I wanted a parent – someone to be proud of me – someone who wouldn't give up on me when I screwed up. I knew the Micahs were like that, it was just difficult to think of them that way, I had only known them for a relatively short time.

"I love you too," Mona said awkwardly. "If I could go back and save baby Claudelle, I would."

"I know," I said, smiling dryly. "You tried at least. Thanks for that."

Mona just nodded and finally dropped her hand, I think to both of our relief. "You know, if you want, you can call me Aunt Mona."

I considered this for a moment. "Aunt Mona?" I asked, testing the name out.

I didn't miss the slight wrinkling of Mona's nose as I said it and I had the same sort of reaction to saying it.

"Or maybe not," Mona agreed.

I laughed and she smiled. Maybe she wasn't the affectionate nurturing aunt, but she was a capable, intelligent person who cared more than she let on. She was a role model – not like Attis. Mona had earned it. I had just given all my respect to Attis without even wondering if he deserved it. There were a lot of things I didn't like about Mona, like her submission to the general's authority, but I had to admit that I admired her strength.

"Now, you should probably get some sleep," she said, standing up and motioning for me to do the same.

"Are you telling me it's my bedtime?" I asked dryly.

"No," she replied. "Never. However, if you don't sleep now you'll probably pass out tomorrow."

"I guess," I said, rolling my eyes and carefully getting off the stool, limping to the door and opening it as Mona watched me go. I appreciated the fact she didn't try to help me out the door. That would've been more than a little embarrassing.

"Goodnight," she called.

"Night," I called back, the door swinging shut behind me.

***

"How did you sleep?" Keel asked, kindly slowing to my pace to walk with me around the busy old province.

"Not great," I said honestly.

Actually, I had hardly slept at all, which was extremely frustrating because I was exhausted. I lay awake for most of the night, my mind busy as my leg throbbed and the sheets felt too scratchy on my skin. *To think I'm complaining about sheets,* I thought wryly. *The Delle from a year ago would have had no respect for who I am now.*

"Was your leg bothering you?" he asked, concern flashing through his grey eyes.

"No, no," I said hurriedly. "It was tight this morning, that's why I'm stretching it now, but it doesn't really hurt."

"Good," he replied, taking my hand and squeezing it.

I raised an eyebrow at him but he ignored me so I conceded.

"I couldn't sleep because I was thinking." I was mildly surprised with myself for offering this information, but it also made me realize that at some point I must have actually accepted Keel into my inner circle – the only other members being Jag, Steffy, maybe Appy and Sacrif, and formerly Attis.

"Me too," Keel said, rubbing his eyes with his free hand.

On closer inspection, there were circles under his eyes and they were rimmed with red. I should have realized that he was exhausted too.

"About what?" I asked.

"About Nanda, and the Micahs. Cursed my father some," he commented, flashing me a quick smile before returning his attention to the path. "I even thought about Attis."

"Attis?" I asked, my voice automatically scornful. "Why him?"

"He did save your life," Keel pointed out, looking troubled in a way that confused me.

I tried to remove my hand from his, but he only held tighter.

"I don't get it, Keel," I said in frustration. "How do you do it? People close to you have tricked you and cheated you, but it doesn't affect how you see the rest of the world at all."

"The rest of the world didn't trick me or cheat me," he replied, still looking bothered. "Just a few individuals living in that world."

"But they *could,*" I pointed out. "Your father, Nanda, and Attis are proof of that. If the people you think care about you most in the world stab you in the back, then what's to stop everyone else from doing it?"

Keel shook his head. I could see the frown on his face. I hated myself for being so harsh, but I couldn't take it back. I had to know how he did it – *why* he did it.

"It's so much easier to keep people at arm's length," I continued, forcing my voice to soften even though I was infinitely frustrated with myself for upsetting him. "Why do you let them in when you know they can hurt you?"

"Everyone hurts someone at one point or another," Keel replied instantly, but he didn't sound fully convinced. There was no thought in his answer.

"But Keel," I persisted. "Human instinct is to withdraw, to protect yourself from being hurt again. For example, you shouldn't trust me at all. I've treated you terribly for most of the time I've known you." My mouth felt dry after I said it, but I knew it was true.

"That's true," Keel said, stopping in front of me, catching my shoulders as I teetered on unbalanced legs.

We fell silent as a group of Gypsies and Provincials shuffled by, deep in conversation.

"But the way I see it," he continued slowly, his eyes meeting mine so intensely that I felt the need to drop my gaze. "If I spend my whole time worrying that people are going to betray me, that I'm going to lose people, then I'll miss the people in my life who I can enjoy – even if it's just for a little while."

"But is it worth it?" I asked, holding onto his wrist partly for balance and partly because I was afraid he might leave. "Is it worth caring about someone if they're going to hurt you?"

"I think if they really care about you," he said slowly, his expression softening, his dark hair falling just above his eyes in a way that I realized I found really attractive. "They'll learn to stop hurting you. That doesn't mean they won't ever hurt you again, but as long as they're *trying* not to and they maybe even make some progress, then yes, I think it's worth it."

I considered him. Keel hadn't hurt me – not really – not like Attis had. I couldn't imagine Keel hurting me. Then again, until recently I couldn't imagine Attis hurting me either. But then, Attis had helped me. He'd found me and bandaged my leg and helped me save Keel and the rest. Why would he do that if he only wanted to hurt me? But he had been working for The Eye the whole time. He never stayed with us because he wanted to. It was just his job. Whenever he talked about our perfect life beyond the horizon, he didn't actually believe we could have that. He always knew he would be returning to his keepers.

"You're thinking about Attis," Keel observed, dropping his hands.

My shoulders felt cold without his hands. I brushed a hand across my forehead to try and clear my thoughts. I watched him walk to a nearby bench and sit down.

"How did you know?" I asked ruefully, hobbling over to sit beside him.

He sighed and looked out over the busy street, swarming with all kinds of people from all different places, the only thing uniting them their common goal. Without that, these people would probably never interact.

"You always look conflicted when you talk about him," Keel said, his stormy eyes darting over to me only for a second. "Like you're hurt and hopeful at the same time."

I nodded and leaned back, pulling my good leg onto the bench so I could hook my arm around my knee.

"Does it bother you?" I asked, wincing even as I said it.

"Does what bother me?" he asked.

The tension in his voice led me to believe that he knew exactly what I was talking about and yes, in fact, it did bother him.

"Does it bother you that I think about Attis so much?" I clarified with a sigh, glaring at the small tear in the knee of my pants. "You seemed uncomfortable when Dr. Reece called him my true love and I know it's obvious that I was really attached to him – but I'm over that and –"

"You're not over it," he interrupted sharply.

I tensed at the change in his tone of voice, my hands instantly folding into fists as I prepared myself for an argument. I expected him to continue, to spout off some inflammatory remark that would have us at each other's throats. The silence stretched between us like a tight rope for several seconds too long.

"Sorry," he finally said.

The tension broke and I could feel both of us instantly relaxing again.

"It's just – Delle, I know you're not over it – him. You might not think you loved him, but I'm pretty sure that you do – or at least you did. I don't know how you wouldn't after everything you did for each other and all the time you spent together."

I remained silent, knowing that his words should be having more of an impact, but somewhere inside of me I had already been suspecting them myself. I was just denying them because I felt that, for all intents and purposes, I should hate Attis.

"It does bother me," he continued. "But not for the reasons that you probably think."

I wasn't sure if he was going to continue. As he remained silent and continued to look out over the Rebels on their ways to complete various duties, I got the feeling that he wasn't intending to continue at all.

"Care to explain?" I prompted, nudging him with my shoulder.

He looked over at me and seemed to consider something important, his eyebrows drawn just slightly together.

"I'll try, but you have to promise to try and not take this the wrong way," he said, clasping his hands between his knees as he looked away again.

"I promise," I responded instantly, leaning closer, wishing he would look at me again. "Go on."

"Look," he started, taking a deep breath. "If I thought that you had feelings for him, but that he had none for you, I probably wouldn't be as bothered. I know that sounds bad." He glanced over at me, probably gauging my reaction, which I was surprised to find was effortlessly neutral. "But I do think he cares about you."

I raised an eyebrow. "You think after everything he's done – turning me in, abandoning our caravan – you think he cares about me at all?"

Keel shook his head in annoyance. "Don't be like that, Delle. Be honest with yourself. You know he must care about you at least in some way. After all, he did tell you how to escape the Runners on that rooftop when he was taken. Then he saved you at the InterLine Complex and to our knowledge didn't tell his troop where to find you. He could have ruined us all then, but he didn't. Surely you can see that if he didn't care about you he wouldn't have done those things."

"Still," I stopped him, frowning. My heart was beating surprisingly fast at hearing the arguments spoken out loud that I had been struggling with in my head. "Even if he does care about me on some deranged, psychotic level, I could never trust him again."

"Maybe," Keel grumbled.

"Maybe?" I echoed, raising an eyebrow.

"You're stronger than you think, Delle," he said pointedly. "I think you have a much greater capacity for trust and forgiveness than you believe – especially where Attis is concerned."

I dropped my forehead to my knee and shut my eyes tightly. Keel's words were bringing up all sorts of feeling and thoughts I hadn't bothered to consider. I just wanted him to stop. I had moved on, hadn't I? I was done searching for the Attis I thought I had known – the one I had depended on – the one that didn't exist. This Attis was someone entirely different.

"I guess it doesn't really matter though," Keel continued, his voice softer.

I could feel him leaning closer to me now. Even without looking up or opening my eyes I could sense him.

"You have the right to feel for him whatever you want. I just have a lot to compete with, that's all," he said, and I could hear the shrug in his voice, the dry amusement.

"There's no competition," I mumbled into my leg, still unwilling to look at him, my mind still filled with unresolved questions about the nature of humanity and betrayal.

"I can't understand you like that," Keel said gently.

I sighed and lifted my head, holding tighter to my knee as I studied my friend.

"It's not a competition because you two are completely different," I elaborated. "Besides that I can't imagine anyone wanting to compete over me in the first place." Keel looked ready to correct me at this point, but I was ready. I held up a hand to stop him and he managed to refrain, though his skeptical expression remained. "The two of you are completely different people and the things I appreciate about you are completely different. When you first joined our caravan, I was worried that you were trying to take Attis's place, but now that I know you it's obvious you never could – and that's not a bad thing," I added hurriedly. "I don't want a copy of Attis – clearly there were a lot of things about him I never knew and he never thought to share with me. I just want the people in my life to be reliable and honest, so as long as you're those things, you don't need to worry about competing. That's all that matters to me."

Keel scrutinized me for a moment. I couldn't tell if he fully believed what I was saying, but he didn't look ready to argue about it, so that was a good sign.

"Alright," he said finally. "I'll try to be as reliable and honest as possible, and hope that's enough to keep me in the game."

"There is no game," I insisted, rolling my eyes as he chuckled at me.

"We'll see," he said mysteriously, stretching and putting an arm around me.

I decided to let the subject drop, not seeing anywhere else it could go at this point. I leaned my head on his shoulder and realized how tired I was. As I blinked sleepily I thought of a question I knew we would hear the answer to soon.

"What do you think they're going to do with Nanda?" I asked quietly, not wanting any passersby to hear.

"I'm not sure," Keel answered, sighing and pulling me closer, leaning his cheek against my head. "Probably keep her locked up until the revolution is over."

I felt sick to my stomach. I wasn't angry at Nanda. I didn't know if I was supposed to be, but I couldn't manage it.

"She just wanted to help Steffy," I said glumly.

"Good motives don't justify shooting friends," Keel pointed out.

"Yeah, but –"

"I know," he interrupted me, smoothing my hair down and kissing my temple. "We'll just have to see what happens."

***

Tac was flooded with new recruits over the next several days. I didn't know where they all came from or why, but Mona was constantly busy. Even when she was spending a brief moment or two with our little family she was distracted, like she was always listening to something none of us could hear. Appy and Sacrif were making preparations to leave with Jorge again, but promised we would all be together soon. I didn't know how we could. I was considered one of the most dangerous Taints in the country, because even though I now had no powers and was constantly suffering from splitting headaches, only the Tinkers and I knew about that. The Micahs were wanted fugitives now because they had harbored me – a wanted fugitive since birth. Still, I was going to hope. They told me that Steffy was doing well and that she was making a lot of progress with the exercises they were putting her through. They assured me that she missed me, but I couldn't tell if this was true or not. I was under no delusions. Children forget things relatively quickly. Hearing about her caused me physical pain, both in my head and heart, but I smiled and nodded and told them to give her a hug for me.

Dr. Reece was going to arrive soon and apparently she had a lot of questions for me. Every time I mentioned anything related to the Rebel cause to Mona, she would change the subject. Sometimes I would catch Rebel officials watching me out of the corners of their eyes as I walked by. I couldn't shake the feeling that they were expecting something of me – there was something no one was telling me. This along with the preparations being made to make another try for the codes left the entire province with an uneasy feeling. Keel was a constant though. We spent a lot of our time together, although I knew that as soon as Dr. Reece arrived that probably would cease to be the case. Fil was quieter than before now, probably shaken by what happened with Nanda. That didn't stop him from being productive though. He had quickly advanced in rank and was dragging Keel along to more military planning sessions than I was secretly comfortable with.

Jag was the main issue though. I rarely saw him and whenever I did it was obvious that he was avoiding me. I wondered if he blamed me for what happened – either with not seeing Attis for who he really was in the first place or maybe just for screwing up the mission to get the codes. He was busy too, which I found disconcerting since he wasn't even a member of the Rebel forces. This was just a stopping point for us. We were just staying here for now, just until an opportunity arose for us to make a break for it. Maybe we couldn't have the perfect life past the horizon like Attis had always ridiculously outlined, but maybe we could find somewhere, a Gypsy camp on the edge of the bomb lands maybe. It didn't have to be perfect. It just had to be safe and I just wanted us all to be together.

Dr. Reece's eventual arrival stirred up quite a bit of commotion. She came fluttering in with her burly bodyguard and her neon dresses trailing through the streets of the province. While I had to give her credit for not turning her nose up at every ramshackle building, it was clear that the place made no impact on her. She seemed to be drifting through, distracted by the mysterious thoughts in her purple head and barely bothering to pay attention to the Rebel officers watching her everywhere she went.

She agreed to meet with the general before meeting with me as per his request, but Mona promised to listen at the door and tell my anything important. It turned out that she didn't have to though, because shortly after Dr. Reece entered the building for her meeting, she insisted I join them. Keel frowned when I told him he didn't need to come, but Fil needed help working out the logistics of a new hospital so Keel agreed to stay behind.

"Ah, hello dear," Dr. Reece laughed as I entered the room, working very hard to conceal my limp. "There you are."

"Hello Dr. Reece," I said civilly. I slowly approached the table where she was seated across from the general who was making a face like he tasted something sour. I nodded at her bodyguard in greeting, but he just raised an eyebrow at me. It was the equivalent of an entire conversation for us. She nodded at the chair across from her, but I ignored the offer and remained standing.

"How are you, Claudelle?" she tittered as I sat down at the general's gesture. "Do tell me, how is Presid's boy? Just as handsome as ever? And what ever happened with that love of yours – Attis, wasn't it?"

"Keel is still handsome and Attis is a conversation I'm not having with you," I said shortly.

"Oh, you're no fun," she sniffed, tossing her lilac hair over a bare shoulder. "But fine, if we must stick to business, I have another proposal for you."

I frowned and glanced at the general to see if she had already run it past him. His expression was indiscernible.

"You see," she began, her voice so wispy I needed to lean closer to hear her properly. "I managed to obtain a sample of Exterophine and while I do plan on figuring out how to reverse the effects, that is going to take me time. And meanwhile, there is somewhere else I think you could be useful, if you are interested in helping your kind after all."

"Useful?" I echoed again, raising an eyebrow.

"Yes," she said, smiling at me with glowingly white teeth. "I believe the only reason this chemical hasn't killed you like it has the others is because the Exterophine isn't the only thing suppressing your powers." She gave me a look like I was supposed to understand where she was going with this. "Your willpower, dear. You trained yourself from a young age to suppress the powers. Like I mentioned before, your self-control is impressive. If you didn't already have that control in place, the sheer force the Exterophine would place on your body would have destroyed you."

"You're saying that because I trained myself to never use my powers, this chemical isn't taking as much of a toll on me?" I clarified, unconvinced.

She nodded. "And of course it's why you were never captured as a child. There is no way any other Taint with powers as visible as yours would be able to travel through the provinces as frequently as you have over the years. I looked at the file that Attis of yours submitted and I know you've spent a fair amount of time running about the more civilized parts of this country – and somehow you have managed to never reveal your powers."

I clenched my fists by my side and scowled at her. I really didn't want to hear anything about the information Attis had gathered on me over the years.

"What's your point?" I growled.

"My point," she said, raising an eyebrow at my frustration. "Is that there are very few Taints in this world who have the control to do that. If you could teach others like yourself how to suppress the powers on their own, they might even be able to live normal lives. More than that, you could prove to the public that Taints aren't volatile time bombs that could explode with unheard of powers at any moment. If you could show the provinces that Taints don't pose a threat, the First Province would lose all the support they've gained by breeding fear of your kind."

"So what do you want me to do?" I asked, still not understanding.

"I want you to teach the other Taints," Dr. Reece said, her yellow eyes glimmering determinedly as she leaned towards me. "I arranged for Taints willing to learn control to arrive here several days ago. You already have willing recruits who want to learn how to control their powers."

"I can't teach anyone," I said, horrified at even the thought of having that kind of responsibility. "I can't even use my powers anymore."

"You don't need your powers to teach them," she insisted, her expression unchanging, her voice stronger than usual. "You're just going to teach them techniques – how you managed to stop yourself whenever you felt the desire to use your powers."

I shook my head, standing up. "I didn't agree to this."

"You would be helping people just like you," Dr. Reece persisted, her eyes flashing coldly at me, a warning not to leave.

"Why do you care?" I asked, crossing my arms. "Why do you care what happens to my kind?"

"Because," she hissed, her polite façade faltering just a bit as she stood up, towering over me in her pointy heels. "Someone very close to me could use the lessons you have to offer."

"You're friends with a Taint?" I asked skeptically.

"Oh, I'm more than just *friends*," she sneered, stepping back towards her bodyguard.

"Is that so?" I responded, glancing over at the general who was watching us over steepled fingers, apparently uninterested in taking part.

"I don't believe," she began sweetly, her voice returning to its tinkling pitch, "That you have met my little brother, Henri."

I cocked my head, confused. Then I realized whom she was gesturing to. I blinked several times.

"*He* is your *little* brother?" I gasped, stepping back to see her enormous bodyguard in an entirely new light.

"Yes," she said, patting his arm and smiling at me. "We were born from the same parents, but I was born without any genetic alterations. That's why I made it my life's work to understand what causes these mutations and how they can be masked."

I observed the quiet man silently. He looked nothing like Dr. Reece. Then again, I had no way of knowing what she truly looked like underneath that wig and make up.

"Do you –" I began slowly, starting to finally work out why she was so passionate about this idea. "Do you want me to teach you how to control the powers?" I asked doubtfully, addressing Henri.

Henri nodded. I wondered if he could speak or if he was mute like Steffy.

"Why?" I asked, testing him.

"So I can control the powers, instead of the other way around," he responded stoically, his voice deep and clear, surprising me, his expression unchanging.

I shook my head and stepped away. I couldn't believe I was considering this. I was supposed to go with the Micahs. I was supposed to see Steffy again. My involvement with the revolution was supposed to be over after I helped Dr. Reece find the antidote.

"I have to think about this," I said, surprised by how cool my voice came across. "I won't agree to anything right now, but I'll give you my answer by tomorrow."

"Of course, dear," Dr. Reece replied, smiling at me charmingly again, like she already knew what I would choose. As I turned to go, she called, "And tell Presid's boy I said hello."

I rolled my eyes and didn't respond, letting the door swish shut behind me. Mona was standing by the door, watching me with wide eyes. I knew she had heard every word. Thankfully, she didn't follow me as I exited the building. I had a lot to consider.

***

Keel and Fil were still in the midst of their planning when I arrived back at the apartment, but they both looked up when I entered. Apparently my expression was intriguing enough because they both turned away from the Tab screen and asked how my meeting went. I considered withholding Dr. Reece's idea from them, but I knew that I needed honest opinions.

"It would mean staying here," I added. "In Tac. Until the revolution is over."

Keel and Fil exchanged looks, but neither of them looked certain of what to say, though they did seem surprised by the revelation about Henri. I sighed again. If Sacrif and Appy had stayed even a day more then I might have been able to discuss this with them. As it was, I would have to make the decision now and inform them of it later.

"I think you should talk to Jag," Fil said, giving me a knowing look.

I nodded. "Probably."

The problem was that Jag didn't make an appearance for hours. No one knew where to find him – or if they did know they refused to tell me. I resolved to wait by the door until he came back. I waited for hours. Everyone had gone to bed by the time the door creaked open and slammed awkwardly shut.

"Hey Jag," I said, surprising him as he turned around.

"Scrap it, Delle," he said, catching his breath. "You scared me. Why are you awake?"

"I just wanted to talk," I said with a shrug, pulling the other stool closer, nodding for him to sit.

Jag sat and considered me quietly for a moment. "I think maybe I should tell you something first."

"Oh," I said, confused. "Okay."

Jag took a deep breath before meeting my eyes intensely. "I'm joining the Rebels, Delle."

I might have stopped breathing for a moment. Or maybe it just felt that way because for a moment the world stopped turning.

"What?"

"It's not really surprising, is it?" he asked, his dark eyes shining in the dim light of the kitchen. "I know it's been pretty obvious I've been interested in the revolution since Sacrif first mentioned it."

I nodded, feeling numb and stupid. Of course I knew this was what Jag wanted all along. I had tried really hard not to see it.

"They assigned me to a mobile unit," he said slowly, watching me to see if I understood. "I'm going to be leaving here. I'll be travelling all over the country for extended periods of time."

"Leaving," I echoed. "Oh."

"I wanted to tell you before now, to give you some kind of warning," he said with a wince. "But after everything that happened with Attis, I didn't want it to seem like I was abandoning you."

The hopeful, worried eyes watching me now were no different than the ones watching me out of a pale, childish face as he sat down to eat his first meal with our caravan. Jag was my little brother. I hated the idea of him being put in danger, but it wasn't as if he was unfamiliar with it. I had put a lot of effort into ignoring every sign of him growing into a self-sufficient adult.

"Of course not," I finally managed, everything falling into place, finding reason and sense in my mind. "I know you wouldn't abandon me, Jag."

"Good," he said, clearly relieved. "I'll still see you, but it won't be often – at least not for a while. There could be weeks or months between, just depending on where we're moving and what we're doing."

I nodded. "And when do you leave?"

"Tomorrow."

"What?" I gasped, flying to my feet. "*Tomorrow*? You waited this long to tell me?"

Jag cringed. "I didn't know how to tell you, Delle!"

"Were you just going to disappear?" I continued furiously. "You were just going to leave?"

Jag rolled his eyes at this. "Of course not, that's why I'm talking to you now. I was going to talk to you in the morning actually because I didn't expect you to be awake when I got back."

I shut my eyes and pressed my fingers against my temples for a moment as the pounding, splitting ache in my head threatened to become unbearable. I waited a few moments, until I was calmer.

"Thank you for telling me," I finally managed, smiling at him ruefully. "I think I knew you wanted to be a part of all this. I just didn't want to think about it because I didn't want to lose you."

"You're not losing me," he said seriously. "I just won't be around as much."

I nodded, noting the question that hadn't left Jag's eyes. "I think you should do what you think is right, even if it means I don't get to see you very often," I admitted, even though it made my stomach twist up to do so. "We'll always be a caravan, right?"

Jag smiled. "Yeah – and a family."

"Good," I replied, smiling back even though there was a burning pressure behind my eyes.

Jag stood up and pulled me into a hug. I hugged him back tightly, wishing safe thoughts for him and praying that no one would even think about trying to hurt him – because if they did I would find them and kill them. When he finally pulled away – long before I was ready to let him go – he gave me a curious look.

"What did you want to tell me?" he asked.

"*Oh.*" My conversation with Dr. Reece and my impending decision came flooding back to me. "Oh, it's stupid now. It's probably a terrible idea. I mean if you're not going to be here, I really don't have any reason to stay."

"Stay?" he repeated, obviously confused. "What are you talking about?"

"Dr. Reece," I said with a sigh, crossing my arms and leaning against the counter. "She wants me to teach other Taints how to control their powers so they can blend in with normal society and convince the Provincials that we're not a threat. She wants me to stay here and train them while she works on the antidote for that stuff the Tinkers gave me."

Jag nodded, his expression thoughtful. He was always such a thinker. Maybe that's why I didn't expect him to be so avid for war.

"It sounds like a good idea," he said, clearly not understanding why I didn't like it.

"Maybe," I hedged. "But if you're not here and neither are the Micahs, then why should I stay?"

"Because right now there are people who need you more than your family does," Jag said. "Or if that's not good enough, because right now you have the opportunity to do something that could help your family if this revolution pans out."

I considered him as my fingers tingled distractingly. "Those are some reasons."

"It's your decision," Jag said, although there was a tone of finality in his voice. "I've made mine."

I nodded, biting the inside of my cheek as I considered my options. Right now I wasn't a huge fan of any of them

"Well, goodnight, Delle," Jag said, surprising me with another hug.

"Goodnight, Jag," I mumbled into his shoulder, hugging him extra tight.

***

Keel stood beside me as we watched Jag's transport turn a corner, rumbling out of sight.

"Mona says he's one of the most talented," Keel commented. "They think he's going to do a lot of good for their cause."

I nodded.

"You okay?" he asked quietly.

I nodded again. "I'll be fine."

"Have you thought about Dr. Reece's plan?" Keel asked, semi-curious, semi-hesitant.

"I have," I replied. "Last night Jag said something that I think is important."

Keel waited for me to continue, as he knew I would.

"He told me that there were people who needed me more than my family did," I said casually, fighting the urge to swallow as I realized what my train of thought was leading up to. "Jag doesn't need me anymore and neither does Steffy – not essentially. Attis never needed me, not really. The Micahs have each other and even though we're family, they have things pretty much under control."

Keel was watching me closely, waiting for me to continue. "And so?"

"And so," I continued. "I've spent my whole life deciding what I was going to do by considering who needed me the most. It's who I am. And even though my family doesn't need me right now, for the first time, I can't just stop being who I am. I should help the people who need me – and right now that's Taints, other people like me who are in just as much danger as I am."

"So does this mean you're staying?" Keel asked.

I reached for my necklace even though it wasn't there because I'd left it with Magely.

245

"At least while they need me," I agreed. "But if you don't want to stay here, you don't have to. I understand there might not be anything here that –"

"Before you finish that sentence and we get into an argument," Keel interrupted me with a grin. "There are actually several compelling reasons I have to stay. Fil and I have been planning that new hospital, and Mona thinks the plan has real potential. I'd like to see it through if we can. I think my mother would have approved. And besides that, there's this crazy, stubborn, beautiful girl staying here that I would really like to spend some more time with."

I rolled my eyes. "I really don't know if Dr. Reece would appreciate that description."

Keel snorted. "I should hope not. I was describing you, anyways."

I crossed my arms and smiled, fighting the enormous grin that wanted to plaster itself over my face.

"I know," I said calmly. "I just wanted to hear you say that."

Keel laughed.

"I guess I'll have to tell the general that I'm staying," I said with a dramatic sigh, scratching at my hand and inspecting my scars. "Do you think he'll be disappointed?"

Keel took my hand and tugged me closer, waiting for me to look up at him before kissing me on the nose.

"Undoubtedly," he confirmed. "But you're basically the most wanted person in the country right now, so I doubt he'd kick you out."

"Being a felon has its perks," I agreed, fighting to stay chipper even though I felt sort of empty with Jag gone.

"Not just a felon," Keel corrected me as we crossed the street, hand-in-hand. "You're a revolutionist now, a true Rebel."

"As are you," I agreed, although my stomach felt jittery at the idea.

I had never intended to be a part of this, but considering I would soon be training Taints the general wanted to use in the revolution, I suppose I was supporting it after all. Besides, whether we won or lost this fight, it would at least be spitting in the eye of the government that had forced my family to take sides. Even if we didn't win, I was all for causing those people as much trouble as possible.

I had spent the last several months of my life in an insane effort to locate the guy I had thought of as my leader and best friend, only to find out that he was a complete fraud. It was time for a new goal – and if that goal happened to cause him a significant amount of discomfort, well that was just an unexpected benefit. The Tinkers had destroyed me when they gave me that Exterophine – they took away a gift I didn't know I had – not even when Richy tried to tell me as much. The least I could do was try and convince others like me that their abilities weren't all that bad – that they had the potential to live normal lives and control their powers. Besides, the sooner this revolution ended, the sooner I could find somewhere that my family could live together. Thinking of it in those terms made me sure of my decision. I was ready to cause as much chaos as it took to bring down the government that had betrayed its people – my family included.

Ash Leigh grew up on the scorching concrete of Ft. Worth, Texas, where she spent most of her life and discovered her overwhelming passion for storytelling. Currently, she splits her time between Portland, Oregon and Phoenix, Arizona. She began writing Gypsy, the first novel of A Tainted Age trilogy, at the age of fifteen. Years later, fueled by her desire to captivate and entertain, she can no less stop writing than she can stop breathing.

**Visit her and learn more about
Traitor, A Tainted Age at:**

ashleighbooks.com

facebook.com/ashleighbooks

twitter.com/Ash_Leigh_123

9 780996 552622